DANTER

Never for an instant had Si Cwan thought he would find himself helpless before Lodec, the Senate Speaker of Danter. The powerfully built Thallonian stood a head taller than Lodec, was younger, in far better shape, and one of the most fearsome and deadly fighters ever bred in the history of Thallonian royalty.

So it was that he had been astounded to discover himself in Lodec's palatial estate being held high up, up off his feet, dangling in the air, as the much shorter Lodec held him there. Unable to draw in air, Si Cwan could only gag. His hands clamped around Lodec's arm, trying to twist it free, but he felt corded muscle beneath Lodec's sleeve that had not been there only a few days earlier.

Kalinda let out an infuriated cry and tried to come to his aid, but the other senators intervened and held her back with no effort at all. . . .

STAR TREK®
NEW FRONTIER

Gods Above

PETER DAVID

Based upon
STAR TREK: THE NEXT GENERATION®
created by Gene Roddenberry

POCKET BOOKS
New York   London   Toronto   Sydney   Singapore

This book is a work of fiction. Names, characters, places and incidents are products of the author's imagination or are used fictitiously. Any resemblance to actual events or locales or persons, living or dead, is entirely coincidental.

An *Original* Publication of POCKET BOOKS

POCKET BOOKS, a division of Simon & Schuster, Inc.
1230 Avenue of the Americas, New York, NY 10020

STAR TREK is a Registered Trademark of Paramount Pictures.

This book is published by Pocket Books, a division of Simon & Schuster, Inc., under exclusive license from Paramount Pictures.

ISBN: 0-7434-1858-1

First Pocket Books printing October 2003

10 9 8 7 6 5 4 3 2 1

POCKET and colophon are registered trademarks of Simon & Schuster, Inc.

Manufactured in the United States of America

For information regarding special discounts for bulk purchases, please contact Simon & Schuster Special Sales at 1-800-456-6798 or business@simonandschuster.com

The Old Father was amused.

From his place of exile, he looked out upon the insanity that his children had wreaked and the havoc that they were in the process of spreading, and he could only marvel at what he beheld. He wasn't certain whether to be proud of them for having learned from him so well, or ashamed because of what they had learned. He opted for both and, since he was vast and contained multitudes, did not consider holding the two to be mutually contradictory.

His children had been very, very busy. They had returned to a cosmos that had considered them legend—gods from the times of ancient Greeks and Romans and Egyptians and Norsemen—and endeavored to gather in one of their own . . . a half-breed, a genetic throwback, who had grown up in the so-called real world under the name of Mark McHenry.

1

McHenry had chosen an odd path, as an officer aboard a spacegoing vessel, the Excalibur. The Old Father remembered when he had first seen such vessels launching themselves into the abyss, with the same verve and confidence that such heroes as Ulysses or the Argonauts had displayed when first taking to sea. Certainly the latter had been as vast and daunting to those explorers as the former was to these intrepid souls. Impressive, the potential for disaster remained equal for both.

And disaster had indeed presented itself. It hadn't seemed so at first. They had been investigating a section of space they termed Zone 18 Alpha. (Funny, the continued obsessions of the little creatures. They needed to name everything. Everything. It had always been that way with them. They could not handle anything, from new lands to new diseases to new offspring, until they found something to call it.) And in Zone 18 Alpha, they had discovered McHenry's former lover, the child Artemis. She desired to take up with McHenry once more. She also desired, on behalf of her kind—the "Beings" was all they referred to themselves as—to allow all races within the United Federation of Planets to partake of the sacred ambrosia. To bestow upon all beings a new, great golden age of health and wisdom and achievement. But McHenry did not trust her, and informed his commander—a noble sort called Calhoun—of his trepidation. This earned him the wrath not only of Artemis but her kin, and the Excalibur was beset by the god children in their stunningly impressive vessels, hurtling through space but looking for all the world like ancient triremes. It was a lively battle, terminated by the *arrival of the* Excalibur's *sister ship, the* Trident, *under the command of one Elizabeth Shelby. But the battle was not without cost, as it appeared to claim two lives: McHenry, and the woman of nearly immortal lineage herself who was named Morgan Primus. Their bodies were burned and wounded nearly beyond recognition, or any sign of life. Although life, as the Old Father had discovered, had a way of constantly surprising one.*

Ah, the Trident. *A vessel with nearly as much stimulating activities as the* Excalibur. *The* Trident *had had its own mission, to travel to the world of the Danteri. The Danteri, an aggressive and combative race that desired to revive the fallen Thallonian Empire, with former royalty Si Cwan as figurehead. The* Trident *had brought the so-called Lord Cwan to the Danteri, along with his sister, Kalinda. There they had agreed to take the Danteri up on their offer, much to the annoyance and dismay of the* Trident *personnel in general and one Robin Lefler—daughter of the deceased Morgan Primus—in particular. But the business of reigniting an empire soured for Lord Cwan . . . particularly when the Danteri speaker of the senate, Lodec, found a new and even more intriguing ally: the god child Anubis, renowned by the Egyptians as the harbinger of death. Anubis, who even now confronts Si Cwan, preparing to remove what might be a potential impediment to the worship that the god children seek as price for their precious ambrosia.*

The Old Father smiled a tired smile to himself. There were other activities as well on board the ships, activities that would lead to nothing but heartache and death, as always. As always. For all their sophistication, for all their advancement, they remained consistently and de-

pressingly the same. No wonder the departed god child Apollo had thought he could compel earlier versions of these space voyagers to bow down before him. For all they thought they had left their primitive origins behind, they had really accomplished nothing but to introduce their own absurdities to a universe that looked on in stunned amazement.

"What fools these mortals be," said the Old Father, and only one heard him, and looked but saw but did not see.

DANTER

NEVER FOR AN INSTANT had Si Cwan thought he would find himself helpless before Lodec, the senate speaker of Danter. The powerfully built Thallonian stood a head taller than Lodec, and was younger, in far better shape, and one of the most fearsome and deadly fighters ever bred in the history of Thallonian royalty.

So it was that he had been astounded to discover himself in Lodec's palatial estate being held high up, up off his feet, dangling in the air, as the much shorter Lodec held him there. Unable to draw in air, Si Cwan could only gag. His hands clamped around Lodec's arm, trying to twist it free, but he felt corded muscle beneath Lodec's sleeve that had not been there only a few days earlier.

Kalinda let out an infuriated cry and tried to come to his aid, but the other senators intervened and held her back with no effort.

Lodec's smile was affixed upon his face, spreading

wider as he drank in Si Cwan's helplessness. "In case you have not yet figured it out, Lord Cwan . . . we were willing to present ourselves as test cases for the ambrosia. And we are able to give firsthand testimony as to its effectiveness . . . as I'm sure you now can, as well. Oh . . . and here is our benefactor now."

A shadow fell upon Si Cwan as he saw a monstrous creature coming toward him. Kalinda had described the being to Cwan as eight feet tall, skin like ebony, face like some sort of vicious jackal's. Evocative of one of the Dogs of War, but far more terrifying. She had not exaggerated in her estimation; he was just as Kalinda had described him, and his eyes burned with fiery scorn as he gazed upon Si Cwan.

Si Cwan fought desperately to break loose, but the inability to breathe hampered him severely. He dangled there from Lodec's grip, helpless as a babe, and the world seemed to be growing dark around him.

"I know, I know," Lodec was saying. "This prospect of 'worship' and such . . . it seems absurd. But Anubis explained to us their specific desires, and we've discussed it, and we felt, truly: What is the harm? The problem was, we suspected that your pride would make it impossible for you to accept, which was why we had to keep you excluded from many of these meetings . . . and it turns out we were correct in our assumptions. But I say again: What is the harm of a bit of worship? We tell them what they want to hear. We have prayer meetings and such . . . and in the meantime they provide us and our allies with this remarkable substance."

Anubis moved closer in toward Si Cwan, an unobstructed path to Si Cwan's face, and his jaws opened wide, and the warm, fetid breath washed over him. And as blackness closed upon Si Cwan, the last thing he heard was Lodec's gently mocking voice inquiring, "Come now, Lord Cwan, honestly . . . would it harm us . . . to gather a few laurel leaves?"

And then Si Cwan was jolted back to awareness when he hit the floor. He had no idea what had caused it to happen. All he knew was that one moment he was firmly in Lodec's grasp, and the next he was on the ground, gasping, the world swimming before his blurred vision.

There was a roaring in his ears from the blood deep within, and then it started to fade, only to be replaced by screaming. It was Lodec's voice doing the screaming, which couldn't have suited Si Cwan more.

What Si Cwan could not comprehend, though, was why Lodec's hand was still squeezing his throat. Then his vision began to clear and he instantly understood. Lodec's hand was no longer attached to his arm.

The senate speaker of the Danteri was clutching the stub of his right arm, staring in horror at the blood which was fountaining from the end of it. His face was becoming a paler shade of bronze, and his eyes looked like they were glassing over. The fingers were still clutching spasmodically on Si Cwan's throat, and the Thallonian quickly pried the hand away and tossed it, still quivering, on the ground nearby.

The other senators had a collectively stunned expression on their faces, but Cwan was also struck by what they no longer had: specifically, Kalinda in their grasp. The Thallonian princess was standing several feet away, and she was holding a golden, shimmering, curved cutting tool. The cutting edge was dripping with a thick liquid that was the same color as the blood pouring out of Lodec's stump, and Si Cwan did not require a map to be drawn for him to figure out what had just happened.

Whereas earlier Kalinda had been tentative and even daunted by the prospect of facing down the difficult Danteri senators in Lodec's home grounds, there was now no trace of fear in her at all. The contemplation of difficulty, it seemed, had been far more problematic for her than being faced with the actual difficulty itself. Now that the danger was thrust upon them, she was completely focused on finding a way out of it, and whatever concerns for herself she might have had been shunted aside.

Si Cwan felt a swell of pride in his sister, even as he wondered where in the world she had gotten the cutting implement from.

The answer was not long in coming as the feral-faced creature called Anubis took a step forward. Kalinda swiveled in place, keeping a distance between the two of them, holding the blade level so that any attempt to come in at her quickly would result in the same sort of dismemberment that Lodec had experienced. Lodec, for his part, had sunk to his knees, his screams reduced to faint whimpers. The other senators made a motion toward her, but a quick flick of the instrument in their direction froze them where they stood. "I'd stay where I was if I were you, Senators," Kalinda said in frozen tones, "lest you lose other, more valuable parts."

Anubis likewise ceased any forward motion, but unlike the others, he did not seem particularly intimidated. Indeed, his red eyes burned again, but this time with what seemed a sort of vague amusement. He spoke, his voice low and gravelly, and his long, pointed teeth clicking together slightly. "That is my scythe," he informed her.

"I know," Kalinda said matter-of-factly. Si Cwan truly admired her icy demeanor, for when she had spoken earlier of merely seeing Anubis in passing, she had had such dread in her voice as Cwan had never known. He suspected it was taking all the self-control she possessed to keep herself together in the face of this . . . this whatever it was. "It was hanging from just behind your hip."

A weapon. He'd had a weapon on him, and Cwan hadn't seen it, else he might have tried to grab it himself. Then again, considering he was being choked at the time, it was probably understandable that he'd missed it considering it was dangling out of immediate sight behind him. But not, obviously, out of Kalinda's sight.

"So you shook free from your captors and grabbed it from me. Very resourceful," said Anubis. He was studying her with such intensity that it seemed as if his gaze were dissecting her. "There is more to you than meets the eye, I suspect."

"And less to you, I'd say," shot back Kalinda. Si Cwan had detected some slight trembling in her hands earlier as she held the scythe, but now it was rock steady.

She abruptly took a step toward Anubis, thrusting the scythe forward. The jackal-headed god did not flinch, but his eyes narrowed in what now seemed annoyance. It appeared that Kalinda's amusement value to him was wearing thin.

"You have potential, child. But not as much as you think." Then Lodec's whimpering from nearby distracted him, and Anubis turned his attention to the injured Danteri with poorly disguised annoyance. "Cease your carrying-on. Pick up the hand. Hold it against your wrist."

Lodec did as he was instructed. He did so very tentatively, however, apparently appalled by the notion of touching his own severed hand. Anubis, seeming for all the world as if he'd forgotten that Kalinda was standing there—or perhaps he simply no longer cared—strode over toward the fallen Lodec and produced a small vial from the belt of his kilt. A thick, viscous green liquid was within, and he upended it so that it poured down upon the separation between hand and arm. Lodec let out another scream then, and this one made the earlier seem a mild squeak in comparison. There was a loud sizzling, like meat being cooked up, and the aroma almost triggered Cwan's gag reflex. He was relieved he was able to squelch it in time; vomiting before one's enemies was never a good idea.

"Stop your yowling," commanded Anubis, and Lodec did the best he could. He sank his teeth into his lower lip and once again confined his pain to whimpering noises. As he did so, however, he was staring fixedly and with amazement at the point where he had pressed his hand against his arm. The tissue appeared to be reknitting, and there was already some movement visible at the ends of his fingers. "You see? You see how we take care of those who treat us properly?" continued Anubis, and Lodec managed a nod. "Good. I do not suggest you forget."

"I will not, High One," stammered Lodec in gratitude.

But Anubis had already forgotten about him, instead turning his attention once more to Kalinda. He cast a brief glance at Si Cwan as if trying to determine whether the Thallonian nobleman was worth further time, and obviously decided he wasn't. "You trade in the ways of the dead, as I do. That gives us some common ground," he growled. "And you did catch me unawares. You tricked me. I do appreciate a good trick, more than any others who live might. But do not, however, think that it gives us so much commonality that I will hesitate to treat you as anything other than an enemy."

"Nor we, you," Si Cwan said, rallying. He moved to Kalinda's side, keeping a wary eye on the other senators. Cowed they might be by current circumstances, but Si Cwan had not forgotten for a moment the inordinate strength that had flowed through Lodec's limbs.

Nearby was a fountain with a statue of a Danteri warrior wielding a sword. Si Cwan did not hesitate. He lashed out with a powerful thrust of his right foot and slammed into the base of the stone sword where it was held by the warrior. The stone cracked under the impact and shattered, and Si Cwan caught the stone sword with one deft grab. It was far weightier than any real blade, of course, but that was all to Cwan's liking. If he swung it, anything of flesh and bone that it came into contact with would instantly be crushed by it. Water gurgled out of the broken-open hole.

"Very impressive," commented Anubis, although he did not sound especially impressed. He was still watching Kalinda warily. "It is a pity. You could have been a most useful ally."

"Oh, I doubt that," replied Si Cwan. He swung the stone sword in a leisurely arc, causing the other senators to step further back. It gave Cwan a good deal of pleasure, seeing them hesitate in that way. If there was one thing he had learned long ago, it was that there was far more to dominating a situation than just having superior physical strength. Not that Cwan was ready to concede that they *were* superior to him. But they were obviously far less anxious to put self-defense capabilities to the test than he was. "I suspect that Kalinda and I would be far too much in the way of independent thinkers to fall in line with whatever it is you're planning. Which, by the way, would be . . . ?"

Anubis made a sound that Cwan suspected was supposed to be vaguely akin to a laugh. But only vaguely. True laughter was infectious. This was a sound that was infectious in the same way that plague was.

"You seek some deep, hidden 'true plan,' " Anubis observed. He was not moving at all now, not flexing so much as a single muscle in his body. If he hadn't been speaking, he would have looked like a statue carved from ebony. "My clan and I have never been anything less than forthright. We wish to provide ambrosia to bring out a golden age of mankind. My kin offered it to your captain . . ." He paused, as if endeavoring to pluck a name out of the ether. "Calhoun," he said finally, as if someone had whispered it to him as a prompt. "He was encouraged to refuse us. That was . . . unwise."

"Unwise. What are you saying?" Si Cwan's eyes narrowed, and he gripped the makeshift sword more tightly.

Suddenly he saw movement with his peripheral vision. Without even taking his gaze from Anubis, he whipped the stone sword around under his arm and slammed it into the pit of one of the senator's stomachs. The man had tried to come up behind him. It had not gone well for him; with one swing, Si Cwan had done the man some serious damage, and he was now on the ground with his arms wrapped around his middle. Si

Cwan suspected he might have broken several of the Danteri's ribs. He did not, however, care. His concerns were focused instead on the implicit threat he had just heard. "In what way unwise?" he continued.

"Let us say they have been dealt with," said Anubis.

"Let us say more than that," Si Cwan said dangerously, and started forward.

But Kalinda's sharp "Don't move, Cwan" froze him in midstep. He looked at her, scowling, and she met his gaze with a warning one of her own. Immediately he realized what she was trying to put across to him: that continuing this challenge was not the wisest course of action. Anubis had made no further move toward them, but he was still coiled, ready to spring. And the fact that one senator was down with some broken bones and Lodec was just recovering use of his hand didn't render the other two less dangerous, or the entire situation less fraught with peril. Also, for all they knew, other senators or even soldiers might show up as reinforcements. Matters were being held together at that moment through only the most tenuous of circumstances, and the more they prolonged it, the worse it would go for them.

"Listen carefully," Si Cwan told everyone standing there, keeping enough edge in his voice to sound as threatening as he possibly could. "We agreed to come to Danter for one reason and one reason only: your desire to create a new Thallonian Empire. You wanted my help for that. But since that time, another . . . option," and he inclined his head toward Anubis, "has clearly presented itself. I would have much preferred that you tell me about it, instead of what you had been doing. The skulking about, the late-night meetings from which I was excluded."

"We . . ." Lodec was trying to push through the pain he was still obviously feeling. "We thought . . . you would not understand."

"Perhaps I would not have. But I understand duplicity even less." He looked at them for a long moment, and then said to Lodec, "You have a private field, do you not?"

"Field?" Lodec, still rubbing the rejoining place of his hand, looked blank for a moment. Then the confusion evaporated. "Oh. A landing port."

"Correct."

Slowly Lodec nodded. "Yes. Yes, I do." He was speaking slowly and a bit sheepishly, as if chagrined that he had been screaming in such an out-of-control manner earlier. "It's . . . one of the perks of being the—"

"I do not care," Cwan interrupted. "You will bring us there. You will give us the fastest shuttle off this rock. And you will allow us to leave unmolested."

"And if they do not?" inquired Anubis. He seemed most intrigued to hear Si Cwan's response.

"Then," said Si Cwan unflappably, waving the stone sword in a decidedly menacing manner, "we shall see if we have a god who bleeds."

A long silence followed, and then came another of those frightening laughs from Anubis that made the listener feel as if bugs were crawling beneath his skin and lodging in various important organs. "Lodec," he said after a moment more. "Give him what he wants."

"But High One!" Lodec began to protest, until a single fearsome glance from Anubis silenced him.

Anubis turned back to Si Cwan as if Lodec no longer

mattered to him . . . which was, very likely, the case. "Believe it or not, Thallonian," Anubis said, "you were of interest to me. I sought to test your mettle. I am . . . unimpressed."

Si Cwan bowed mockingly. "I shall endeavor to live with the disappointment of failing to impress you."

Paying no heed to Si Cwan, Anubis shifted his gaze to Kalinda. "She, on the other hand, has potential. Vast potential. It might be best for you to remain here, young Kalinda."

"I go where Si Cwan goes," she said defiantly.

He shrugged almost imperceptibly. "That is your choice, child. I think it an unfortunate one, but I will not tamper with your free will. None of my brethren will. We are gods, not monsters."

"Despite all appearances to the contrary," Si Cwan said sharply. "And you won't tamper with free will? From what you're saying, you attacked friends of ours simply because they were exercising their free will in deciding not to trust you and your . . . ilk."

Anubis' teeth flashed. For half a heartbeat, Si Cwan thought he was going to have a fight on his hands, and he wasn't ecstatic about the likelihood of triumphing in it. But Anubis promptly calmed himself; it happened so quickly that very likely Cwan and Anubis were the only ones aware of the flash of temper. "There is free will," he said in a soft voice that sounded much like a growl. "And then there is lack of respect. Blasphemy, if you will. All living creatures have the gift of free will. But we need not tolerate blasphemers. Any more than you, 'Lord' Si Cwan, tolerated insurrection in your days as a noble of the Thallonian Empire."

"You know nothing of me, nor of what I did or did not tolerate."

"A pity," said Anubis, his eyes blazing brighter, "that we will not have the opportunity to learn. Know one thing, however," and he shifted his gaze toward Kalinda, "my scythe must be returned before your vessel will be permitted to leave. It is my property. You may not depart with it."

"Odd," commented Kalinda, "that you don't try to come and take it back yourself." She idly whipped the blade through the air.

"Odd to you. Not to me. But then . . . we have been known to move in mysterious ways."

And with that comment, Anubis turned his back to them and walked away as if they were no longer of any interest to him. Si Cwan watched him go. He did not move like anything remotely human. Indeed, it almost seemed as if he had no mass whatsoever. For an instant, Si Cwan wondered if perhaps Anubis wasn't there at all. Perhaps he was a hologram of some sort. But he quickly discarded the notion. Si Cwan had spent a good deal of time on the holodeck of the *Excalibur*, running through various combat scenarios. And no matter how realistic his opponents had seemed, his senses were never deceived. He was able to discern between that which was living and that which was manufactured. If nothing else, they tended to move with machinelike perfection. No matter how sophisticated the computer program, there were still limits as to what it was able to replicate in terms of movement.

Anubis, no matter how bizarre his appearance, was definitely living. A living what, Si Cwan could not begin to say.

The Thallonians were escorted to the landing port by a stonily silent group of senators. Lodec was still waggling his fingers, obviously to make certain that they were fully functional. Every so often he would toss an angry glance in Si Cwan's direction. Cwan resisted the temptation to put his fist through Lodec's face . . . particularly considering that it wasn't long before that Lodec had been lifting him off his feet as if he were a child. Truth to tell, he wasn't all that anxious to have another run at Lodec; not until he had a clearer idea of just what had happened and how it had come to pass. His only priority at that moment was getting Kalinda out of there.

There were several vessels sitting in the port, and Lodec made a sweeping gesture. "Choose one," he said, his voice even. "If I select one, you may suspect some sort of treachery."

"Don't concern yourself about that, Lodec," replied Si Cwan. "At this point, no matter what you say or do, I will suspect treachery . . . very likely because you are, in fact, a traitor."

"Why? Because circumstances caused me to break my word to you?" He made a scoffing noise. "A traitor is someone who acts contrary to the best interests of his own people. You are simply put out because I acted contrary to *your* best interests. That does not concern me in the least."

"Concern yourself over this, then, if you wish." He leaned in toward Lodec, keeping a firm grip on the stone sword. "This is not over."

"I hope not," replied Lodec with a very unpleasant smile. "I would dearly love to have a rematch with you,

Si Cwan . . . preferably without your little sister to step in and save you."

Reflexively Si Cwan started to take a step forward, but Kalinda put a firm hand on his arm that stopped him. He forced a nod in acknowledging that departure would serve them far better than continued conflict. He chose a runabout at random and then had Lodec start it up. The reason for his caution was obvious: Lodec might have some sort of fail-safe built in that would cause the thing to blow to bits if anyone other than Lodec endeavored to depart with it.

Lodec then stepped out of the runabout, but turned and called, "Lord Cwan! I believe you have something that the great Anubis requested be returned to him."

"Oh yes. So he did." Standing in the entrance to the runabout, Si Cwan extended a hand to Kalinda. She hesitated briefly, but then handed the scythe over to her brother. He held it a moment, feeling the heft and balance. "An impressive implement," he said . . . and then with a quick, smooth motion he sent it hurtling at Lodec.

The Danteri senator let out a shriek but was rooted to the spot as the blade whipped through the air at an angle. It landed exactly where Si Cwan intended it to, thudding into the ground directly between Lodec's legs. Lodec looked down at the still quivering handle, the blade buried in the ground.

Si Cwan grinned broadly, and then turned and saw the disapproving scowl on Kalinda's face. Without a word he pushed the button that caused the door to iris closed. "That was unnecessary," she said as Si Cwan went straight over to the guidance consoles.

"I found it to be very necessary."

The runabout lifted off and seconds later the small craft was angling skyward. Si Cwan was watching the sensor readouts carefully, concerned that Danteri vessels would be launched in pursuit with the intention of blowing them out of the sky. Kalinda obviously shared the concerns as she asked, "Are we being followed?"

"Not so far," said Cwan. He shook his head. "This is going to be embarrassing."

"Embarrassing?" Kalinda said in bewilderment. "How would it be . . . ?" And then she realized and, despite the seriousness of their situation, she couldn't help but smile. "Ahhh . . . Captain Shelby."

He nodded. "She's going to laugh in my face. She tried to warn me. She cautioned me against accepting the Danteri offer. It was my own ego running rampant."

"She said that?"

"No, I said that. That is, I say that."

"Oh, Cwan." She went over to him and rested a hand on his shoulder. "You did what you thought was right. All the reasons you gave her were good ones. We are who we are. We are Thallonians, the last members of our line. All during our time on the *Excalibur,* you've put yourself forward as 'Ambassador,' but really, that's just been a polite fiction. The truth is, you haven't been representing anyone or anything except yourself and your own interests. The Danteri offer was simply too good to pass up."

Slowly he nodded. "And would you mind saying all that to Captain Shelby?"

"Out of the question. She'd laugh in my face."

The response prompted a genuine chuckle from Si Cwan, but it died in his throat as the warning lights suddenly snapped on and a shrill alarm sounded within the runabout.

"We have a problem," grated Si Cwan.

"What is it?!" Even as she asked, Kalinda was clambering into a seat and strapping herself in. But the response was forthcoming before Si Cwan could respond as the runabout shuddered violently. *"Did we hit something?"*

"No, something hit us," he shot back. "Their ground cannons, most like. We've been targeted. Apparently Lodec desired to give us a parting gift."

"I don't think Anubis is going to like that."

The runabout trembled once more under another violent impact. "His likes and dislikes will be somewhat moot if we're smashed to bits."

"Does this vessel have shields?"

"The standard astro-nav shields to deflect debris and particles. Nothing meant to withstand the direct pounding of surface-to-air weaponry." His fingers flew over the controls and the runabout banked sharply.

"What are you doing?!"

"If we can't survive direct hits, then the best thing to do is be where they're not shooting until we're out of range."

Under Si Cwan's deft handling, the runabout darted to the right and left. Ground blasts erupted in the air around it, the shock waves battering the ship mercilessly even when the cannons missed. The higher into the atmosphere they went, the thinner the air became and the less of a problem the near-hits were. But Si Cwan wasn't thrilled with the way the runabout was maneuvering. He suspected that some of the guidance systems had been damaged by the assault. He didn't tell Kalinda that, however, seeing no point in worrying her.

Reaching escape velocity, they pulled free of the gravity of Danter, and Si Cwan and Kalinda shot each other a look of relief just before one final, stray shot slammed into them squarely, sending all their nav systems completely off line and the runabout whirling helplessly into the depths of space.

EXCALIBUR

i.

"I CANNOT DETERMINE a cause of death."

In the sickbay of the *Excalibur,* Mackenzie Calhoun stared with incredulity, first at Dr. Selar and then at the unmoving, charred body of Mark McHenry, laid out on a diagnostic table, and then back to Selar. "What the hell do you mean, you can't determine it?" demanded Calhoun. "Look at the man! He's got a burn mark through his chest the size of a cannonball!"

Selar frowned. "The size of a what?"

Calhoun was about to reply, and then thought better of it, particularly since he saw that others in the sickbay were reacting with surprise to his raised voice. They looked bedraggled, shell-shocked. Sickbay was crammed to overflowing with the injured; everyone from every shift, and everyone who had ever wielded any sort of medical instrument in their life, had been pulled in to deal with the damage the ship had sustained in the battle with the Beings. People were battered, burned, moaning and waiting for painkillers to kick in. They were lying there waiting for skin grafts to take, or sleeping and in stasis, waiting for their bodies to stabilize so further work could be done on them. And everyone, everyone who was conscious was looking at him, and he felt as if there were accusatory stares . . . or hopeful? Or desperate? Looking to him for salvation or explanation or something, anything. *What the hell do they want from me? What am I supposed to be? Made of stone?* Then he drew in a deep breath, steadied himself, found a calm center, and focused once more on Selar. As frustrating as Vulcans could be at times, he had to admit that their capacity for maintaining calm in the face of difficulty was something he occasionally envied. "I'm simply asking," he said, "how it could be unclear what caused Mr. McHenry's . . . demise."

"Because I am not entirely certain that he is dead."

Once again Calhoun found himself staring at Selar in total confusion. "I would have thought," he said, "that the lack of life signs in his readings would have been sufficient to establish that."

"Ordinarily, yes. But Mr. McHenry is . . . less than ordinary. And more."

He rubbed the bridge of his nose, feeling the onset of a thumping headache. "That much, I'll agree with. So lay it out for me, Doctor. What are you saying?"

"There's no deterioration of his cells," she said, circling the bed on which McHenry was stretched out. "No cellular degeneration. Oh, there's been catastrophic damage to his body, there is no disputing that. But . . ." She paused and then looked up at Calhoun. "You will think I am joking."

"Trust me, the odds of my thinking that are minuscule at best."

She nodded and then said, "From all accounts, some sort of massive surge of energy leaped out of the conn station and lanced through Mr. McHenry. Morgan Primus . . ."

"Also known as Morgan Lefler . . . Robin Lefler's mother."

"I know who she is, Captain," said Selar with raised eyebrow. "Morgan Lefler endeavored to intercept the energy surge, and was killed instantly. I could not say for certain, however, that McHenry was killed as well. I do not know whether the blast of energy drove his life from his body . . . or if his life was pulled from his body before the blast struck."

Calhoun shook his head in confusion. "Isn't that just semantics?"

"I do not know," she said, and pushed a strand of stray hair from her face. She was actually starting to look as if the pressure of the situation was weighing upon her. "I simply . . . feel as if I am missing something."

"What are you missing?"

"If I knew the answer to that, Captain, then I would no longer be missing it," she replied matter-of-factly, and with the air of someone who did not suffer fools gladly. "All I know is that something is not right with McHenry's body. It is as if . . ."

"As if time has frozen around it somehow?"

She considered that, looking as if she wanted to dismiss the notion out of hand owing to its inherent absurdity, but at the same time finding a measure of explanation there. "Somewhat . . . yes. The effect is not dissimilar from a medical cellular stasis field. But such things cannot be generated by nature."

"Doctor," Calhoun said tiredly, "we are part of nature. You and I and everyone on this ship. Nature made us. We are capable of generating it. Therefore, nature can generate it. It's just that, until now, it's been done with mechanical aids. But if something can be done with mechanical aids, then it stands to reason that the possibility exists it could be done without them as well."

Selar considered that. "Interesting, Captain. There are times where you would make a passable Vulcan."

"Thank you."

"There are some who would not consider that a compliment."

"I choose to take it in the spirit it was meant. So . . . what do we do with Mr. McHenry?"

"I will be moving him to a separate, private observation room," Selar said, studying him thoughtfully. "Nothing is to be gained by having him continue to remain here. It is disconcerting to the other patients." She eyed him. "Captain, you may want to consider some rest for yourself."

"I'm fine," he said dismissively. "What are you doing?"

She was holding up a medical tricorder and aiming it in his direction. "In addition to my observations of your having sustained multiple contusions and lacerations, you have also a broken rib, a hairline fracture of the clavicle, and a mild concussion . . ."

"I'm Xenexian, Doctor," said Calhoun. "I can take a lot more punishment than humans . . . or Vulcans, for that matter."

"I think it would be wise," she said, "if you did not inflict an excessive amount of punishment upon yourself in order to prove that point."

"What does that mean?"

"I believe the statement speaks for itself."

Before he could push it further, his combadge beeped. He tapped it. "Calhoun here."

"Captain, this is Burgoyne," came the voice of the Hermat first officer. "You wanted a shipwide status meeting as soon as we had in reports from all decks and departments. If you would—"

"Burgy?" said a puzzled Calhoun, firing a look at Selar. Her face was impassive. "What the hell are you doing on duty? You have a broken leg. You should be up here. Why isn't s/he up here?" he demanded of Selar.

Before Selar could reply, Burgoyne said, "Selar treated me and I felt it imperative I return to duty."

Calhoun let out an impatient sigh. "Fine. Department heads in the conference lounge in—"

"The conference lounge was badly hit, sir. Recommend the team room."

"Fine. Team room in twenty minutes. And after that, Burgy, bed rest for you. That's an order."

"Aye, sir. Burgoyne out."

Calhoun ended the connection and shook his head. "Running around with a broken leg. What is s/he thinking?"

"Have you considered the likelihood, Captain," Selar pointed out, "that my mate is using you as a role model for how s/he is expected to conduct hirself."

Calhoun looked at her in surprise. "You know, Doctor . . . I could be wrong, but I believe that's the first time you've ever referred to Burgoyne as 'your' anything."

"I still make certain, Captain, that it does not recur," she said archly.

He turned away, but instead of heading to the team room, he crossed the sickbay and returned to a bed he'd visited when he'd first arrived there.

Moke, his adoptive son, was lying there, staring up into space. Calhoun's heart went out to the boy, seeing how banged up he was. Apparently he had taken a spill down a Jefferies tube during all the commotion when the ship had been under attack. The boy had been brought into the sickbay convinced that he was never going to walk again, and Calhoun's heart had been in his throat until it had been discovered that he'd just pinched a nerve in his spine. It hadn't taken Selar long to set things right, but she was keeping him there a few hours more for observation.

The boy was staring fixedly up at the ceiling, and didn't even seem aware that Calhoun was standing there. That concerned the captain greatly. He took Moke's hand, listening to the steady thrum of the monitoring devices. "Moke? You're going to be fine. Remember, I told you earlier, you're going to be fine?"

Moke said nothing. Just continued to stare. Calhoun started to worry that, despite Selar's earlier assurances, the boy had sustained some sort of brain damage. Then Calhoun caught a glimpse of his own reflection in the metal surface of the monitor. He looked as bedraggled as Selar had said. He hoped that hadn't scared Moke. Doing his best to be of comfort, he squeezed Moke's hand even more tightly. "Moke . . . I know you had a scare. But really . . . everything's fine now."

"No. It's not."

It was a very, very faint whisper that escaped from between the boy's lips. He spoke with the air of someone who knew without reservation that matters were going to go from bad to worse, and was only trying to figure out just how to impart this information to others. "It's not going to be fine. It's going to be worse. A lot worse."

"Who told you that?" Calhoun said with a faint tone of scolding.

Moke looked as if he wanted to answer, but wasn't able to bring himself to do so. Prodding a bit more determinedly, Calhoun repeated, "Come on, Moke. Who told you that, huh?"

"Nobody. I just know. The Dark Man wouldn't be here if everything was going to be all right."

Calhoun had no idea what the boy was talking about. He leaned in closer to Moke. "What Dark Man? What are you talking about . . . ?"

But Moke would not respond, and not all the urging from Calhoun could get him to do so. So it was that Calhoun left sickbay feeling as if he knew even less than when he'd arrived . . . and with the uncomfortable sensation that something he didn't understand could turn out to prove very, very dangerous.

ii.

Robin Lefler paced the shattered bridge of the *Excalibur,* watching in mounting frustration as Ensign Beth labored under the still-sparking remains of the conn station. The monitor screen, which had gone on and off line repeatedly since the battle had concluded, was back on at the moment. However, the view of the starfield before them was still a bit fuzzy, as was the view of the *Trident.*

She still couldn't quite believe the timing of it. When she'd been aboard the *Trident,* on her way back to the *Excalibur,* she had thought nothing could distract her from the foul mood enveloping her since Si Cwan had elected to remain on Danter. The entire voyage back, she had done nothing but dwell on his lack of gratitude, on his frustrating inability to realize her interest in him, and now . . . this? To try and restore the Thallonian Empire? Had he learned absolutely nothing in his stay aboard the *Excalibur?* Well, obviously not. Obviously not.

But she had been startled from her ennui by the call to battle stations that had been sounded in the *Trident* upon her approach to the *Excalibur.* Since she'd been aboard merely as a passenger rather than an officer, she didn't have a battle station per se. Consequently, she'd felt an overwhelming sense of helplessness, particularly when she'd realized that it was her home ship that was under attack. She'd stood at the deserted Ten-Forward (since the recreation area obviously wasn't heavily populated at times of crisis) and stared out the window in fixed astonishment as she'd witnessed the *Excalibur,* punctured, battered, saucer separated from the main hull and both of them badly injured, under attack by . . .

She still couldn't wrap herself around it.

And then the call had come in . . . the call about . . .

She looked at the ops station, which had been occupied by her mother such a short time ago, and all she could think of was how she had resented Morgan because of it. Her mother had subbed in for her, and it had angered her. All she could reflect upon was the time wasted through harsh words and . . .

She pushed it away, unable to deal with it, and instead focused her irritation on the hapless Ensign Beth. "What's the problem here?" she demanded finally.

"I'm working on it," Beth said testily, craning her neck out from under the unit. Her face was as smeared with grime and soot as anyone else's, and her normally curly hair had flattened out from the sweat that was dripping off her. There was an array of tools to her right.

"That's what you keep saying. That's what you've *been* saying . . . !"

The others on the bridge were going about their tasks as best they could, but the dispute over by the conn station was starting to catch their interest. "You think you could do better?" demanded Beth.

"I think a trained chimp could do better!"

Beth, infuriated, threw down the spanner she'd been holding and started to rise, but managed to strike her forehead on the underside of the conn station. She fell back as a thin stream of blood began to trickle down the side of her face. *"Dammit!"* she snarled.

"Oh, that's perfect!" snapped Lefler. "That's just—"

"That's enough."

Lefler didn't have to turn to know that it was Soleta's sharp voice that had intervened. The Vulcan science officer was approaching, moving with impressive grace over the debris, stepping around maintenance crew members who were in the process of clearing it away. "Do we have a problem, Lieutenant?" she demanded evenly of Lefler.

" 'We' are less than satisfied with the speed that the repairs are being accomplished," Lefler replied.

Beth was about to respond, but Soleta silenced her with a look. "That's as may be, Lieutenant," she said. "Ensign Beth, however, does not answer to you. She answers to Chief Engineer Mitchell. If you have any concerns—"

"But—"

Soleta spoke right over her. "—then I suggest you bring them to Mr. Mitchell, who will, I assume, give your complaint the deepest consideration right before he tells you to go to hell."

Robin stepped in close, fuming, and the two women faced each other just before a loud, high-pitched whine filled the bridge and sent them clapping their hands to their ears. Soleta was the hardest hit, staggering, as her sensitive ears sent the science officer to her hands and knees. *"What in the world is that?!"* she called out.

Trying her best to shake it off, Robin made it over to the ops station. "It's the ship's computer!"

"Shut it down!"

"I can't shut down the ship's computer from ops! It has to be done at the computer core in engineering!"

"I *know* that!"

"Then why did you tell me to shut it down!"

"Because I can't think!" shouted the obviously exasperated Soleta. "Bridge to enginee—"

And then, just like that, the noise stopped.

Robin sagged against ops, waiting for the ringing in her head to cease. Soleta eased herself into the command chair, putting her hands out to either side in a way that indicated that the world was whirling around her. "I did not need that," she announced. "Beth . . . run a systems analysis and full diagnostic immediately. If we have another virus in the computer, I will personally use the Vulcan death grip on whomever put it there."

From over at the tactical station, apparently unfazed by the earsplitting sound that had been emanating from the computer moments before, Zak Kebron rumbled, "There's no such thing as a Vulcan death grip."

"I'll invent one for the occasion," replied Soleta.

Drawing in air unsteadily, Robin turned to Soleta and said, "Why have Ensign Beth run the systems diagnostic? I can do it . . ."

"No. You cannot. Not in your current state of mind."

Robin's face colored; she felt the sting of blood rushing to her cheeks. "I don't see who you are to . . ."

"Robin," Soleta replied, her voice imperturbable, "I am that deadliest of combinations: I outrank you, and I am your friend."

"You're my friend?" Robin said dryly.

Soleta seemed to shrug with her eyebrows. "In the sense that we see each other every day and I do not find your presence repulsive, yes." Then, more softly, and with what seemed genuine sympathy, she said softly, "We've helped each other in the past, you and I. Believe it or not, I'm helping you now by telling you to get off the bridge and take some time. Take as much as you need."

"I don't—"

"You do. Go to your quarters. Go to the holodeck."

"The *holodeck*. This is hardly the time for recreation."

"Perhaps it's exactly the time. Just . . . go. Be anywhere but here. If a situation arises, I promise you that you will be summoned instantly."

"But Soleta, I don't think that . . ."

"Robin," sighed Soleta, "leave before I have Mr. Kebron carry you out bodily."

"Can I?" inquired Zak. "I'm bored."

"Fine," Robin said in exasperation. Maintaining as much of her dignity as she could, she crossed quickly to the emergency stairs, since the turbolift had been unreliable at best. She clambered down and out of sight of the bridge . . .

. . . and for a moment, she almost lost her grip on the ladder.

She wondered what could possibly have caused her to do so, and it was only at that point that she realized her body was seized with great, racking sobs. Desperate not to slip off, she threw her arms around the ladder, clutching it like a lover, and she dissolved into tears while chewing on her lower lip so as not to let her sobs echo up and down the passageway.

iii.

Elizabeth Shelby was shocked at how wan and exhausted her husband, Mackenzie Calhoun, appeared.

She'd been sitting in the team room, along with Dr. Selar, Commander Burgoyne, Lieutenant Soleta, and Chief Engineer Mitchell. They all looked tired and shaken by what they'd been through, but that didn't surprise the *Trident* captain particularly. They were all fine officers; she knew, having served with all of them. They'd had a hell of an experience, though, and she couldn't blame them at all for looking tired, even a bit forlorn.

She was not expecting it from Calhoun, however. It wasn't simply that he was her husband and therefore she anticipated a certain level of performance from him. It was because, in all the years she'd known him, he was one of the most unflappable people she'd ever encountered. Not only did stress and difficulty not impede him, but he actually seemed to thrive on it.

Not this time, however. When Calhoun entered, there was a haunted look in his face, in his eyes, such as she had never seen. He covered it very quickly; when the others began to rise in response to his entrance, he gestured for them to remain seated with as much calm and control as he always displayed. They'd never have known there was anything wrong. But Shelby did.

"Thank you for coming, Captain," he said with impressive formality. She'd been expecting his typical, offhand "Eppy," his abbreviation for "Elizabeth Paula." He knew she hated it and derived perverse delight in employing it whenever possible. "And I should add," he continued, "that the thank-you is on behalf of everyone aboard this ship . . . or what's left of this ship," he added ruefully. Immediately he turned to Burgoyne and Mitchell. "Damage report."

They proceeded to give him a blow-by-blow description of everything that was wrong with the *Excalibur*. It was a staggering list. The Beings had done an astounding amount of damage, up to and including punching a hole in the saucer section that was sealed off by automatic forcefields. "With all of that," Mitchell commented, shaking his head, "it's a miracle we were able to rejoin the saucer and hull sections as smoothly as we did."

It had seemed a good idea, a smart tactical move.

Separate the saucer from the main hull and then fly both into battle, with Calhoun (and Morgan Lefler assisting) employing a new holographic technology that enabled them to be on both the saucer section and the battle bridge of the main hull. Unfortunately, it had backfired . . . or else it simply had not been enough. The damage sustained by both vessels had shorted out the holotech, and things had gone downhill from there. . . .

Maybe it wouldn't have if you'd been there.

As Mitchell and Burgoyne continued their report, it was all Shelby could do to banish such thoughts from her mind. Calhoun was a brilliant captain, leader, and tactician. There was no reason whatsoever to think that, if she'd been along for the ride, she would have been able to accomplish what he hadn't.

Except you did. They ran when you showed up. . . .

"Only because I had another starship," she said.

That brought conversation screeching to a halt as they all look at her in bewilderment. "I . . . beg your pardon, Captain?" asked Burgoyne.

"Nothing." She waved it off dismissively. "I was just . . . thinking out loud."

Calhoun nodded, looking as if he wasn't paying all that much attention. "Dr. Selar . . . total damage?"

"At last count, eighteen fatalities, forty-seven injured. Considering the violence of the attack, we must consider that number to be extraordinarily low."

"Almost miraculously," said Burgoyne.

"Miraculously," Calhoun said distantly. "Burgy, we've lost eighteen crewmen and we're only a few notches above dead in space. This isn't exactly the time to start dwelling on the mercies of the almighty."

Burgoyne looked in confusion at the others. "My apologies, Captain . . . I didn't mean to—"

As if Burgoyne hadn't even spoken, Calhoun said, "Repair estimates."

"Hard to say, Captain," Mitchell told him. "Until we get in to a starbase . . ."

"We're not going to a starbase."

There was a stunned silence around the table. "Captain," Soleta said cautiously, "Starbase 27 is reachable, particularly if the *Trident* takes us into warp-speed tow."

Shelby nodded. "That's certainly doable. Not the best thing for standard practice, but once we put tractor beams on and get moving, and we don't go above warp three . . . provided Burgy and Mitchell think the ship's up for it structurally."

"We should be able to hold her together," said Mitchell. "The question is—"

"Excuse me," Calhoun said, his voice far sharper than it had been before. "I believe I'm still in the room. Furthermore, I believe I've already addressed the idea. We're not going to a starbase."

"But Captain . . ." began Burgoyne.

"For future reference, Commander, those are two words that should never be combined in the same sentence . . . especially at the beginning."

Shelby saw the stunned look on Burgoyne's face, and on Mitchell's. Soleta and Selar, naturally, managed to maintain inscrutable expressions, although Shelby fancied she could see a flicker of surprise in Soleta's eyes.

Calhoun leaned forward and said, "This is the part where you say, 'Yes, sir.' "

"Yes, sir," Burgoyne immediately replied.

Nodding once, Calhoun continued, "We came to this area of space because we detected energy surges that we now know were created by the Beings. We're not going to run off because we got our eyes a little blackened . . . particularly considering that, for all we know, they're still out there, waiting to see what happens next. Well, if they're going to keep an eye on us, we're keeping an eye on them as well. And we can't do it if we're sitting in drydock at Starbase 27. Captain Shelby, I take it that the *Trident* can extend whatever aid is required in terms of effecting repairs?"

"Whatever is required, yes," Shelby said carefully.

"Very well. Chief, I want you to put together a complete list of what you're going to need to pull this ship together again. Manpower, hardware, the works. Have it for me within the hour."

"Within the—?" Then Mitchell paused, the expression of shock on his round, bearded face subsiding, and he simply said, "Yes, sir. Within the hour, sir."

"All right. Dismissed."

Everyone except Shelby began to rise, and she said, "Captain . . . a moment of your time? To discuss logistics."

Calhoun nodded, and the others filed out. Shelby watched sadly as Burgoyne limped away with hir leg in a massive brace. The brace was humming softly, resetting the bones even as s/he walked. Still, considering the fluidity with which Burgoyne customarily moved, it was a depressing thing to witness. On the other hand, at least s/he was still alive.

Calhoun sat again once they were alone, his fingers

interlaced, his face grim. "I didn't get a chance," he said, "to formally thank you for your timely—"

"Fine, glad to help, now what do you think you're doing?" demanded Shelby.

He stared at her blankly. "What?"

"What. Do you think. You're doing?"

"Are you questioning my command decisions, Captain?" It sounded as if he didn't know whether to be amused or angry, and settled for a combination of both.

"No, I'm questioning your sanity," she said, and rose to come around the table to him. "Mac, you can't do it. You can't make the kinds of repairs this ship needs out here in the middle of nowhere."

"You said you would provide whatever was required . . ."

"That's right," she said, "and right now what's required is some common sense. Your crew doesn't need to try and stitch the *Excalibur* back together against such odds when it's not necessary."

"I don't think I need to be lectured by you, Eppy, as to what my crew needs or doesn't need, particularly since you're no longer a member of this crew."

She blinked in surprise. "And what is *that* supposed to mean? What, are you now saying you resent me for getting my own command? Is that where this is going?"

"No, what I resent is having you second-guess me . . ."

"And what I resent is seeing one of the most intelligent men I've ever known thinking with his wounded pride instead of his head!"

"This has nothing to do with my pride."

"Mac, it has *everything* to do with your pride," she said, her voice a bit softer but still firm. She half sat on the table, facing him. "You absolutely despise the idea of limping back in to a starbase seeking help, because the truth is that you think you're better and smarter than the entirety of Starfleet and you see it as some great loss of face, admitting you need help from the fleet. It's ridiculous. Starfleet is a resource, and it's madness not to take advantage of that resource."

Calhoun said nothing; simply stared into space. Shelby knew that look all too well. He was going to say something; he was just going to take his own sweet time saying it.

When he did, it was with a long, frustrated sigh. "I got my ass kicked, Eppy."

"I wouldn't say that . . ."

"No?" He looked up at her.

"No. Well . . . not to your face."

It was intended to provoke a smile from him. It didn't succeed. Instead he drummed his fingertips on the table. "I've had setbacks, Eppy. Don't think that I haven't. Going all the way back to my warlord days on Xenex . . . it's not like I won every battle. But this was . . . this was different. When I was fighting to free Xenex from the Danteri, my fellow Xenexians came to me of their own free will, and we were battling for a common cause. Here, though . . . most of the people on this vessel were assigned. They're doing a job, and trusting me to keep them safe so they can do it. I let them down."

"You did the best you could."

"You know better, Eppy," he said chidingly. "I've never settled for 'the best I could.' That's a way of finding an excuse for not getting the job done."

"Not always. And no one thinks the less of you."

"I do."

"Well, now you're just getting into self-pity."

His eyes flashed with temper, which she was actually happy to see since it seemed more like the fiery Calhoun she was used to. "Have you ever known me to feel sorry for myself?"

"No. That's why I'd rather not start now."

For a moment, the old scar that lined the right side of his face flared a bright red . . . and then just as quickly subsided. "I wasn't feeling sorry for myself," he said softly, sounding just ever so slightly like a recalcitrant child. Despite the gravity of the situation, she couldn't help but smile.

"If it makes you feel any better," she pointed out, "it took no less than gods to kick the ass of the great Mackenzie Calhoun."

He rose from his chair to look her eye-to-eye. "They weren't gods," he replied. "They may be many things . . . energy beings, creatures of incalculable power . . . but they aren't gods. That much I know. And if they aren't gods, I can find a way to kill them."

"Mac . . ."

"They die, Eppy."

"Mac . . ."

"Eppy," and his voice became low and angry, but the anger wasn't directed at her. It was instead focused on the entities out there, somewhere in the void. "Eppy, I sat in my ready room and talked to Mark McHenry, and he told me these . . . Beings . . . are not to be trusted. In the privacy of that room, he expressed an opinion, nothing more. And he died for it, and Morgan died for it, and other good people died for it. These creatures don't walk away from that. I don't care if they're some advanced species. I don't care that they claim they can present us with some sort of 'golden age.' I don't want to study them, or understand their point of view, or try to comprehend their alien thought process. I don't care that our mandate is to seek out new life and new civilizations, because we sought out that new life, and it wasn't civilized, and it killed us, and I'm going to kill it back. And don't you for a moment think you're going to talk me out of it."

"I wouldn't even begin to try," she sighed. "On the plus side, I suppose this beats you feeling sorry for yourself. I do feel constrained to point out, though, that if you have any intention of taking on these individuals, you're going to want your ship at her best. Not held together with spit and baling wire. You're going to have to make some choices in terms of your priorities."

Before Calhoun could reply, the door chimed. "Come," called Calhoun.

Chief Engineer Mitchell entered, looking slightly apologetic as he did so. He had a padd tucked under one arm.

"That was fast," said Calhoun.

"I figured getting you at least a partial list to start might be a good idea, sir," said Mitchell. He sounded very tentative. That was quite a departure from Mitchell's normal convivial and wryly sarcastic attitude.

"Smart thinking, Chief." He took the padd from Mitchell and studied the specs on it carefully. His eyebrows knit and he shook his head. "I'm disappointed in you, Mitchell," he said finally.

Mitchell looked utterly crestfallen, and even Shelby was surprised at Calhoun's cavalier dismissal of the work done so far. "I . . . beg your pardon, sir?"

"Well, I should hope you would. Look at this. The amount of work that will be required to get this ship back into fighting shape, and you're trying to figure out ways to do it while we're sitting here in the middle of space. It's absurd. Obviously we're going to have to get to a starbase and have this attended to. I would think . . . what?" He looked to Shelby with an innocent expression. "Starbase 27? I think that would work. Don't you?"

"I think Starbase 27 would probably suit your needs, yes."

Mitchell's face became a mask of deadpan. "Perhaps the *Trident* could tow us there."

"That's a clever notion, Mitchell," said Calhoun, his face no more expressive than Mitchell's. "I wish I'd thought of it."

"Don't worry, sir. I suspect you will." He turned to leave, paused, turned back, and said with mock seriousness, "I just want you to know, Captain, that it's moments like this that remind me why it is that you're my role model. Brilliant idea, going to Starbase 27."

"That's why they pay me the big money, Mitchell," said Calhoun.

Mitchell bowed deeply, like a courtier, and left the room. After he departed, Calhoun reached over and took Shelby's hand in his. "Thank you."

She waved it off dismissively. "I didn't say or do anything you wouldn't have come up with yourself, eventually."

"That's true," he said. Then he drew her to himself

and kissed her. She felt as if she were melting against him, and then he drew back and looked into her eyes. "I hate to admit it," he said softly, "but in some ways . . . I do hate that you got your own command. Then again, you'd probably never have married me if that hadn't happened, because you would have felt uncomfortable being subordinate to me in the workplace."

She ran a hand against his cheek. "Mac, my love . . . if it's of any consolation, I never felt subordinate to you."

"Ah. That would explain all the cases of insubordination."

"Indeed."

"I think," he said after a moment, "I'm going to address the troops. They could probably use it."

"That's a good idea. When did Mitchell come up with it?"

That time he did laugh, and it sounded good. But the laughter was tinged with sadness . . . and she still saw the anger in his eyes.

At that moment, despite their power, she wouldn't have wanted to be the Beings for all the world.

iv.

Robin Lefler stood in the middle of the holodeck without the faintest idea of why she would want to be there. The vastness of the unactivated room made her feel all the more lonely.

She walked slowly around, her hands draped behind her back, trying to think of some scenario to activate. Nothing came to mind. Instead she just kept dwelling on her own insignificance and isolation, and all the things she should have said and wished she had, but now would never have the opportunity.

"I . . . don't understand," she said finally. "She . . . she wasn't supposed to die."

"Came as a surprise to me as well."

She jumped, her heart almost coming out her throat, and she whirled and saw her mother standing behind her. Morgan was utterly untouched, unblemished by any marks or burns. She smiled at Robin in that way she had, and that was when Robin realized that, of course, she was a hologram.

That had to be it. That was why Soleta suggested she go to the holodeck. She'd arranged for a holoprogram depicting her departed mother. She'd wanted Robin to have the opportunity to say whatever it was she wanted to the "face" of the dearly departed. It was morbid in a way . . . but also kind of sweet.

Still . . . it wasn't her. Not really. The entirety of her mother's personality . . . how could it possibly be encapsulated into some computer relays?

It's the best you're going to get.

Well, that was the bottom line, wasn't it. It was the best she was going to get. So she might as well do as much as she could with it.

"Hi, Mom," she said sadly, and she was surprised how her voice was choking up just from greeting this representation of her mother.

"Hello, honey. Surprised to see me?"

"Kind of. But kind of . . . not. Mom . . . you . . ." She steadied herself. "You told me you couldn't die. That you were immortal."

"Imagine my surprise," she said dryly. "In point of fact, Robin, I never said I *couldn't* die. I simply said there was nothing on Earth that could kill me. Remember? That's why I left Earth. To see if I could find something that could end my ages-long existence. I guess I found it." She laughed with a touch of bitterness. "That's how it always goes, isn't it. You stop looking for something, and bam, it comes looking for you." Then she looked sadly at Robin and took a step toward her, resting a hand on her shoulder. It felt so real. Of course it was supposed to. "I'm sorry, Robin. I mean . . . I lived my life. Hell, I live a hundred lives. But this must be so hard on you. First you lived for so many years, thinking I was dead, and then we found each other . . . and look what happened. Maybe it would have been better if we'd never met."

"Oh, no, Mom!" Robin said firmly, shaking her head. "I wouldn't have given up the time we had for anything. Not for anything."

"Even our vacation to Risa?" She rolled her eyes. "What a debacle that was."

"I know. But if I have to be stuck with someone on a world undergoing a complete disaster, I'd want it to be you."

"Thank you, sweetie." She patted Robin's cheek. "I'm reasonably sure there's a compliment buried in there somewhere."

Robin laughed. She had to admit it was a hell of a program. Soleta had absolutely nailed her mother's personality. "Look . . . Ma . . . I . . ."

Abruptly there was a shrill whistle piped through the intercom system of the *Excalibur,* a distinctive tone that went all the way back to the earliest sailing vessels. "Attention all hands. This is the captain," came Mackenzie Calhoun's voice.

"Oh, God, is it another battle alert?" moaned Robin.

"No," Morgan replied briskly. "Aside from the *Trident,* long-range sensors say we're alone."

She glanced at her "mother" in confusion at that, but then Calhoun continued, "After analysis of our current condition, it has been decided that the *Trident* will use her tractor beams to tow us to Starbase 27. Anyone requiring more medical care than we are presently set up to accommodate will be able to find it there, and the base has already been notified of our needs and will be prepared to deal with them. This has . . ." He paused, and then continued, "This has been a difficult chapter in the life of the *Excalibur.* But this ship is about far more than the vessel itself. It's about the crew working upon her. A crew that can deal with hardships and challenges better than any other crew I've ever worked with. Better than any other crew that's currently in Starfleet . . . although I'd suspect Captain Shelby might have something to say about that." He waited a moment, as if allowing for unseen laughter to subside. "The point is, I could not be prouder of any crew than I am of the way that this crew came through the fire and the fury of what we encountered earlier. We have sustained losses. We have sustained damage. It has not been the first, and I daresay it won't be the last. But this crew, this collection of dedicated people, can handle anything that's tossed at us and come back for more. I know that in my heart, just as certainly as I know that—in the end—we will triumph. We will be victorious. Our honored dead will not be forgotten, and I swear to you . . . there will be justice in their names. Captain out."

There was silence for a time and then Morgan said thoughtfully, "Well, he's not exactly Winston Churchill, but he certainly gets his sentiments across."

"Yes, he certainly does." She took a deep breath and let it out. "Mother . . . there's things I want to say . . . but I don't know how to say them, and I'm thinking this might not be the right time. Not when I'm busy wiping tears out of my eyes just looking at you."

"Oh, honey," said Morgan, and she reached for her.

It was more than Robin could take. She knew that Soleta had meant well, but this was simply too much. "End program," she said.

And Morgan blinked out of existence.

Robin Lefler ran out of the holodeck then, moving so quickly that she wasn't around to see Morgan Lefler flare back into existence, looking around with her hands on her hips and an annoyed expression on her face.

"Well, now that was just *rude*," she said to the empty room.

TRIDENT

i.

HE WAS COMING TOWARD HER, as clear as anything, he was right there in her quarters with her, and he was unmistakably, irrefutably real even though every aspect of her senses told her that it was just a dream, it had to be a dream, it couldn't be real, because her senses were her greatest asset and they were never mistaken, just never, and she'd had dreams before, many many times, and this wasn't like those, this was something very different, and it was Gleau, all right, Lieutenant Commander Gleau, the science officer who had used his abilities upon her, the "Knack" his people called it, and undercut her willpower so that she had willingly given herself over to him and now he was coming toward her again, and she was backing up, backing up, and suddenly there was no more room to back up, she was right against the wall, and she wanted to attack but she couldn't, she was paralyzed, she wanted to leap, she wanted to charge right at him, but she was rooted to the floor, her claws furled, and she was trembling, but not with desire, with fear, and Gleau was drawing closer still, and she saw that sparkle in his eyes that had at one time excited her, but there was no excitement in her now, just terror, just stark, stinking terror, and she tried to call out for help but she couldn't because her throat was constricted and there was nowhere to go and nowhere to run, and he was right there in front of her, and God, this wasn't a dream, it was real, it had to be real, it felt real, and he leaned in close with that frightful smile upon his face and he whispered in her ear, and his breath was warm and creepy, and he said, I'm going to kill you, you know that, don't you, because of what you did to me, because you went to Shelby, because you told her that I used the Knack upon you, and now I was forced to take an oath of chastity for as long as I'm on this vessel, and it's your fault, all yours, and don't you know they're laughing at me behind my back, and pointing and looking at me with utter contempt, and it's all your fault, M'Ress, all yours, I've lost face because of you, and no one does that to me, no one, not the greatest enemy that the Federation might have and certainly not some furry-skinned little nothing from another time and place, oh yes, M'Ress, you are going to die, I will come for you when you least expect, and I will kill you, yes, I will, and the best part it, I will get away with it, yes, I will, because no one will believe your warnings and no one will accept that you're in danger and when it does come, when I do kill you, it won't even look like a murder, and everyone will just stand over your body and shake their heads and say, Well, it's a pity about her, but really, she never did fit into this time and place, so it's probably better that she's gone, just gone, good-bye, M'Ress, your time is running out, you can't escape it, you can't escape me, farewell, M'Ress, farewell you little—

She woke up screaming.

ii.

Kat Mueller persisted in not being a morning person.

Indeed, that was why she had always been happy being an executive officer, the Starfleet equivalent of the first officer who operated on the nightside. (Indeed, considering her ability to perform on three hours' sleep, she was on call day and night for the *Trident* and consequently retained the rank of XO on her new ship.) She knew intellectually that there was no reason for her to feel preference for one time over the other. They were, after all, on a starship, bereft of natural light, having to depend upon dimming and rising of the onboard lighting to simulate a night/day shift. But night had always been her first, best love, going back to her childhood. Considering it was that ingrained, it was too late to fight it.

So as a general rule of thumb, Mueller tried not to deal with anything that looked as if it was going to be particularly challenging or aggravating when she first came on duty. Not that she wasn't capable of doing so. She had a basic way of handling it, which was to present an outer demeanor that came across as if she were paying attention. Meanwhile, inside she just kept thinking, *Go away, please, just go away,* but no one could ever discern that.

Therefore, given her preferences, she would just as

soon not have dealt with Lieutenant M'Ress first crack out of the box. But M'Ress had been insistent that she needed to speak with *someone,* and Mueller had the distinct feeling that if she didn't handle it, the Caitian would take it upon herself to go to the captain. Certainly M'Ress seemed agitated enough to do so.

Mueller had been in her office when M'Ress had first shown up. Mueller preferred to ease into the day by spending an hour or so dealing with routine problems, ship's issues, and such in her office, which was attached to her main quarters. It was not the general style for first officers to be anywhere but on the bridge; however, Shelby didn't seem to mind.

On the one hand, she was concerned over what had M'Ress so worked up. On the other hand, she didn't really care all that much and would just as soon have shut her down and sent her on her way. But she had given in to the inherent responsibility of her rank, and also to innate curiosity. As soon as M'Ress started talking, however, Mueller was regretting her decision . . . particularly since it was early in the morning.

"Let me see if I understand this," said Mueller, leaning forward, fingers interlaced and hands resting on the desk in front of her. "You're saying that Lieutenant Commander Gleau . . . 'haunted' you somehow? And while doing so, threatened your life?"

"I am saying that he projected himself into my mind and, while there, issued threats against me, yes." M'Ress spoke with total conviction.

Mueller suspected M'Ress had no clue how ludicrous the things she was claiming sounded. "Do you have any clue how ludicrous this sounds?" asked Mueller.

M'Ress stared at her blankly. "No."

Well, that confirms that. "Lieutenant," she said carefully, then paused, and refocused her attention on her computer monitor. "Computer."

"Working."

"Access records, Selelvian race. Question: Do Selelvians possess any powers of thought transference, astral projection, or mind-meld?"

"Negative."

M'Ress started to interrupt, but Mueller raised an index finger to quiet her and continued, "Question: Is a scenario in which a Selelvian inserts himself into someone's dreams consistent with any known capabilities possessed by that race?"

"Negative."

But M'Ress was simply shaking her head. "That doesn't prove anything."

"It doesn't?"

"Commander, right up until Captain Kirk saw one on the *Enterprise* viewscreen, the ship's computer at the time would have answered 'negative' as to whether the Romulans were an offshoot of the Vulcans."

Mueller shrugged. "Technically, it might simply have replied with 'Unknown.' "

"All right, but the point is—with all respect to the far-reaching capabilities of Starfleet records—the computer only possesses data of that which is already known. If the Selelvians are capable of doing what I know Gleau did to me, and they've kept it a secret, then naturally the computer won't tell you any different."

"I believe, Lieutenant," Mueller said frostily, "I know the capabilities of a starship's computer."

"I didn't mean to imply . . ."

"In fact," she continued, "I would daresay that just about every person who first set foot on this ship knew the capabilities of a starship's computer, with the sole exceptions of you and your fellow displaced associate, Lieutenant Arex."

M'Ress's mouth became a thin line, and the tips of her fangs showed. It wasn't threatening, but she was clearly upset. Not that Mueller was particularly bothered by that. "Commander . . . I'm not insane."

"I didn't say you were."

"I know when I'm dreaming."

"I should hope so."

"And what happened to me . . . what happened last night . . . it wasn't just a dream. It was a deliberate threat, planted there by Lieutenant Commander Gleau. Truthfully, I don't know whether he meant it or not . . ."

"Well," said Mueller in mock relief, "it's a relief to know that he's got that degree of leeway."

". . . but his intention was still clearly to upset or terrorize me in a way that would leave him with apparently clean hands."

Mueller sighed heavily. "Lieutenant, what would you have me do?"

"Bring him in. Question him." She pointed at the monitor on Mueller's desk. "The computer can detect when someone's lying. Ask him if he attacked me in my dreams. See what he says."

"Lieutenant . . ." Mueller felt like tearing out her blond hair, but she continued to keep her hands firmly on the desk in front of her . . . although her fingers were interlaced so tightly that the knuckles were turning white. "Lieutenant, the fact that we have devices on this vessel that can tell when someone's lying doesn't mean we can employ them whenever we wish. There are still Starfleet rules and guidelines, and a fundamental respect for right to privacy."

"What about *my* right to privacy?" she asked in exasperation. "How can I have any privacy from someone who invades my sleep?! You have to ask him—"

"I have no basis on which to do so! Don't you understand that?" The instant Mueller's outburst flew from her lips, she was irritated with herself that she had allowed it to happen. She was normally proud of her ability to keep her cool, probably stemming from her German upbringing. M'Ress, for her part, looked unruffled. Mueller almost admired her for that. Almost. "I can't," she continued, having brought herself under control, "simply start grilling Starfleet officers for no reason."

"There is a reason."

"So you say."

"I would have thought that my saying so would have been enough."

"Lieutenant," she said with forced calm, "if you said to me that you witnessed an incident, that would indeed be more than enough reason for me to pursue it. But the bottom line here is: *You had a bad dream.* Believe it or not, Lieutenant, we don't all operate autonomously here. We have logs to keep, procedures to follow. Do you seriously expect me to list in the official Starfleet recording of my activities, 'Cause of action: Time-displaced Caitian had a bad dream'?"

It seemed to Mueller as if M'Ress's hackles were starting to rise. With others, that was merely a broadly descriptive term. For M'Ress, it was literal. A low hum was coming from her that sounded like something that was the opposite of a purr. "Permission to speak freely."

She leaned back in her chair, her interlaced fingers now resting comfortably in her lap. "Knock yourself out."

M'Ress looked momentarily bewildered. "You want me to . . . what?"

"Permission granted," she said with a sigh.

Nodding and looking slightly relieved, M'Ress said, "Commander Mueller . . . I am not like you."

"A cursory glance would have tipped me to that," deadpanned Mueller.

M'Ress ignored the sarcasm. "To be a human . . . it's as if a large bag has been draped over your senses. You depend entirely—almost exclusively—upon your eyes. Your hearing is muffled, your taste is limited, and don't even get me started on your sense of smell."

"I'll make sure not to. Is there a point to this anywhere in the offing?"

"The point is that I have a far clearer sense of the world, and everything in it, than you." She leaned forward, looking like a caged puma. "And not only that, but I have a very clear sense of myself. I know what dreams feel like. I know how ephemeral they are in a way that you never could. And what I experienced was not ephemeral. It was not a passing fancy conjured by stray neurons. It was real. What happened was real. His threat was real. And you have to do something about it."

Mueller leaned back in her chair, nodding, her interlaced fingers now resting in her lap. "I very much appreciate your candor, Lieutenant. I really do. Allow me to repay that candor with some of my own."

"Hurt yourself."

"What?" Mueller stared at her blankly, but then comprehended. "You mean, 'Knock yourself out.' "

"Yes. That."

"All right." She smiled in a way that wasn't reflected in any other part of her face. "From the moment you came aboard this ship, Lieutenant, you have received special treatment. That angered me, and continues to anger me. You have special circumstances. That's nice. I don't give a damn. Every single person on this ship has their own 'special circumstances.' Oh, maybe they aren't the same as yours. Maybe not everyone fell through a time-travel device and wound up in a future century. But you know what? To all of those crew members, their problems and considerations and 'special circumstances' are as overwhelming and catastrophic to them as yours is to you. And none of them have received any sort of special dispensation. None of them are being held to a different standard. The fact is, you shouldn't be here, Lieutenant. The Starfleet of which you're a part is, literally, history. The ships you served on are relics, the people you served beside are dust, and the knowledge in your head is so antiquated as to be useless. At the very least, you should have been required to attend Starfleet Academy all over again. And if that was too much to demand of you, then perhaps you didn't deserve to go back out into space in the first place.

"You know what, though? Starfleet didn't feel that way, nor did Captain Shelby. Because of that, I was given orders and I have followed them. And you were placed in a position of authority in the science department that I did not feel you were entitled to. Then you became romantically involved with your superior officer, only to purport that you did not do so of your own free will. You claim *you* were harassed, yet *he* was the one who was mercilessly hounded by you and forced to sign an onerous pledge of chastity. And that apparently is not good enough. You now have the temerity to come to me and give me a flimsy story which has Lieutenant Commander Gleau rooting around in your brain and making death threats. Has it occurred to you, Lieutenant, that Gleau simply might not be thinking about you at all? Or perhaps that's the problem. Perhaps you actually, in some perverse way, actually want his attention, but have no idea how to go about getting it. I don't know. I don't pretend to understand your motivations, Lieutenant, but what I do understand is that your flights of fancy are taking up an inordinate amount of my time. Get me a witness that Gleau came toward you with a knife and threatened to turn your pelt into a hat, and I'll take action. But save the spooky bedtime stories for someone who doesn't think you've been treated with entirely too much favoritism already."

M'Ress's eyes had grown steadily wider and wider throughout Mueller's speech. There was a long silence after Mueller finished talking, and when she was finally done, M'Ress spoke. Her voice was low and choking, as if it was taking everything she had to suppress her genuine reaction to Mueller's harsh words.

Instead she just said, "I . . . appreciate your telling me exactly how you feel."

"Do you."

"Oh yes. Yes, you've done your utmost to make me feel welcome in this time."

"See, that's where the problem is," Mueller informed her. "It's not my job to make you feel welcome or coddle your neuroses. It's my job to help maintain the smooth running of this vessel and carry out the captain's desires." She paused and then added, "You are, of course, welcome to go to the captain if you are dissatisfied with my feelings on the subject. After all, you went to her when you were convinced that Gleau had 'taken advantage' of you."

"I went to the captain in that instance because I thought what Gleau was doing was a shipwide concern," M'Ress said slowly. "This, however, is far more personal to me. It's my life at risk, and no one else's. I thought therefore that it would be more appropriate to follow the chain of command and report directly to you."

"That's very considerate of you," Mueller told her. "And you're not going to go over my head now?"

"No."

That genuinely surprised Mueller. "No?"

"No." Whatever flashes of anger M'Ress had been displaying before were now so thoroughly reined in that Mueller saw no sign of them. "One of two things will happen. Either the captain will be forced to overrule you, which would be a most uncomfortable position for both her and you to be in, and I would just as soon not place her in that predicament. I have too much respect for the office of the captaincy to do that. Or else she will simply let stand your decision, in which case I will have wasted both my time and hers. So I see no point in either course."

"May I ask what you intend to do?"

"Whatever is necessary."

"And what might that be?"

"I don't know, Commander," said M'Ress matter-of-factly. "I haven't decided yet." She paused, and then asked, "May I leave now?"

"You came of your own will. Feel free to depart the same way."

M'Ress nodded, rose, and walked out. Just before she departed, she flipped her tail in a way that made Mueller wonder if it was supposed to be some sort of obscene gesture. But she couldn't think of any way to ask.

She leaned back in her chair, drumming her fingers thoughtfully on the tabletop.

iii.

Somehow when M'Ress got into the turbolift, she knew Gleau would be there. She didn't know how she knew; she just did. The turbolift had slid to a halt and when she stepped in, there he was. "Deck nine," she said. The doors hissed shut and the lift continued on its way.

"Lieutenant," he said with a slight nod of his head.

"Lieutenant Commander," she replied. Then she saw his small smirk. "What?"

"How nice that you are still capable of acknowledging ranks."

She didn't look at him. Instead she stared fixedly at the door even as she said, "I know what you did. Last night. To me."

"To you? I was in my quarters," said the Selelvian. She didn't have to see him to know that he was smirking. "Why, did something happen to you last night?"

"You threatened to kill me."

He sounded dumbfounded when he said, "What are you *talking* about?" He was certainly one hell of an actor.

"You threatened to kill me. Other people know. So if anything happens to me, suspicion will fall on you."

"Let it," he said flatly. "Let it fall where it will, because I would be exonerated should anything transpire, since I've no intention of killing you or anyone. I certainly hope you've no intention of spreading even more vicious rumors about me than you already have."

The doors opened. "My intentions are to step off this turbolift and go about my job."

"If you're so unhappy here, Lieutenant, you can always apply for a transfer."

That caused her to turn and face him. "You're not going to force me to run," she said. "That's not going to happen. I won't run."

"As you wish. Of course, you could consider walking very, very briskly." And the doors closed, obscuring his smiling face.

EXCALIBUR

i.

MARK MCHENRY WAS SCREAMING as loudly as he could, but he was the only one who was hearing himself.

He could hear himself produce sentences. He heard his voice calling out the names of every single person on the ship that he could think of. He gave the Federation Oath of Allegiance. He began reciting everything he remembered from the Starfleet Handbook for Cadet Protocol. He sung every song he knew, which happened mostly to be show tunes. He began rattling off the names of planets and star systems, and that took him a good long while. He did it all for two reasons: in hopes that someone would hear him, and to keep him from going completely out of his mind.

The former was not occurring, and he was beginning to have serious doubts as to the latter.

The oddest thing about his predicament was that he was able to see. He didn't know how that was possible, considering that he sensed his eyes were closed. Nor was he able to move a muscle of his body. Yet he felt as if he were outside of his body and inside all at the same time. But he wasn't so far outside that he was able to move from where he was.

He could "see" the sickbay all around him. He had been staring at it helplessly for a couple of days, seeing all the injured crewmen brought in and treated by an increasingly exhausted medical staff. People kept glancing over at him, staring at him as if he was some sort of truly piteous thing. Then he sensed himself being lifted up, relocated to another part of sickbay . . . probably so his continued presence wouldn't keep upsetting people. He could see all around sickbay, but he could not see himself. And McHenry was beginning to think that maybe, just maybe, that was a fortunate thing. These were Starfleet veterans, after all, accomplished and experienced crewmen. So if even they were daunted by his looks, then he must have looked pretty damned unpleasant.

Only one individual, aside from Dr. Selar, regarded him for any length of time, and that was—of all people—Moke.

Moke had approached him early on in McHenry's imprisonment, staring at him thoughtfully. It was as if Moke was trying to see past the shell that was containing McHenry, and into the man who was trapped within. McHenry had never noticed before how deep, even endless the boy's eyes appeared. He seemed to have what once would have been called an "old soul." McHenry called Moke's name as loudly as he could, and just for a moment he thought there was a flicker of recognition from the boy. But the recognition, if it was there, was quickly replaced with a look of caution. McHenry had no idea why the boy was reacting that way. It was almost as if he was afraid that someone might notice.

Then Moke walked away, and McHenry screamed after him. Then he began to sob piteously in frustration, and he'd never been more glad and relieved that no one could see him or hear him.

He lost track of the amount of time that he'd been there, trapped, restrained. Once upon a time, back in the dark ages of humanity's medical knowledge, a person could have something called a "stroke." A blood vessel in their brain would burst and they would become virtual prisoners in their own bodies. Cybershunts, of course, had long ago cured such physiological mishaps, relegating them to the same bin where other ailments such as smallpox, cancer, and AIDS had been deposited.

It gave McHenry a feeling for what it must have been like to live back then and suffer such hideous mishaps. He wondered how in the world anyone had ever lived their lives, knowing that at any moment they could be transformed into this . . . this state of nonbeing.

McHenry lost track of time. He had no clue how long he had existed in this twilight state, or whether he would continue to do so. He did, however, begin to notice a few things as he turned his attention inward.

He wasn't breathing.

His heart had stopped beating.

I'm dead . . . oh my God, I'm dead . . . well, this just stinks.

But it made no sense. If he was dead, why was he still lying around in sickbay? Since when had sickbay become a morgue? Were they . . . were they going to shoot his body off into space? Was he going to just float around forever in the depths of the void, an eternal prisoner in his own corpse? The airlessness of space would likely preserve his body under eternity. Of all the ways he had envisioned his demise and final fate, somehow he had never seen this.

For some reason, he'd always imagined that he would die while having sex. He wasn't sure why he'd thought that. Perhaps it was just wishful thinking. Have one's heart give out at just the right moment. Go out with a bang. It was the sort of stuff of which Starfleet legends were made. He was wistful for the days when he thought his passing would involve something as trite as that.

Day turned into night and into day and into infinity, and he was suffering from both a lack of, and too much, sensory input. As always, he was able to divine his literal place in the universe. The *Excalibur* was definitely moving. It was doing so slowly, cautiously. He began to get the feeling that the great starship was being towed, although he wasn't certain how he knew. He made some mental calculations, visualized their course and where it would take them, and concluded that they were heading toward Starbase 27. They must have been fairly badly hurt if they required aid at a starbase. Furthermore, he knew Captain Calhoun. Calhoun was a proud bastard; if he admitted that he needed help, they must have taken quite a pounding.

What had Artemis and her pals done to them?

"We gave you a beating, you pack of ingrates."

Mark McHenry let out a yelp and jolted in shock and jumped up . . . all in his head, of course. In reality, his body remained exactly where it was, unmoving, unresponsive. His thoughts were scrambled after days (weeks? months?) of lack of focus, and it took him a few moments (minutes? hours?) to string together words into a coherent sentence. *"Who is that? Is that you, Artemis?"*

"Of course it is. Who else would it be?"

"You bitch. If I could just get my hands on you, I would—"

"You would what?"

He had no sight, and yet she moved into his sight line. She was smiling at him, looking as strikingly beautiful as she ever had. Her more-than-human beauty still chilled him, although it was a far colder chill than he'd known in his youth. When she had first come to him, he had found it all exciting and amazing. He'd been too young to understand, and then when he'd become a teen and she had introduced him to other "aspects" of male/female relationships, he'd been filled with a sense of wonder and amazement.

Now she just scared the crap out of him . . . although there was a large measure of anger in him as well. Because of her and the other Beings, he was in this predicament. . . .

"Because of us, you are all that you are," her voice came, penetrating deep into his mind. Her lips didn't move. Her eyes were luminous, her thick hair cascading around her shoulders. *"The great Apollo lay with your ancestor, and his godhead is carried within you. You do not truly think you would have achieved your current greatness and position if the aura of Apollo did not surge within you, do you?"*

"My current greatness and position? My current position is prone, and my greatness is somewhat dimmed by the fact that I'm DEAD, YOU BITCH!"

She circled him, and for some reason no matter where she was standing, his viewpoint of her was exactly the same, unchanging, unvarying. *"You're not dead, my love. Not exactly."*

"Well then what, exactly, am I?!"

She was smiling. The charming facial expression would have chilled him to the bone, had he been able to feel any sort of sensation. *"Why should I tell you, dear one? After all, you'd have no reason to trust me, would you. That is what you told your own captain, is it not? That my kind are not to be trusted. Of course, you are an extension of my kind as well, so what does that say for you?"*

"Artemis . . . if you can get me out of this . . . please . . ."

"Offering me prayers?" She laughed softly. *"My, my, that does bring back a wave of nostalgia. And tell me, Marcus, honestly,"* and she leaned in closer to him. He would have felt her warm breath upon him provided he could feel. He wanted to scream, to claw his way out of this . . . this shell of whatever he was. But all he could do was lie there and continue to die, if that was indeed what was happening to him. *"Tell me . . . aren't you the least bit interested to know what it's like to be prayed to? It's quite a heady sensation, you know. It lifts you up, it makes you grateful to be alive . . . provided you are, indeed, alive . . ."*

"What do you want?" he said coldly.

"To help you. That is all."

"And how do you propose to do that?"

"Simplest thing in the world, Marcus. All you need to do is give yourself over to us, freely and of your own will. It's such a little thing, really. In fact, I can't believe

*that you've delayed this long. That's all I've ever
wanted. You know that, don't you?"*

"Be one of you, you mean."

"Yes, of course."

*"One of a group of creatures who assaulted our
ship?"* he said, and he wasn't sure if his voice was getting louder, rising with anger, but he certainly felt angry
enough to be causing that to happen. *"Who put a hole
through us? Who killed us? And why, exactly, should I
join with a bunch of murdering bastards like you?"*

Her face darkened. Literally darkened. He could see
shadows creeping across it as her quiet fury grew. *"Need
I remind you, 'my love,' that you are not in the best position for displaying such an attitude. I am the one who is
showing generosity at the moment. I could leave you to
rot. Perhaps that's what I'll do. That would do you some
good, I think. To just lie there, unmoving, trapped for all
time. Caught in a stasis of your own making, that you've
neither the puissance nor the knowledge to comprehend.
Or better still . . . I could end you right now. I'm not certain which would be preferable. Leave you to your condemned uncertain state of helplessness, or . . ."*

"Leave him alone!"

The unexpected voice jolted both of them. McHenry
didn't turn—that wasn't an option—but it was as if his
mind's eye shifted around, and suddenly he was looking
at a boy. For a heartbeat he didn't recognize him, and then
he saw it was Moke. The captain's adopted son was
standing perhaps three feet away, still favoring his injured leg even though it was mostly healed by this point.
He was trembling, although McHenry couldn't immediately discern why, and he was pointing straight at Ar-

temis, and shouting, "Get away from him! You . . . you get away!"

"Moke!" McHenry's desperate mind reached out. *"Moke, can you hear me?! Tell them I'm alive! Tell them to do something! Tell them—"*

Moke gave no sign that he had heard McHenry's silent plea. Instead he was still looking at Artemis, and he was advancing on her, his pointing finger shaking without letup, and he cried out, "You've hurt him enough! You've hurt all of us enough! You just . . . you leave him be! Leave all of us be!"

Her attention attracted by his shouts, Dr. Selar came over to him. Her face was impassive as always, but her voice carried with it a distinct sound of annoyance. "Moke, you should not be back here."

"Make her go away!" Moke demanded, and he was continuing to point at Artemis.

Artemis appeared completely disconcerted. Seeing her that way was something of a first for McHenry. Until then, she had always been completely in control of whatever situation she had thrust herself into. By rights, if Moke was any sort of irritant to her, she should have been able to dispose of him with a wave of her hand. Instead she was rooted to the spot, staring at the dark-eyed boy and apparently unable to do a damned thing about him.

Selar's frustration was mounting, although again she kept it in check. "Moke . . ."

"You will be worshipped, Marcus," Artemis said, sounding arch even though there was a tinge of desperation to her voice. *"You will be worshipped with us . . . or cast adrift on the byways of space, to spend eternity as you are now. Those are your only choices."*

"Make her go away!" Moke repeated.

"To what 'her' are you referring?"

"Her! The god lady! She's standing right there, in front of Mr. McHenry!"

And something within Selar, some fundamental intuition, told her that these were not simply the ravings of an annoying child. Her eyes narrowed, her interest obviously piqued, as slowly she said, "What god lady, Moke? Where? Describe her to me."

"She's gone."

And indeed she was. McHenry felt at once a swell of depression, and yet a simultaneous glee in that Artemis had apparently been chased off by this . . . this kid. *"Great job, Moke!"*

Moke did not respond. He was frowning at the air where Artemis had been, but he was not reacting in any way to the silent shouts coming from McHenry. Again and again, the frustrated navigator tried to get the boy's attention, but there was nothing. Not the slightest acknowledgment that McHenry was there.

Here McHenry had felt a brief swell of hope, only to see it being crushed as Selar said, "What about Mr. McHenry. Do you see anything unusual about he himself? Or just the woman standing near him."

"There is no woman," Moke said. He was tilting his head slightly, like a dog trying to home in on the distant trill of a sonic whistle. It might have been that he was, on some level, perceiving McHenry's cries for help, but was unable to discern exactly what they were. "And he's just . . . lying there. I think."

"Yes. Yes, he is," Selar said, looking with detachment at McHenry. "Moke . . . we shall reexamine that leg to ascertain the quality of the healing, and then we will speak to the captain about what you think you saw."

"I know I saw her," said Moke, but he allowed himself to be led away, leaving Mark McHenry crying to the emptiness within himself.

ii.

For Robin Lefler, it was as if her life had moved into slow motion.

First, it had taken seemingly forever for the *Excalibur* to be towed into drydock. Once there, the damage to the ship had been so comprehensive that additional crewmen and members of the engineering corps had been called in to aid in the rebuild. They'd been laid up for two weeks as it was, and the estimates for bringing the ship back up to working order were elongating.

Some of the ship's personnel had been put on temporary transfer to the *Trident,* which was continuing to patrol the area. Apparently the Beings had not shown their collective glowing faces again in the immediate vicinity. That, however, did not automatically mean anything. Who knew what they were up to?

As for Robin, there was an emptiness within her that she simply could not shake. She spent most of her off-duty hours in the team room, staring vacantly into glasses of synthehol and making polite chitchat with those people who opted to swing by and extend their condolences. A small, quiet ceremony had been held for the mortal remains of a supposedly immortal woman, Morgan Primus Lefler. Her body had then been placed into a photon torpedo casing and fired into the vastness of space. By this point in time, Robin imagined, it had been caught in the gravity field of a star and likely been pulled in. So . . . that was that.

Except it wasn't. She felt as if Morgan was still there with her, watching over her, whispering consoling words to her as she dropped off to sleep. She would have hoped that it would have eased her loneliness; instead it made it all the more painful.

With her off-duty hours stretching to infinity in the team room, Robin began spending more and more time at her post. Her continued presence started eliciting comments, but Robin turned a deaf ear to them all. At Burgoyne's urging, Calhoun considered ordering her to take time off. Ultimately, he decided against it.

"Everyone deals with grief in their own way, Burgy," he had said. "Who am I to decide what's right and wrong for Robin Lefler? Besides, we're stuck here at starbase. It's not as if we need her at peak performance because we're about to head into battle. We have some margin for error."

And so the bridge became Robin's second home as she did all she could to try and bring operations systems back up to speed. During those times where repairs called for the ops station to be offline, she would just sit there and stare out at the emptiness of space, picturing her mother's coffin tumbling away toward its fiery fate at the heart of a star.

"Wake up."

The words jolted Robin from her reverie. She rubbed her eyes and leaned forward at her post, realizing to her chagrin that she had indeed fallen asleep. Robin turned in her seat to see Soleta staring down at her with that vague Vulcan annoyance she so easily projected. "Ohhh God," muttered Robin, stretching her arms. "Falling asleep at my post. I'm turning into McHenry."

The moment the words were out of her mouth, she felt mortified. Soleta's face was like an expressionless mask. Zak Kebron, still at his post even though there was no need for him to be, looked up but said nothing. The rest of the bridge was filled with techies working on bringing systems online, and the name of McHenry meant nothing to them, but even they sensed that the mood on the bridge had abruptly shifted.

"I'm sorry. Sorry, folks," Robin said with genuine chagrin. "I . . . it's . . ."

"It is difficult to think of him as gone?" asked Soleta quietly.

Immediately Robin nodded, feeling a rush of relief. "Yes. That's it exactly."

"Understandable. Particularly considering the curiosity of his 'corpse' in the sickbay."

Robin shuddered at that. The entire thing had taken on an air of ghoulishness. Starfleet had even sent someone from the surgeon general's office, and she hadn't been able to make any more sense of it than Selar or her people. It seemed that McHenry's body was caught in some sort of . . . of cellular stasis, as Robin had heard it (admittedly thirdhand). There had been a brief hope that some sort of miracle might occur, that a regeneration of the cells would commence. Such had not been the case. He was just lying there. Starfleet had requested the body be turned over to them for more detailed analysis, and Calhoun had point-blank refused. That she had heard about firsthand, specifically because everyone on the bridge had heard Calhoun's raised voice from within his ready room . . . a certainly unusual-enough occurrence.

"You people can't seem to determine whether he's alive or dead!" he'd said loudly and clearly. "Until such time as you do, he's still under my command, even if he's just lying there. And there is where he's going to stay until we get this sorted out." Perhaps realizing he'd let himself get too loud, Calhoun had promptly reined himself in and the rest of the conversation was lost. The end result, though, was that "there" was indeed where McHenry had stayed.

Now Robin looked up at Soleta and shook her head in bewilderment. "Do they have any clearer idea of what's happened with him than they did before?"

"None," said Soleta. "It is . . . perplexing. I . . ."

She looked briefly uncomfortable, and Robin frowned. "What?" she asked in a lowered voice. "What is it?"

Soleta glanced right and left, seemingly ill at ease over the prospect of anyone else listening to her lowering her guard, however incrementally. But the rest of the bridge crew had returned to its respective duties and was paying no attention. "It is most illogical for me to find it frustrating . . . yet I do. I have known McHenry for many years, going back to the Academy. I dislike the current situation, and I am increasingly of the opinion that, if I can find some way in which to take a hand, I am obligated to do so. I have not yet determined, however, what that might be."

"It sounds to me like you actually might have determined it, and just don't want to think about it."

Appearing momentarily amused, Soleta replied, "You are most perceptive for a human."

A muttered curse came from across the way at the engineering station. A cybertech named Devereaux was working on it. Although he was in his twenties and purportedly quite brilliant (having spent his internship at the Daystrom Institute), he looked to Robin as if he was about twelve years old. Not surprising; most of the best and brightest computer experts looked like juveniles.

Soleta, who had been leaning over, stood. "Problem, Mr. Devereaux?" she inquired.

He scowled at her. "The mnemonics in your whole computer system are still off by a huge margin."

"How so?" She glanced at Robin and said, "The system has been functioning in a satisfactory manner, has it not?"

"Aside from when it screamed a few weeks back, yeah," Robin replied with a shrug.

"Yeah, well, it shouldn't be. The rhythmics are completely out of whack."

"Rhythmics?" asked Robin.

"Lord, don't they teach you people anything?" Devereaux said impatiently. "Rhythmics are . . ."

"Rhythmics are the electron flow of a computer's 'thinking,' " Soleta cut in, not even bothering to glance in Devereaux's direction.

"Right, except computers don't actually think," said Devereaux. "They process information, but draw no conclusions, nor do they have personalities beyond what we program into them to give a semblance of personalities. So the rhythmic for a computer is very, very consistent. It never changes, because it doesn't react to anything."

"And that is not the case here?" asked Soleta.

He shook his head vigorously. "They're all over the damned place. It's like the computer is . . . I don't know. Studying its own databases. Trying to comprehend what it knows rather than just regurgitate on command. Except it's impossible. The only time I've ever seen anything like it is in textbooks."

"So you're saying it's a textbook case?" Robin asked, confused.

"History textbooks. The M5 computer. A computer that Richard Daystrom had imprinted with human engrams. That had these kinds of hiccups . . . except this is a hundred times worse. I just don't get it."

"I am certain," Soleta told him, "that you will figure it out."

He gave her a sour look that indicated just how much her confidence in him meant before returning to work.

Leaning back in toward Robin, Soleta said softly, "You have detected nothing unusual in ops?"

"All systems seem normal," replied Robin. "Then again, I'm not running the sort of detailed analysis that he is." Then she chuckled and added, "Maybe I should ask my mother for guidance."

"Your mother?" Soleta's eyebrows came together in a puzzled frown. "Is that some manner of intended jest?"

"No, I . . ." Robin's cheeks colored slightly. "Not at all. I'm sorry, that probably sounded a little weird."

"Just a touch," Soleta acknowledged.

"I was just thinking about that program you created for the holodeck. It seemed so . . . so realistic. So much like her. And since she always seemed to have all the answers . . ."

"Wait." Soleta's head was cocked like a curious bulldog. "What are you talking about?"

"I know, I know," sighed Robin. "I should have thanked you for it ages ago. I'm sure you went to a lot of work for that, and I'm sorry, I simply got distracted with all of the . . ."

"Robin," Soleta said firmly, placing a hand on Robin's shoulder to command her attention. "I have no clue as to what you are referring."

"When you suggested I go to the holodeck a few weeks back," Robin reminded her. "And the holoimage of my mother was waiting for me. The one you put together."

"I put together no such thing."

"You did! You must have!" Her voice was getting louder, once again attracting attention. "I mean . . . why else did you suggest I go to the holodeck if you didn't have that waiting for me?"

"Because the holodeck can be a diversion. That's all," Soleta said. "I had no ulterior motive other than to suggest you engage in some pastime that you might find amusing."

'So . . . so what are you saying? That you didn't . . . ?"

"I believe," said Soleta with careful patience, "that I have said this far more times than should be necessary."

"Well then who . . ."

Her voice trailed off and very slowly, she looked at the ops station. She felt a pounding beginning in her head as matters that seemed too insane to contemplate began to occur to her. "It couldn't be," she whispered.

"What could not be? What are you . . . ?" And then Soleta's mind went in the same direction as Robin's, and she likewise was stunned at the notion, although the shock did not register as openly on her face. "You . . . are not insinuating what I think you are . . ."

"Devereaux!" Lefler suddenly called, and she didn't realize she was standing even as she rose and backed away from the ops station. "Stop fiddling with the computer systems a minute!"

"Fiddling?" He sounded very put out. "I would hardly term what I do fid—"

"Just shut up!" She licked her suddenly dry lips, cast a quick glance at Soleta, who nodded in encouragement, and then called, "Computer."

"Working," came the familiar computer voice. Except for the first time, Lefler noticed it sounded a little . . . too familiar.

Her mouth started to move, to try and form the next words, but nothing emerged at first. And when it did, it was as a strangled whisper. "Mother?"

Silence from the computer.

All eyes were on Robin as she took a step forward, cleared her throat, and said more loudly this time, "Mother? It's me. It's Robin. Mother . . . if you can hear me . . . say something."

Another pause, and then . . .

"You really need to do something about your hair, dear," came the slightly disapproving voice of Morgan Primus from the computer console. "Mourning is all well and good, but you don't have to let yourself go to seed because of it."

The world went black around her, and for the first time in her life, Robin Lefler passed out dead away from shock.

RUNABOUT

SI CWAN STARTED TO WONDER what was going to get to him first: the damage to the runabout's life-support system, or the deathly quiet.

Ever since the runabout had torn away from Danter, Kalinda and he had known that there had been systems damage from the farewell shelling they had taken. They had managed to keep the engines going, and between those and the simple tendency of objects in motion to stay in motion, they had continued on a fairly straightforward heading away from Danter.

They had watched for any signs of pursuit for the longest time. It wouldn't have been all that difficult for anyone chasing them to catch up in fairly short order. The ship was barely able to attain warp speed, and even then it couldn't maintain it very long without sustaining serious structural damage. No one, however, did. For a time, Si Cwan wondered why, and then it occurred to him: He and Kalinda simply weren't important enough to go after. It was a harsh realization for him to come to, and irrationally he almost wished that they had come in pursuit and blown them out of space. Better to be dead than ignored. Then he realized what he was thinking and cautioned himself not to repeat his sentiments to Kalinda, lest his sister give him that dead-eyed stare she used to indicate she thought he'd just said something amazingly stupid.

It was not long after they had made their initial escape that Si Cwan realized his ruminations about oblivion being preferable to obscurity might be coming to unfortunate reality. The systems-wide damage they'd sustained was worsening at an exponential rate. The runabout was simply not on par, in terms of quality, with similar Federation equipment.

The first thing to develop problems was the replicator, which would be providing them with food and water for however long they were out in space. Neither Si Cwan nor Kalinda were technicians; nevertheless, they did everything they could to effect repairs with the help of oral computer instructions. This worked right up until the moment when the computer suggested they slam their heads repeatedly into the console, then blow open the hatch and go for a long walk, at which point they realized the computer systems were malfunctioning.

So they eked out what they could from the replicators whenever they could get them to work in some sort of spotty fashion, and that kept them going for quite a few days until the air started feeling thick. It was at that point they realized the air purifiers were going offline. They weren't running out of air, but the toxins from their exhalations were being filtered out at a slower and slower rate. The Thallonians realized it would be only a matter of time before they were unable to function or even breathe.

They minimized their activities. Both of them were trained in deep meditative techniques, and they reached into that training in order to minimize both their breathing and their movements around the cabin.

Si Cwan had no idea how long this situation went on, because the chronometer had started counting backward. For a while he'd hoped this was indicating that they were, in fact, going back in time. That, at least, would be interesting. Eventually, he had to settle for the realization that something else was broken on the runabout.

Along with the navigation system, of course. Never had Si Cwan so wished for the presence of Mark McHenry. That amazing conn officer somehow always just knew where he was in the vastness of space, with or without guidance systems. Si Cwan, however, was not quite as blessed. He had a general idea of the star systems, but navigation was more than just being able to pick out stars unless one was interested in heading into a collision course with a sun. It meant being able to know precisely where a planet was in its orbit in order to find it. Otherwise solar systems could be mighty big affairs while trying to locate one particular sphere. And that was information Si Cwan simply didn't possess. Nor did he know where particular man-made outposts or space stations might be.

Besides, it wasn't as if the ship's engines would have been up for the voyage even if he knew precisely where to go. They were coasting well enough with occasional warp-speed thrusts, but the aim was to conserve energy in the engines because who knew when those might go?

The com system went shortly thereafter, so any sort of distress signal was moot. There would have been an automatic distress beacon on a Federation runabout, but he didn't know if a Danteri craft carried such equipment. Ultimately the entire question was likely moot. Even if it did have such equipment, the way things were going it would probably be broken.

And so they sat in the runabout.

And sat. And sat.

Because the *Excalibur* so routinely interacted with other vessels, and because there was so much to occupy one's time on the great starship, and because the ship went so damned fast, Si Cwan tended to forget just how gargantuan and empty space truly was. At first he had told himself that they couldn't possibly travel for too long without running into another ship that would be able to provide them succor. Now, however, so much time had passed that he was starting to wonder if the opposite was true. If they would, in fact, ever see another ship for the rest of their lives . . . however long that might be.

Every so often in the endless floating haze of their existence, he would glance over at Kalinda and smile, or give her an encouraging nod. At first he had been filled with confidence that they were faced with only a temporary inconvenience. That confidence eroded as time passed, although one could never have known it from the way he continued to look in a positive manner at his sister. What choice did he have? Focusing on the growing likelihood that they would not survive their predicament wasn't going to help anything.

But the silence was just . . . just staggering.

Naturally there was no sound in airless space. On a day-to-day basis, the *Excalibur* was filled with noises, ranging from the distant thrumming of the engines to conversations, laughter, argument, and so on. Here, though, there was nothing. Endless nothing. He thought he was going to go insane.

So he was slightly startled when Kalinda abruptly said, after who knew how long, "We're not getting out of this, are we." There was no whining or fear in her voice. She was very matter-of-fact about it.

He supposed he shouldn't have been surprised at that. She was, after all, someone who seemed to have extended congress with the spirit world. Kalinda tended to view death as an extension of existence rather than the end of it. Si Cwan didn't find that view comforting, unfortunately.

He wanted to lie to her. To tell her that everything was going to be okay, and that she shouldn't worry her pretty little bald red head. But he couldn't bring himself to do so. He had too much respect for her to insult her by feeding her cheery fabrications just to spare her feelings.

"I don't know," he said truthfully. He was surprised to hear his voice coming out as a sort of croak. That made sense. They hadn't been talking all that much. The smart thing would be to refrain from talking now as well, but dying in the vacuum of space was pointless enough. Dying in silence while waiting for it to happen seemed a true exercise in futility. "I admit, matters look bleak. But they're not hopeless."

She stared out through the front viewing port at the vista of emptiness before them, that stretched to infinity without the slightest hint of another ship in sight. "Not totally hopeless."

"No."

"But significantly hopeless."

He sighed and nodded. "Of sufficient significance as to warrant consideration, yes."

The silence settled upon them once more as Kalinda absorbed his opinion . . . an opinion that, on some level, she doubtless already knew.

"Any regrets?" she said abruptly.

He blinked. "Excuse me?"

"Any regrets. Over your life. All the decisions you've made."

"Ah." He could smell how stale the air was, and he was feeling light-headed besides. Every instinct told him that it was an obscene waste of resources and energy to be holding a conversation with Kalinda under these circumstances. But he couldn't bring himself to tell his sister to be quiet. For all he knew, this might be their last conversation. "Well . . . obviously I regret the decisions that have brought us to this pass."

"Really? I'm surprised. I mean, I personally thought this was your best decision ever."

He laughed softly at that. "I see your powers of sarcasm remain undiminished."

"I've worked hard to make it so. It's comforting to know all that effort hasn't gone to waste."

"Is there really any point to examining regrets?" He sighed. "Really. Wouldn't it be preferable to dwell on all the positives?"

"I don't see the point of that. Dwelling on positives would simply be an exercise in self-congratulations bordering on eulogizing. Pondering the things you've done wrong is more forward-thinking. It allows you to consider different directions you might take in the future . . ."

"Presuming we have one."

"Well, that's implicit, yes."

He had to admit, he liked her thinking. Dwelling upon roads not taken, things one might do differently. "I keep thinking about the fall of the Thallonian Empire," he said after a time. "I find myself wondering if there isn't more I could have done. Some action I could have taken that might have prevented it."

Kalinda shifted in her seat and rested her chin thoughtfully on her hand. "I'm not entirely sure what you could have done. Matters certainly spiraled out of your control."

"That's the point. I should have found a way to maintain control."

"I don't know if that would have been possible, Cwan, even for you."

"Yes, well . . . that's the aspect of 'regret' that's the most problematic. Determining what and what not to blame oneself for." He paused, and then smiled. "You'll think it's ridiculous."

"What? What's ridiculous?"

"It's trite."

"Cwan! Everyone regrets something. If you can't be honest with your own sister when death may be galloping toward us, when can you?"

He sighed. "Women."

"You regret women?" She looked at him askance. "Cwan, is there something you've not been telling me until now?"

"What are you . . . oh. No, not that." He smiled. "Nothing like that. It's more a case of that, in the entirety of my life, I've never had a genuine, long-lasting, relationship with a woman. I've had affairs, dalliances, to be sure. But the women who approached me when I was a nobleman of Thallon always seemed to do so because they were attracted to the power I wielded. I was never certain they felt anything for me, myself. Since the collapse of the Thallonian Empire, there haven't really been opportunities to explore any sort of extended relationship with a woman. Again, a dalliance here and there."

"Really? Who?"

"Kally," he admonished her, starting to feel a bit uncomfortable. "This is becoming unseemly. . . ."

"I was just curious. If you're ashamed . . ."

"I'm not ashamed!"

"Well?"

He sighed. "The executive officer of the *Trident.*"

Kalinda looked stunned. *"Her?* You became involved with her?"

"You sound shocked."

"I *am!* Aren't you at all concerned about Captain Calhoun's feelings?"

Si Cwan stared at her blankly for a moment, and then said impatiently, "The *executive officer,* Kalinda. Not Captain Shelby, Calhoun's wife."

"Oh." She looked confused. "Isn't the executive officer the same thing as the captain?"

"No."

"Oh. Then who . . . ?"

"Mueller. She's the executive officer."

"The blond woman with the scar?"

"If you must know, yes. Her."

"Poor choice."

Si Cwan was taken aback by his sister's offhand dismissal of Kat Mueller. "You speak to me of poor choices? You, who became involved with a meandering, shiftless rogue?"

Immediately he regretted saying it, but before he could even apologize, Kalinda said heatedly, "You will not talk that way about Xyon. He was Calhoun's son, and brave, and he saved my life, and I know you never liked him, but you don't get to say such things about him."

"I'm sorry."

"You just don't get to say them."

"I *said* I'm sorry, Kalinda. Now, please . . . it seems pointless to argue during what may well be our final moments."

Obviously she felt the truth of what he was saying, but nevertheless his comments about Xyon obviously rankled. "All right. Fine. And I . . . suppose I shouldn't have acted that way about the executive officer person. But really, Cwan, how you could have missed the obvious choice in your own life . . ."

"What obvious choice?" he asked.

"Robin Lefler, of course."

"What do you mean?"

She stared at him with unrestrained incredulity. "What do I *mean?* Si Cwan, the woman's *in love* with you."

He outright laughed at that. "Kally, don't be absurd. . . ."

"It's not absurd! I can *see* it! In the way she talks to you, looks at you. For as long as I've been with you on

Excalibur, I could tell she had the deepest of feelings for you. I always just assumed that you knew, but didn't reciprocate. It never occurred to me that you were just oblivious to it."

"Kalinda . . ." The very notion was so ridiculous that he didn't even know where to begin. "Kalinda, Robin was assigned to work with me as my aide, that's all. Now I suppose it's natural that, when two people work together, deeper feelings can emerge, but it's artificial. It's not real. It's just a result of proximity."

"I know the difference between artifice and reality, Cwan. I . . ."

Abruptly she stopped talking, seeming short of breath. He swiveled his chair to face her, took her by the arm, called her name. His lungs were starting to feel heavy, his head lighter than before. Everything suddenly seemed very amusing for some reason, but he couldn't for the life of him imagine why. He realized distantly that this wasn't something that had occurred all of a sudden. It had gradually been building toward this point, and he was simply becoming aware of it.

He visualized his willpower as a sword, hacking through the fog that was hanging over his ability to concentrate. There was a tight squeezing on his hand and he realized it was Kalinda. Odd. He'd forgotten she was there for a moment. "Don't say anything," he told her.

She ignored him. "Robin loves you, Cwan," she said, fighting to enunciate each word. "It's real. And pure. And genuine."

"Kally . . . she doesn't even like me."

Kalinda smiled at that. "You don't have to like someone to love them, Cwan. That's . . . the funny thing about love . . ."

He nodded, supposing that she was right. He wanted to ask her about things that she might have regretted, might have done differently. It seemed only fair. He called her name, softly first and then more loudly, but she wasn't responding. She looked exhausted. Or maybe . . .

He shook her. She responded, but very limply, her hand trying to brush away his in annoyance. He had a dim sense that a good deal of time had passed since she'd last spoken, but he couldn't be sure. He couldn't be sure of anything, except that he was actually starting to hear the pounding of his own heart.

I wonder how things could possibly get worse, he said, except he wasn't certain whether he'd uttered the words aloud or just thought them.

Si Cwan became convinced that he was starting to hallucinate, because it seemed as if space itself was wavering in front of him. Then he leaned forward, blinking his eyes furiously, rubbing at them. He wasn't wrong; something was occurring dead ahead.

Except it had nothing to do with space itself. Something was materializing in front of them. A vessel of some kind, with great flared wings and some type of extended "neck," but it was like none he'd seen before, and yet the markings of it were familiar as well. He fought with his floating mind to focus on what was happening, sift through the knowledge there and pull up an answer to what he was witnessing.

The ship was slowly coming toward them, and he pushed away random images of Robin Lefler—he couldn't even recall why he was thinking of her—to arrive at a realization that did not exactly fill him with cheer.

"Romulans," he whispered. "You know . . . the 'how can it get worse' thing . . . that was intended to be rhetorical . . ."

And as the oncoming Romulan ship bore down on him, he slipped away into blackness.

EXCALIBUR

i.

ONE OF THE ADVANTAGES Mackenzie Calhoun had found to being captain was that people and situations tended to come to him. Whether he was seated in his command chair, gathering senior crew in his ready room, or summoning pertinent advisors into a conference lounge, he was the one around whom others gathered. There was a certain elegance to that status.

So it was an unusual sensation for Calhoun to be pounding down the corridors of the *Excalibur* in response to an urgent summons from Holodeck A. Soleta had summarized the situation for him, and it barely made any sense to him. But he knew that he had to see it for himself. As a result, crewmen were greeted with the unaccustomed sight of their captain running fast past them. Some of them seemed compelled to say "Hello, sir," or something similarly innocuous. Calhoun ignored them all, hoping that he wasn't going to be putting people's noses out of joint, and promising himself he wouldn't worry about it too much.

He skidded slightly as he rounded one corner, righted himself before he could take an undignified tumble, ran halfway down another corridor, and arrived at Holodeck A. The doors slid open and he entered without having any real idea what he was going to be witnessing.

Robin Lefler was there, looking as if she'd just been whacked in the face with a tree branch. Soleta was endeavoring to maintain her customary inscrutability, but she was a bit easier to read than Selar was when it came to Vulcan dispassion, and so Calhoun could see that she was quite shaken. Also there was Burgoyne, who must have come as a result of being summoned by either Lefler or Soleta—the latter, most likely—since hir status as the most knowledgeable engineer on the ship might well be of use.

And, as advertised, Morgan was standing there as well, her arms folded, looking extremely impatient. The holodeck appeared shut down, its crisscrossing yellow lines along the floor and ceiling as always. Yet there was Morgan, big as life . . . or, in this case, a semblance of life.

The moment Calhoun entered, she turned her full attention to him. "You *jettisoned* my *body?*" she said with open incredulity. "You authorized that, Captain? Did it never occur to you that I might not be finished with it?"

Calhoun stared at her for a long moment and then, without looking away from her, addressed everyone else standing there. "If this is a joke, it's in exceptionally poor taste."

"It's no joke, Captain," Soleta informed him. "She's in the computer system."

"She *is* the computer system," Burgoyne amended.

"Her engrams are imprinted throughout the database of the *Excalibur.*"

"Can we purge the system and reboot?" asked Calhoun.

The question appeared to jolt Lefler from her stupor. *"No! You can't!"* she said, turning to Calhoun.

"I think I can," he countered. "I think I have that right, what with being captain and all. . . ."

"What a staggeringly disheartening lack of curiosity on your part, Captain," said "Morgan." "Somehow I expected more of you. You disappoint me."

It was a disconcerting sensation for Calhoun. He'd never been scolded by a hologram before. "Number one, I can live with disappointment. Number two, I haven't made any decisions yet as to how I'll handle this. And number three," and he looked to Burgoyne, "what exactly *is* this . . . this? It's not really her . . . is it?"

"That's open to debate," Morgan said, and before Calhoun could cut her off, she spoke right over him. He was so taken aback that he said nothing, just listened. "Remember we were hooked up to those devices during the time that the saucer section was separated from the main hull. The things that enabled us to have holographic bodies on the battle bridge while we were connected to them, via relays, from the saucer section bridge."

"Of course I remember," he said, taking care not to address it by name. Doing so gave it a status and hold on reality that he wasn't at all prepared to provide.

"Well, when my body got hit by the energy surge blasting out of McHenry's station, my mind was still literally in two places at once. So I became sort of," and she shrugged, "stuck. I'm in permanent limbo here."

"We have to do something," Robin said urgently.

"Can't we do something? We can . . . we can go try and find her body . . ."

Morgan took a step toward her and Robin reflexively moved back, obviously still spooked about the entire matter. The simulacrum of her mother stopped in its place and smiled understandingly. "Honey . . . the forces that combined to put me in this position were a one-in-a-million combination. I doubt they could be duplicated. And truthfully, even if my body could be found—which I doubt—it's beyond the ability of medical science to revive."

"We could clone it! Or . . . or re-create her body somehow using the patterns stored in the memory buffers of the transporter! We could—!"

"Robin, I prefer things remain this way!"

Her statement clearly floored Robin Lefler, who visibly staggered from her mother's words. Calhoun and Burgoyne exchanged surprised looks, and Calhoun stepped forward. He extended an arm toward Lefler, who was looking as if she was having trouble keeping her feet. She wasn't to be faulted. Granted, she was a Starfleet officer, trained to handle just about everything. But this was really a bit much. "What are you saying, Morgan?" asked Calhoun.

"Captain," she sighed, "in case you'd forgotten, when you first met me, I was trying to find ways to end my too-long life. I was bored. Bored beyond imagining. The only thing that's made my existence bearable in the past months was my being with Robin. Truly, sweetie, you've been a rock."

Robin was just shaking her head. Perhaps she thought that, if she did so sufficient times, this entire insane situation would simply go away.

"Still, the boredom, the day-to-day routine . . . it's weighed heavily on me," said Morgan. She was strolling around the interior of the holodeck, hands draped behind her back, and if Calhoun hadn't known otherwise he would have sworn that Morgan Primus was right there with them in the flesh. She spread her arms wide, as if to encompass the entirety of the ship. "But this! This is . . . this is *amazing!* I'm everywhere in the ship, all at once! I have a storehouse of knowledge and information at my fingertips . . . virtually speaking. The engines are a part of me, and so is the navigation system, and the weapons and defensive capabilities, and the sensors, and . . . it's . . . I can feel the vacuum of space against me, and I move through it like a swimmer through water. I . . ." She stopped, searching for words. "For all I thought I knew, for all the understanding I thought I had of the universe . . . it's been nothing. *Nothing!* It's like I've been living my entire life with a sack over my head. And now that sack is removed, and even though technically I'm dead, I'm more alive than I've ever been. I'm . . ."

She stopped in front of Robin, and Calhoun could have sworn there were actually tears welling up in Morgan's eyes. "It's like I'm in heaven and still with you, all at the same time. This is . . . this is a miracle, honey. It's a miracle. Can't you celebrate it with me?"

"How?" The word was torn from Robin's throat, and Morgan stepped back, clearly surprised. "It's . . . perverse! What am I supposed to do, huh?"

"What are *you* supposed to do?" Morgan looked perplexed. "Well, for starters, you can be happy for me. . . ."

"Happy for you?! *You're dead!* I mean," and her hands flapped about helplessly, "I mean . . . you say you aren't! But you don't *really* know that! Not really! You could be a . . . a glitch! A weird computer glitch of some sort, that *thinks* it's really my mother, but you're no more her than . . . than . . . than something really innocuous that I can't think of right now!"

Morgan made a loud huffing noise, which was an impressive achievement to Calhoun considering he knew she didn't need to breathe. "Robin, your mother is *not* a glitch."

"And what am I supposed to do?!"

"You said that."

"I *know* I did, but I don't have an answer!" Her voice began to crack, and it seemed as if the stressed lieutenant was speaking as much to herself as she was to the image of Morgan that stood before her. "Don't you get it? First I mourned you when I was a kid, thinking you were dead. Then I find out you're not dead, that you're some sort of eternal being . . . except then you die, and I mourn you a *second* time! Except, y'know, ta daa! You're back a third time, maybe, we think maybe you are, or at least a part of you is, and you have no idea what this is doing to me! It's *tearing me apart,* Mother! This isn't how it's supposed to work! Someone dies, you mourn them, you move on! That's how it works! That's how nature set it up!" And her desperate frustration spilled over into anger. "Oh, but not you, no, no! Not Morgan Primus Lefler Whatever-the-hell-your-name-is-this-week! The laws of nature aren't laws for you, no! They're like . . . like suggested guidelines that you just get to ignore!"

"Robin," Calhoun said gently, trying to rein her in. "This isn't the best—"

For the first time in her life, Robin Lefler completely ignored her captain, so focused was she on the subject of her rage and confusion. "I mean, is this just some sort of big game to you? See how many times and how many ways little Robin can mourn your passing so you can show up again! How am I ever supposed to have any sort of closure? Ever get on with my life? Your loss is this . . . this huge, gaping wound in my soul, and you just never get tired of opening it!"

"How dare you!" bellowed Morgan . . .

. . . at which point, every single system in the *Excalibur* went dead.

The holodeck plunged into darkness, and from the startled shouts and exclamations on the other side of the holodeck door, it was evident that the lights had gone out in the corridors as well—and, quite possibly, throughout the ship. All the constant hums of machinery which had become second nature to life on the starship now ceased, and suddenly the ground went out from under Calhoun's feet. In the darkness he heard outcries or gasps of annoyance from the others in the holodeck. Everyone was floating. The artificial gravity was gone along with everything else, and he realized it was only a matter of time before general life support became a problem.

And then, before Calhoun could even bark an order—although, truthfully, he didn't have the faintest idea what to say given the circumstances—the gravity and all the other systems snapped back on. Calhoun thudded to the floor, as did everyone else around him. He was grateful that the lights were the last things to be restored, so that no one else saw the utterly undignified manner in which he had hit the ground.

An instant later, Morgan snapped back into existence as well, looking utterly chagrined. "Captain, I am *so sorry*," she said. "I had no idea the ship was that keyed into my moods. I wasn't trying to hurt anyone, honestly. I would never do that."

"I believe you," said Calhoun, dusting himself off as he got back to his feet. "Still, you see the hazard that the current status quo represents."

"Yes," Morgan said slowly. "I . . . I do. Perhaps you *should* try to find a way to purge me from the computer system. Reboot everything. It . . ." She cast a glance at Robin, but couldn't sustain eye contact. "It would probably be best for all concerned. I won't trouble you again."

Obviously she was waiting for Robin to raise a protest, as she had when the possibility of her mother's erasure had first been brought up. This time, however, Robin remained stonily silent, staring fixedly at the floor in front of her.

"Morgan, wait!" Calhoun abruptly said. "There's . . . something I need to ask you."

She raised an eyebrow and remained where she was. "Yes?"

He took a deep breath. "The other day, Moke claimed that he . . . *saw* . . . Artemis standing over McHenry's body. That she was talking to him in some manner."

Soleta's head whipped around upon hearing this. "I was unaware of that, Captain."

"It wasn't a science matter, Soleta, and it was inconclusive at best," he said, looking at her oddly. "Dr. Selar brought it to my attention. It didn't occur to me that you needed to be informed."

"Nevertheless, Captain, it would have been preferable if you—"

"Lieutenant," Calhoun said sharply, "can this discussion of interdepartmental communication wait until after I'm finished talking to the dead woman?"

Immediately abashed, Soleta said, "Yes, sir. Of course."

"Thank you. So . . . Morgan," and he turned back to her, "I suppose what I'm asking is—"

"Is McHenry in here with me?" she asked.

"Basically, yes."

She shook her head. That simple gesture struck Calhoun as intriguing, because a computer's impulse would have been to verbalize a negative response. But Morgan was still thinking like a human . . . possibly because she was still human? It was all a bit much for Calhoun to take. "His consciousness wasn't 'in transit' as mine was, Captain."

"Then why would Moke have seen Artemis speaking to McHenry's body?" Soleta demanded.

Morgan shrugged. Calhoun couldn't quite believe it. Yet another human gesture. What the hell had happened here? "There are several possibilities. In no particular order of likelihood, the first is that somehow, in some way, McHenry is trapped in his own sort of 'twilight' area. The second is that Moke imagined it somehow. Am I correct in assuming, from the way you phrased the question, that no one beside Moke claimed to see the Being?"

"No one else," confirmed Calhoun.

"Why would Moke be able to see Artemis at all?" Burgoyne spoke up, scratching hir chin thoughtfully. "It doesn't make sense, Captain."

"No. No, it doesn't. Then again, nothing in this entire

damned thing has since Artemis first set foot aboard this ship," Calhoun said in annoyance. "Morgan . . ."

She was gone.

"Morgan!" Calhoun called out, his voice echoing through the room. Still no response. Slowly Calhoun looked at Soleta. "Do you think she . . . ?"

"Did away with herself in some manner?" asked Soleta. "I do not know, sir."

"No. She didn't," Robin said with certainty. There was an almost demented gleam in her eye. "She most definitely didn't. She wouldn't make it that easy on me." Her voice began to rise. "Noooo, she always comes back. Always. That's how she operates. I used to think she loved me, but now I know. I know beyond any doubt: She's *trying to drive me insane!"*

Calhoun was in front of her then, gripping her firmly by the shoulders. "If that's the case, it appears she's succeeding," he said grimly. "Robin, when was the last time you had any sleep?"

"Sleep is for lesser mortals, sir," she told him, her eyes looking glazed.

"Lieutenant." Calhoun cast a glance over to Soleta. "Be so kind as to escort Lieutenant Lefler to her quarters and make damned sure she doesn't emerge until she's had at least twenty-four hours' sleep. We're in orbit around a starbase; I doubt there'll be a matter of such urgency that we can't survive without Robin Lefler for a while."

"Captain," said Robin, "that won't be necessary."

"Your opinion is noted and logged. Soleta . . ."

"I'm not going!" Robin said with raised voice.

"Lieutenant," said Calhoun, and there was no trace of humor in his tone, "I did not issue a request just now.

You cooperate with Lieutenant Soleta, or I will have Mr. Kebron come down here, knock you cold, and carry you bodily to your room. Not only will *he* do as ordered without question, but he'll probably welcome it as a means of breaking up his day. It's your call, Lieutenant."

Robin looked as if she was about to make some sort of reply, and then wisely thought better of it. Mustering as much dignity as she could, she squared her shoulders, pivoted on her heel, and walked out of the holodeck with Soleta at her side.

As soon as she was gone, Calhoun called softly, "Morgan? If you can hear me . . . return now."

Nothing. No response, either out loud or in the form of Morgan shimmering into existence. There was just the silence of the holodeck and an uncomfortable cleared throat from Burgoyne.

In spite of the seriousness of the situation, Calhoun couldn't help but laugh slightly. "Just when you think this business can't get any stranger, eh, Burgy?"

"Captain," replied Burgoyne, "I'm a multisexual being who is mated with a Vulcan with whom I conceived a child that is aging at an exponential rate. My threshold of strangeness is far, far higher than yours."

"So noted," Calhoun said, glancing around the holodeck and wondering if Morgan was watching the entire exchange.

ii.

Soleta had not been able to bring herself to look upon the body of her fallen coworker and longtime associate,

Mark McHenry, because—and she hated to admit it to herself—it had simply been too upsetting a prospect.

It was a frustrating admission for Soleta to make. Despite her half-Romulan heritage (the fact of which she tended to keep to herself), Soleta made every effort to conduct herself with the demeanor and dispassion of a full-blooded Vulcan. In her heart, she knew that she didn't always succeed, but she certainly tried her best.

Despite that, she had found herself much more upset over the demise of McHenry than she had anticipated. She looked back at their days in the Academy together and realized with a sort of awe just how remarkably young they had truly been . . . which was impressive in retrospect considering that, at the time, they had felt very old and grownup. She marveled retroactively at her ignorance, and couldn't help but wonder how she would feel when she was much older about the way she was at this particular moment in time.

Presuming she lived to be much older.

Well, that was it, wasn't it.

McHenry was the first person whom Soleta had lost whom she had considered a true contemporary. It wasn't only the loss of a fellow crewman; it was a stark reminder of her own mortality. And considering that ideally her life span would be far longer than that of a human, the prospect of dying at such a young age was a truly daunting one.

Even though the situation involving McHenry's body was of scientific interest, she had nevertheless given it a wide berth. She had told herself there was no reason, really, for her to get involved. It was more a medical proposition than anything, and Dr. Selar had a handle on it. She also knew that Starfleet Medical was endeavoring to get involved, and that Captain Calhoun was insisting that McHenry's—corpse, or whatever it was—stay right where it was.

Now, though . . . now she could ignore it no longer. Because having learned what Moke had claimed to have seen opened a door to possibilities that Soleta wasn't able to close again.

What if Moke had been right? What if Artemis really had been there, invisible to the eyes of everyone else in sickbay? Soleta's mind was racing even as she headed to sickbay. If that was the case, though, why had Moke been able to see her when no one else could? Well, there were several possibilities. Perhaps the fact that he was a child had something to do with it. Or Moke's particular species, perhaps. He wasn't human, after all, or Vulcan, or a member of any race currently serving aboard the *Excalibur*. So perhaps his brain waves had a unique signature of some sort.

Bottom line, there were all sorts of possibilities. But the possibility that loomed most large for Soleta was the notion that maybe, just maybe, Artemis had indeed been there and speaking to McHenry because he was, in some manner, alive. If that was the case, and Soleta did nothing about it, then she would be abandoning McHenry at a time when he needed her more than ever before.

She entered sickbay and attracted no notice at all. Selar was busy consulting with a med tech about something or other, and that was fine with Soleta. She strongly suspected that, if she asked Selar's permission to do what she was intending to, Selar would not only turn her down flat, but ban her from sickbay for anything short of Selar's head falling off.

She had no reason to know where McHenry's body was, and yet she found it with no problem, secluded off at a far end of sickbay. She glanced right and left before stepping into the small chamber, and then looked up at the life readings. Nothing. Straight negatives across the board. He was dead; there was no doubt about it. Not even the most minimal of brain activity to indicate anything other than that her old associate was dead.

And yet . . . and yet . . .

She stood over him, licking lips that had suddenly gone bone dry. The thought of what she was about to do horrified her to the core, but she could see no other option. She took a deep breath, let it out slowly, and then reached into her own mental center and calmed herself. She slowed her breathing, even her heart, penetrating to the peaceful nucleus of her very being so that she could find the inner strength to do what she needed to.

Her long fingers fluttered, hesitated. Preparing to send her mind into what might well be a dead brain was the psychic equivalent of plunging one's unprotected hands into raw sewage. The very notion was repulsive; most schools of teaching of the Vulcan mind-meld absolutely forbade it. It was considered a perversion of a very sacred technique. To engage in it was to taint one's very *katra,* perhaps beyond reclamation.

Soleta took a deep breath, clearing her mind, shoving aside any hesitations. Entering a mind-meld, even a routine one, could be fatal if there were any doubts. And this was certainly anything but routine.

She slowed her breathing, let her consciousness begin

to slip away, malleable, flowing like water, envisioning the mind of her subject as a receptacle into which she could pour her essence. Her initial skittishness evaporated, simply because she didn't allow for it to exist. Instead, having resolved to do what she felt needed doing, she remembered one of the most important rules of a mind-meld: Confidence. Confidence at all times that one would accomplish what needed to be done. Confidence in one's sense of self, in one's ego. Because to lose confidence was to risk being pulled into the mind of the other, and having an exceptionally difficult time finding the way back. Considering the nature of the other in this case, Soleta could not afford to engage in the endeavor with anything other than total commitment and a certainty that she would be able to achieve her goal.

She eased herself in, at first slightly tentative, like a bather dabbing her feet into a pool of icy water. Then she took a breath, fully committed herself, and eased her mind into

Nothing, there were nothing there, just black void, just emptiness, he was gone, that's all, simply gone, and it was madness for her to be there, she knew it, this was an unnatural act she was engaging in, an exercise in necrophilia, there was no point to this at all, Mark McHenry was nowhere to be found, his soul had wandered away, gone to wherever such things went, and this was perverse, this was a sick exercise in, wait, what's that, just up ahead, she sensed something, something in the blackness that surrounded her, something in the void that seemed to whisper to her and urge her to come forward, deeper, and there was a soft glow from so far away, so very far, far away, and in the times that she had performed a mind-meld before, she had undergone some difficulties and taken on some challenges, but she had never seen a mind so far removed, she had never needed to probe so far into the very essence of another being, this was no mind-meld, this was no blending of minds, no halfway meeting, this was Soleta thrusting the entirety of her essence as far as she possibly could, and for a heartbeat, a heartbeat she could actually hear, she hesitated, and then she shrugged the hesitation away like an old coat and literally/virtually swam through the blackness, envisioning herself as a swimmer, which was a good trick considering she couldn't swim, and she plunged forward and down, her arms swinging in great arcs, her legs scissoring, and the chill invaded every aspect of her essence, and down further she went, the cold everywhere now, seeping in through her imaginary bones, slowing her imaginary joints, and down further into darkness until she reached the point where she was sure she would never be able to return and still she went, and she heard him, an unimaginable distance, crying out to her, calling her name, seeking succor, and she tried to call back to him but her lungs were paralyzed and might actually have collapsed in her virtual chest, and she reimagined herself, she saw herself as a being of purest light in the darkness, because she was confident in her goal and knew that she represented the forces of light and purity and goodness, and she was not going to leave him behind and she was calling to him, and he was answering . . .

. . . and the deaths were there, the dead Romulans, and it all came spinning back to her, when she had gone to the Romulan homeworld, to carry out the last bidding

of the Romulan bastard who was her father, and that last bidding had turned out to be a sinister trick into which she had guilelessly walked, and the result had been an explosion that had killed dozens, maybe hundreds of Romulans, and it was all her fault, and she had run away without taking responsibility, which was certainly consistent as she had hidden the true nature of her heritage from Starfleet, so who was she to pretend she had clean hands, who was she to present herself as some sort of heroine coming to save the day, and all the fears and uncertainties hammered into her, pounding her back, and she sensed that they were coming from somewhere else, originating from some source that stood between her and McHenry, and McHenry was crying out to her, begging her not to leave him, and she thrust forward as hard as she could, but for every action there is always an equal and opposite reaction, as science officer she knew that, and this was no exception, for as she tried to lunge forward, to impart a fragment of her own essence to aid McHenry in the dark prison of the soul where he was being kept, the horror of what she had done, the screams of dying Romulans, the searing of their flesh from their bones, the blood, the gore, the suffering and agony, it all came at her in one great black rush and then Soleta's own screams were mingling with the Romulans', and it was horrible, just horrible, and she wanted to die, wanted to end herself right there, right then, just drive a psychic knife deep into her own katra *and terminate the suffering and the guilt, and the blackness spun around her like an ebony tornado, the whirling both trying to pull her down and push her up, and she felt herself being torn apart, just shredded, just . . .*

. . . SOLETA, SOLETA NOW, COME TO ME NOW . . .

. . . and Soleta tumbled backward, her arms waving about helplessly, trying to grab handholds on empty air. She collapsed, and the only thing that prevented her from hitting the floor were the strong arms of Dr. Selar.

"You are out. You are out. It is over," Selar kept saying, and Soleta looked around to see the confused and concerned expressions of medical technicians. For a heartbeat she forgot where she was, and then remembered. Sickbay. McHenry.

"McHenry," she whispered, and her voice was raspy and constricted. "McHenry . . . he's in there. He's . . ."

"Calmly, Lieutenant," Selar said to her, and then Soleta felt the push of something against her forearm, and the telltale hiss of a spray hypo. "Calm yourself." Waving off the other technicians, Dr. Selar eased Soleta over toward a diagnostic table and helped her lie down on it. Whatever the drug Selar had pumped into Soleta's system, it was obviously working, as Soleta's pounding heart and scrambled mind began to relax and settle into their more normal patterns.

Selar glanced up at the readings and nodded in mute approval of what she was seeing. "Now then, Lieutenant," she said, "would you mind telling me what you thought you were doing?"

"Mind-meld . . . with McHenry . . ."

If Selar felt any revulsion at the concept—a revulsion that would have been as culturally ingrained in her as it would be in Soleta—she covered it with her customary aplomb. "That was ill advised" was all she said.

"I had to try. Had to see if he was there."

Selar pursed her lips slightly, obviously considered a

dozen rebukes she could have said, and just as obviously set them all aside. Instead she simply asked, "And was he?"

"I . . . believe so."

Just as Selar did not permit annoyance to play out on her face, neither did she allow excitement or hope. But there was a brief flash of both of those in her eyes. "Did you communicate with him? Did he provide any guidance?"

Soleta tried to shake her head, and found it too much effort. Instead she just said, "I . . . I wasn't able to. It was as if . . . something was blocking me. I tried to bring him out. Impart to him some of my own . . . vitality."

Selar raised an eyebrow. "What are you saying? That you endeavored to convey some of your own life essence to him? Do you have any comprehension how dangerous that is?"

"If I did not before, I do now."

"Lieutenant," Selar said stiffly, "you are not to attempt such a thing again. Not ever. Not in my sickbay. Not on any vessel on which I am CMO. Is that understood?"

Soleta's gaze fully focused on Selar for the first time. "You pulled me out. You brushed your mind with mine . . . and pulled me out."

Selar gave the closest equivalent of a shrug in her bodily vocabulary. "You have . . . extended yourself in the past to me, when I required aid. I have not forgotten that. As a fellow Vulcan, and as ship's chief doctor, I can do no less. Nevertheless . . ."

"I should never do it again." This time she managed a nod. "I won't. But . . ." She sounded close to despondent. "What of McHenry?"

"What of him? Do you believe your . . . rash . . . behavior had any sort of result?"

And as the full effects of the sedative took hold of Soleta, she closed her eyes and whispered, "I have no idea," before drifting to sleep.

iii.

Mark McHenry stood in the middle of the corridor outside sickbay and stared at his hands, his feet, his body.

He was there. He was alive. He was whole.

"All right, Soleta!" he shouted with more joy than he'd ever displayed in his entire life.

At that moment he heard a cry of "Xyon! Get back here!" And here, around the corner, came Xyon, the young son of Dr. Selar and Commander Burgoyne. He was literally galloping down the hallway on feet and hands, like a small ape. Moke was directly behind him, having agreed to undertake the not inconsiderable responsibility of keeping an eye on the irrepressible half-breed child.

Xyon blew right past McHenry without a second look, but Moke skidded to a halt. His eyes went wide as he stared at McHenry.

"Moke! I'm back! Everything's okay!" said McHenry.

Moke threw himself against the far wall, as if he needed the corridor for back support. He slid slowly along it, easing his way past McHenry while never taking his eyes off him. McHenry stared at him in bewilderment. "Moke? What's wrong? It's me, Mark McHen—"

And with a terrified yelp, Moke dashed off down the hallway in the same direction as Xyon had gone, limping ever so slightly, but otherwise moving with a great deal of speed.

"—ry," he finished, not comprehending what could possibly be wrong.

Then he looked down.

And saw no shadow.

Other crewmen were walking casually past him, paying no attention to him. Quickly McHenry stepped into the path of one of them, and they walked right through him without slowing.

"This can't be good," said Mark McHenry.

"It gets worse," said a low voice from behind him.

He turned and saw an elderly, bearded man with one eye standing directly behind him.

"Much worse," said the one-eyed man.

TRIDENT

i.

KAT MUELLER STRODE into Captain Shelby's ready room with her customary confident stride, but her face was a picture of concern. Shelby looked up as Mueller draped herself across the nearest chair and said briskly, "Our attempts to reach Si Cwan on Danter have proven unsuccessful."

"Damnation," muttered Shelby, shaking her head, and tilted back in her chair. "This is the most insane thing I've ever heard. And I'm someone who witnessed a giant flaming bird hatching out of a planet."

"I might agree with you, Captain, if I had the faintest idea of what we were talking about."

Shelby winced, chagrined that she had overlooked the obvious. "My apologies, XO. You're usually so on top of matters, that it literally didn't occur to me I hadn't told you the latest intel from Starfleet." She leaned forward and rested her interlaced hands on the desktop.

"While we've been out here, looking for signs of the Beings . . . apparently they've been setting up shop on Danter."

"Set up shop? In what sense?"

"According to Starfleet, they are offering ambrosia—the legendary food of the gods—to the Danteri. Supposedly they are out to bring a new golden age to Danter."

"In short," said Mueller, "they've offered the Danteri the exact same deal they were putting forward to Captain Calhoun . . . except the Danteri have taken them up on it. But how does Starfleet know of it?"

"Apparently they haven't been doing much to keep it a secret," Shelby told her. "Word's leaking out to neighboring worlds. There's a good deal of interest, but the Danteri are playing their hand rather closely. Supposedly the Beings were rather 'put off' by the initial reticence Mac displayed. So they're carefully regulating the availability of ambrosia, endeavoring to restrict it to those who are considered 'worthy.' "

"And the Danteri are worthy?" asked Mueller with raised eyebrow and a look of tolerant amusement.

"Apparently so." Shelby blew air impatiently between her lips. "I can only think that Mac would have a fit over that. After all, the Danteri were the original conquerors of Mac's people, the Xenexians, before Mac organized the revolt that threw them off Xenex. I doubt he'd be pleased to know that the Danteri have formed an alliance with the creatures who brutalized the *Excalibur.*"

"On the other hand," observed Mueller, "he might

find some amusement in the notion that the Danteri are lapping up his leftovers."

"Yes. Yes, that might appeal to his sense of the perverse. Still, my major concern now is Si Cwan and Kalinda."

"Why should it be a concern?" asked Mueller reasonably. "They knew the risks they were taking in getting involved with the Danteri and taking them up on their offer of a new Thallonian Empire. If the Danteri had abruptly switched allegiances, and Si Cwan has become so much excess baggage, I don't have a good deal of sympathy for him."

"I find that an odd attitude for you to have, XO."

"Why?"

"Because"—Shelby shifted uncomfortably in her seat—"well . . . not that it's any of my business . . ."

"You're the captain of the *Trident*. Everything is your business," Mueller said primly.

"Yes, well . . ." She cleared her throat. "My understanding, from what I've heard—not that I listen to gossip, of course—"

"Of course."

"—but I'd heard that you and Si Cwan were . . . romantically involved."

Mueller shook her head, strands of her blond hair swinging around her face. She brushed them back and readjusted the bun she kept the rest of her hair tied in. "That is not accurate."

"Ah. O—"

"We simply had sex."

"—kay." She blinked. "Having sex isn't the same as being romantically involved?"

"Not if you do it correctly," said Mueller.

"Sometimes, XO, I really don't understand you."

"I assume you're referring to those times that I get completely drunk and start speaking only in German," Mueller said. When Shelby offered a guttural laugh at that, Mueller permitted a small smile, and then continued, "Are we to return to Danter then?"

"It was my first impulse," Shelby said. "But Starfleet wants *Trident* to remain here."

"Here? In the middle of nowhere? Captain, with all respect, that's absurd. We've been surveying the sector, trying to find a trace of the Beings. If we now know they're involved in planetary politics on Danter, why stay here?"

"Exactly the question I posed to Starfleet."

"And their response?"

"They told me they wanted *Trident* to remain here."

Mueller grunted at that. "Why am I not surprised."

Suddenly the com unit whistled in the ready room. "Hash to Captain," came the voice of the *Trident* ops officer, Romeo Takahashi.

Shelby immediately noticed that his customary leisurely (and most likely affected) drawl was absent, and that promptly got her full attention. If Hash was all business, something was up.

"Shelby here."

"Captain, you might want to get out here. We got a Romulan ship decloaking a thousand kils to starboard. And it ain't like any Romulan ship I've ever seen."

"Shields up," Shelby said immediately. If a Romulan ship was dropping its cloaking device, that could easily be a precursor to an attack, and she was not about to take the chance that it was otherwise. She was on her feet even as she snapped out the order, and Mueller was preceding her out the door.

ii.

It was a Romulan vessel, all right. The markings, the general shape were most distinctive. But Hash had been absolutely on the money: It was like no other Romulan ship that Shelby had ever seen. "XO?" she floated the unvoiced question, since Mueller was generally rather on top of things such as odd bits of knowledge.

Mueller simply shook her head, even as she took her post at the second-in-command station. "Unfamiliar with it, Captain."

"Talk to me, people. What have we got?"

Arex was positioned at tactical; the Triexian was running scans with his three capable arms moving in all directions at once. "Energy pattern is definitely that of a Romulan ship, Captain . . . as if the presence of a cloaking device wasn't sufficient."

"Weaponry?"

"Two heavy-duty plasma cannons, a photon torpedo array . . ."

"Are they running weapons hot?" asked Shelby, her gaze fixed on the newcomer.

"Negative, Captain. They're just sitting there."

"It's not a warbird . . . it's not a bird-of-prey," Hash was muttering. "What the hell is it?" He glanced at Mick Gold, the conn operator who was seated near him. Gold, a slender young black man who was rarely at a loss in coming up with arcane facts, simply shrugged.

The turbolift doors hissed open and Lieutenant Commander Gleau entered. The science officer took one look at the monitor screen and said in surprise, "I'll be damned. A bird-of-paradise."

All heads snapped around and looked at him. "A *what?*" demanded Shelby.

"That's what Starfleet calls it," said Gleau, heading over to the science station. "We don't know what the Romulans call it. I've heard it described, but never actually seen it. There's only one in the Romulan fleet. It belongs to the emperor."

"The *Romulan* emperor?" asked Hash.

Gleau looked to the ops officer with a slightly withering glance. "No, Lieutenant, the emperor Julius Caesar."

"Belay the sarcasm, Gleau," Mueller snapped.

Gleau bobbed his head slightly in acknowledgment, but still had that smug expression on his face.

"What would the Romulan emperor be doing out here?" Shelby wondered.

"I doubt he's aboard," said Mueller. "If the emperor were going somewhere, Romulan protocol would certainly require an escort."

"My surmise as well, Commander," said Gleau. "I'd theorize that it's serving to transport someone whom the emperor holds in high regard. To attack the bird-of-paradise would be regarded as tantamount to an attack on the emperor himself, and would earn the enmity of the whole of the Romulan empire."

"It'd be a more daunting message if more people

knew what the damned thing was," muttered Shelby. "Arex, see if you can raise them."

"Unnecessary, Captain. They're hailing us."

"Are they?" Shelby shrugged. "Well, then . . . let's see what they have to say."

The screen wavered for a moment, and then a face filled the screen. It was not, however, the face of a Romulan, even though the angled eyebrows and pointed ears gave him a passing resemblance to one. But he was most definitely a Vulcan, and a rather aged one at that. The sides of his hair were streaked with gray, and he carried his solemnity like a great cloak.

Shelby had risen from her command chair and was about to speak when she heard a startled gasp from behind her. She half-turned to see that Arex was staring at the screen in more than just astonishment. He was gaping in what could only be shocked recognition.

The Vulcan tilted his head slightly in mild confusion. When he spoke, his voice was low and gravelly, and there was just a touch of wry amusement in his tone. "Lieutenant Arex?"

Arex managed a nod.

The Vulcan continued, "You are a long way from home, Lieutenant."

"I could say the same of you, Mr. Spock."

"Indeed. However, I believe it safe to say that I am somewhat the worse for wear."

"Mis . . . Ambassador Spock," Shelby automatically corrected herself. "You have us at a bit of a loss, sir. May I ask what you're doing out here, aboard what we believe is a personal vessel of the Romulan emperor?"

"You may indeed," replied Spock. And then he waited, eyebrow raised in a minuscule fashion.

Shelby moaned inwardly. His reputation for precision and proper phrasing of language was obviously well earned. "What are you doing out here, Ambassador?"

"Rendezvousing with you, Captain. Starfleet tends to be rather . . . cautious . . . in any of its communiqués that involve me. My ongoing work with Romulus and striving for reunification with my own people remains a matter of some delicacy. I will tell you more once I am aboard *Trident*."

"Very well. Send coordinates through and we'll be more than happy to beam you aboard."

The arched eyebrow went ever higher. "I am always wary of humans who are 'more than happy,' Captain. Such excess rapture often leads to most unhappy outcomes."

"I will remember that, Ambassador," said Shelby, trying not to smile at the gravity which the Vulcan imparted to every pronouncement, whether it be Starfleet directives or grammatical commentaries.

"In addition, Captain . . . I believe I may have something that belongs to you."

"Something that . . . ?"

And Shelby was dumbfounded as Spock stepped slightly to one side, to reveal Kalinda and a slightly abashed Si Cwan standing near him. Si Cwan bowed slightly in a vaguely mocking greeting.

"*Si Cwan?*" said a surprised Kat Mueller. "We tried to get in touch with you on Danter, and couldn't!"

"A most logical outcome," Spock observed, "considering that they were aboard this vessel."

"We were forced to depart Danter under less-than-ideal conditions," said Si Cwan.

Kalinda added helpfully, "If you can term a stolen runabout that was so badly shot up the entire thing was breaking down as 'less-than-ideal.' "

"I think that would qualify, yes," said Shelby. "Ambassador Cwan . . ."

He raised a hand and, looking a bit pained, said, "Captain . . . if you're planning to say 'I told you so,' at the very least do me the courtesy of waiting until I'm there rather than broadcasting it."

"I had no intention of saying that, Cwan. Prepare for beam-over. Shelby out." She turned and asked, "Arex? Have you got their coordinates?"

"Just coming through from the bird-of-paradise now, Captain."

"Good. Feed them down to the transporter room. XO, Arex, with me. Gleau, you have the conn."

"Captain," spoke up Arex, "might we include Lieutenant M'Ress in the welcoming party. Both she and I have significant past history with the ambassador."

Shelby cast a quick glance in Gleau's direction, but the head of science—to whom M'Ress reported, when she wasn't busy reporting about him—simply shrugged noncommittally.

"Very well," said Shelby. "Have her meet us there."

And as Shelby moved toward the turbolift, Mueller falling into step alongside her, the executive officer said in a low voice, "Si Cwan, against your best advice, gets involved with the Danteri and a passing Vulcan has to save his ass, and you have no intention of saying 'I told you so'?"

"I said I 'had' no intention," Shelby assured her. "That's because I didn't know we were going to run into him again. But I *have* that intention now."

"Did I ever tell you how much I look up to you, Captain?" asked Mueller.

"Not nearly enough, XO," said Shelby as the turbolift doors closed around them. "Not nearly enough."

EXCALIBUR

i.

MOKE'S HEART WAS POUNDING as he sprinted down the corridor, moving so quickly that he actually went right past Xyon. The younger child, apparently in response to the pounding feet behind him, came to a complete halt. He turned and waited and then sat there in surprise as Moke barreled past without even slowing.

"Moke?"

The calling of his name was small and innocent and filled with confusion. It instantly caught Moke's attention, and he skidded to a stop. He looked back at Xyon, who was working on forming his lips into the perfect shape for repeating the word. "Moke?" he said again.

It was the first time that the child had uttered Moke's name. Moke walked toward him slowly, pushing his hair out of his eyes, and hunkered down in front of him. He tapped his own chest and affirmed, "Moke."

"Mooookkke," said Xyon, dragging it out, and then

bounced up and down on his buttocks while singsonging, "Moke Moke Moke Moke Mooooookke."

For an instant, Moke forgot to be afraid, and in that selfsame instant came to the startling realization that not only didn't he have to be afraid, but he was tired of it. He had been running from that dark, one-eyed man. Now he'd run from the specter of Mark McHenry. There was something bizarre going on aboard the *Excalibur,* something of which only he seemed fully aware.

He'd gone to his adoptive father, to Mackenzie Calhoun, and told the captain what he had seen. Calhoun had seemed either skeptical or uncertain as to what was to be done. Either way the end result was the same: nothing.

But when he had challenged that invisible woman, that Artemis, she had vanished the moment he'd stood up to her. That should have told him something, except he'd been too upset to fully comprehend it. Now, though, he did, or at least understood it to the degree that he was going to try and act upon it.

Some of that resolve came from the way Xyon was looking at him. The pointy-eared child, whose face was a general mix of the features of both Burgoyne and Selar, obviously trusted Moke implicitly. He drew his perception of the world through Moke's eyes, and Moke wasn't about to make Xyon afraid of that which was around him.

He held out a hand firmly. "Come on, Xyon," he said.

The small boy placed his hand in the elder's, wrapping his tiny fingers around Moke's. They got up and Moke headed back the way he'd come, shoulders squared, determined to deal head-on with whatever might be waiting for him. It particularly helped when he reminded himself that his strident finger-pointing had made the god lady go away when she was clearly trying to bother poor Mr. McHenry.

Indeed, there was no reason at all for Moke to have run from McHenry. He'd just been caught by surprise, that was all. McHenry had been coming right at him, gesturing frantically, and something within Moke had just cried out, "Enough!" And off he'd run. But that wasn't going to be the case anymore. Moke was going to handle it. He could handle anything. Besides, the bottom line was that Mark McHenry was a friend. It wasn't as if he was that intimidating dark man with the one eye. . . .

Moke rounded the corner and saw McHenry right where he'd left him.

He was talking. As had consistently been the case, Moke saw the mouth moving but was unable to hear any words.

The thing was, McHenry was speaking with the one-eyed man.

That was enough to freeze Moke where he was. As much as he had stood up to Artemis, as much as he had overcome his initial fright and gone back to see McHenry, he wasn't prepared for the sight of this dark-some man standing right there, big as you please, in the corridor. Others were walking right past him without batting an eye. No one could see either McHenry or him. But Moke could, and—screwing his courage up—he stamped right toward the two phantoms and said loudly, "You go back where you came from!"

The old man and McHenry both looked straight at Moke. McHenry seemed startled, while the old man . . .

He actually smiled.

It was the first time he'd genuinely smiled at Moke,

and for no reason he could account for, Moke actually found the smile reassuring. The beginnings of a wild thought began to formulate in Moke's mind. He'd spent so much time being startled by this imposing and fearsome individual, that he'd never considered the possibility that this . . . this *person* . . . might actually be friendly somehow.

The old man said something to McHenry, and suddenly he turned and walked right through the nearest bulkhead. McHenry glanced at Moke, shrugged, said something although Moke couldn't determine what, and followed the old man through the wall.

"Get back here!" shouted Moke. *"Get back here!"*

A bewildered Xyon tugged on Moke's pants leg. Moke looked down at him and Xyon, again working meticulously to form the words, carefully enunciated, "I here!"

"I wasn't talking to you, Xyon," Moke said, but he had to laugh as he said it.

And then, to his surprise, McHenry reemerged from the wall. He glanced left and right, then looked straight at Moke and put a single finger to his lips, as if shushing him. Instantly, Moke understood: McHenry wanted him to keep quiet over the fact that Moke had seen him.

This immediately struck Moke as wrong. He felt as if he should go straight to Calhoun and tell him exactly what he'd experienced. As if sensing what was going through Moke's mind, McHenry shook his head with even greater vehemence and again pressed his finger to his lips. The aggressive manner in which McHenry made it clear that he was seeking Moke's silence gave Moke the impression that something very major was at stake. That by going to Calhoun and trying to improve matters, he might instead turn around and make things much, much worse.

Moke felt torn between his loyalty to Calhoun and the desperate urgency in McHenry's face. Finally, deciding to err on the side of caution, Moke nodded once and mimicked the "shushing" gesture McHenry was giving him. McHenry let go a visible sigh of relief, which didn't make a whole hell of a lot of sense to Moke. If McHenry was some sort of disembodied ghost, what did he need to be breathing for? But there was certainly no way he could pose such a question to the officer, and even if he did, he wouldn't hear the answer.

And then Moke saw something he really didn't understand in the least. As McHenry slipped through the bulkhead once more, a pair of darkly feathered birds flapped in through one side of the far wall and passed through the same bulkhead that McHenry had gone through. Quiet as shadows, as empty of substance as smoke, they were there and then they were gone, and so was McHenry.

Moke looked down at Xyon. "Just when you think things can't get any stranger around here."

At which point Xyon suddenly flashed perfectly formed, sharp little teeth, took two quick steps, and vaulted upon Moke like an attacking panther.

ii.

Mark McHenry stood just outside sickbay, staring in wonderment at himself, still trying to process how people could possibly be walking through him without even knowing he was there.

"I don't believe this."

"It gets worse. Much worse," came a grim voice from near him.

He turned and found himself staring at the strangest individual he'd ever encountered. He seemed to defy the very concept of life, instead shrouding himself in darkness. He wore a cape with the hood pulled up, and sported a dark red beard with streaks of white and gray. Most strikingly, he had only his right eye. Where the left would have been was just darkness. A man, definitely a man, shrouded in darkness, with a single streak of what appeared to be blood in the right corner.

"Who are you?" demanded McHenry.

"Don't you mean, *What* am I?" He spoke in a voice rich with amusement. Except McHenry was absolutely in no shape to be amused.

"I think I know the question I wanted to ask," McHenry retorted.

"I don't believe you do, actually," said the old man, and his voice seemed vaguely patronizing, but also—strangely enough—comforting in a way. As if McHenry was talking to someone who really, truly comprehended all that was going on . . . and that would be a nice change of pace. All too often, McHenry couldn't shake the feeling that he was perpetually one step ahead of everything going on. "The 'who' of me is of so little importance," the old man continued. "Of far greater concern to you—or, at least, it should be—is what sort of creature am I, where are we, and how do we get out?"

McHenry tried to come up with some snappy response, but none really suggested itself. His shoulders sagged in defeat as he said, "All right, fine. Any of those questions, then."

"That would be acceptable. However, I think it would be best if we conducted our discussions in private."

"Private?" said McHenry, stunned. "How much more private does it have to be? No one can freakin' see us!"

"He can," said the old man, indicating someone standing nearby. McHenry looked to see where he was pointing, and was surprised—but somehow not too surprised—to see a wide-eyed Moke standing and staring straight at him.

"How?" demanded McHenry. "How is he able to perceive us?"

"I told you your initial questions were worthless. Already you ask more interesting things. And you shall learn the truth of them . . . but not here. Come."

And without another word, the strange man walked straight through the nearest bulkhead.

McHenry did not hesitate to follow him, and found himself passing through an unoccupied quarters. The one-eyed man was just ahead of him, and McHenry said—to himself more than anything—"At least Moke will be able to tell them I'm all right. Not that I'm sure I *am* all right . . ."

Immediately the old man turned to face him, and it seemed as if thunderheads were drawing in around him. The room appeared to darken, and even though McHenry was insubstantial, he still felt a sudden drop in temperature. There was a distant rumbling, and the old man said, "It's too soon. Far too soon. Everyone is not in their ideal position yet. If he speaks of his prematurely, it could have dire consequences."

McHenry had no reason to believe the man, and yet he instantly did. With but a thought, he slid his way back through the wall and saw that Moke was still standing there. "Don't tell anyone you've seen me, Moke," he said, and made a great show of giving the universal sign for keeping a secret.

Moke seemed not to comprehend, however, and McHenry repeated the gesture, this time with an even greater show of force. He only wished he could do more in terms of communication than this frustrating pantomime.

But then Moke nodded and clearly appeared to understand what it was that McHenry was trying to put across to him. McHenry grinned, nodded approvingly, said, "Thanks! Hope to see you later!," and moved back through the bulkhead into the empty quarters.

As he did so, he heard a high-pitched "cawing" almost directly in his ear, and reflexively flinched as what appeared to be two powerfully built black birds—ravens, if he wasn't mistaken—hurtled directly past him and landed on the shoulders of the old man. Insanely (as if this entire thing wasn't insane already) they seemed to be whispering in his ear, their beaks clacking together as they "spoke."

"I see," said the old man, and "Good."

"They talk?" asked a stunned McHenry.

The old man allowed a vaguely patronizing smile. "Yes. Just not to you. All right, my pets, well done. Go to, go to." Obediently, the ravens lifted off his shoulders and flapped away, back out through the wall.

"You said you were going to tell me what's happening. So fine. How am I walking through walls? Why can no one see you and me."

Still smiling, the old man appeared to sit. There was

no chair under him, but he adopted a distinctively reclining posture nevertheless. "You've been imprisoned," he said, "trapped, as it were, in a sort of . . . how best to put this? A sideways dimension. Some manner of psychic energy surge catapulted you here, would be the best way to describe it. There are other ways, but they're far more technical and, frankly, quite boring."

"All right . . . that explains why I'm here. Actually, it doesn't," he realized, "but it's probably as close as I'm going to get. But what about you? Why are you in this 'sideways' dimension?"

"Ah. I was incarcerated here by my fellow entities . . . the race whom I believe you know as 'the Beings.' "

"You're one of them?"

"Not just one. The greatest of them!" he said with a grim smile that indicated massively wounded pride over having been cooped up in this semi-existence. "No one of them could possibly have overcome me and put me here. It took their combined efforts. It was quite a surprise, really. I'd never seen so many of them agree on something before. On the one hand, I should be angry over it. On the other . . . it's quite flattering, in a perverse sort of way."

"You're flattered that you're imprisoned?"

"Well, I *did* say perversely." The old man chuckled. "We are a perverse lot, we gods . . . or Beings, or whatever we're calling ourselves now. Sex with siblings, sex with mortals, sniping and plotting against each other. And yet, despite all that, we were worshipped. Indeed, our sins were exalted, made the stuff of legend. I've always thought humans did so in order to make themselves feel better about their own shortcomings. They reasoned that if we, in our divinity, could be base in our actions, then that excused any sins they might commit. How could they reasonably expect more of themselves than they expected of us?"

"All right," McHenry said slowly. "That makes sense . . . even if none of the rest of this does. But that still doesn't explain—"

"I was the last, you see," the old man continued, as if McHenry hadn't spoken.

"The last?"

"The last god to leave the Earth." His voice seemed to carry the sadness of the ages in it. "I had different priorities, you see. To the rest of my kind . . . it was all about them. It was all about having the humans of your world worshipping us. They felt that humans were there for us. Only I believed that we were to be there for them. The only one who was anywhere close to my view on the subjects was poor, tragic Apollo . . . and even he had an ego that superseded his wisdom.

"Eventually, humans had less and less need for us. They turned their interests elsewhere. To gods who were more . . . unknowable. Or gods who, if abominations were committed in their name, would not be inclined to come down to earth and destroy the perpetrator with bolts of lightning. Besides, I've always thought," he said in amusement, "that they came to know us too well. You cannot worship that which you know; it's antithetical. Familiarity breeds contempt, not adoration. Instead of being gods, we were more . . . celebrities. And humans must always tear down their celebrities. It's just the nature of the species."

"And . . . you were the last one to leave?"

"Yes," the old man sighed. "Curiosity kept me, I suppose. That, and a desire to be a source of inspiration for humans rather than an object of reverence." He looked to McHenry and amusement twinkled in his eye. "You still need to know who I am, don't you. You humans— even half-humans, such as yourself. You still need to apply names to everything so you can comprehend it."

He sagged heavily into a chair. How he could possibly do that, McHenry didn't know. For that matter, McHenry had no clue why he wasn't sinking through the floor if he was supposed to be without bodily form.

"I have a variety of names," he said at last. "Some called me Zeus. Others, Jupiter. The Norse called me Woden. They named days after me, planets after me. Very flattering, actually. The Egyptians dubbed me Amen-Re. Takami-Musubi is what the Japanese called me. Elegant language, Japanese. Elegant people. Always liked them. And so many more, big and small. From nations to tribes, they all knew me."

McHenry's eyes widened. "You were . . . you were a sky god? A creation god? But . . . you were one of the greatest gods of all! You were . . . you were big!"

"I'm still big," rumbled the old man. "It's creation that's gotten small."

"And . . . how long did you stay around? After the others left?"

He shrugged his broad shoulders. "A while. For entities such as I, we don't tend to pay all that much attention to the passage of time. Monitoring that is much more the province and interest of mortals than us. One century is like five is like ten. It matters little to me. Although I will say that in my last centuries on Earth, there was very little call for most of my incarnations. The name applied to me most often during that time was Klaus."

"Klaus?" McHenry looked at him dubiously. "I don't remember any god named Klaus."

"I wasn't seen as a 'god,' per se. More as a charitable sprite. I must say, I rather liked that time of my life. I dealt with children, mostly. Saint Klaus, I was. Those were good times."

"Saint Klaus . . . wait. *Santa Claus?*" he said suspiciously. "You're telling me you were Santa Claus?"

"That was one version of it, yes."

"Santa Claus. With the red suit and the presents and coming down the chimney? You must be joking."

"Do you find that so difficult to believe?"

"Well . . . yes! You're Zeus and Odin and Santa Claus all rolled into one? How ridiculous is that?"

"I feel the need to point out," the old man said airily, "that someone who is currently existing as a disembodied spirit is hardly in a position to question the little absurdities that life presents. All those names aside, I find that after all this time, I simply prefer to be called the Old Father. It's certainly descriptive enough."

"You know," McHenry said at last, "I really, really hope I'm dreaming all this, because it's too insane to cope with if I'm not."

"You're not," the old man assured him, and he now had a grim demeanor to him. "Would that you were. But you're not. This is the truth of it: My brethren, my 'associates,' shunt anyone to this dimension whom they believe can cause trouble. Then again," he said reflectively, "I suppose it's somehow appropriate that they keep me locked away like this . . . considering that it was I who had kept *them* imprisoned for so long."

"You did?" McHenry began to pace, no longer dwelling on mundane matters such as how he was able to move about in relation to physical objects. "This isn't exactly the story they were telling us."

"Well, of course it wouldn't be, would it." He snorted derisively. "Do you think they would want you to know? Can't blame them, really. More than a century, I kept them tightly bottled up, like the Earth legends of genies in lamps . . . which originated with us, I might add."

"Of course," said McHenry with a helpless gesture. "I'm starting to think everything from the common cold to Fermat's last theorem came from you people."

"I would not call us 'people,' really."

"It doesn't matter," McHenry told him, beginning to feel impatient. He didn't know *why* he was impatient. It wasn't as if he had anything else to do or anyplace else to go. It was probably a holdover from his annoying human condition. "So why did you do that? Keep them under wraps?"

"They wanted revenge. For Apollo."

"Revenge?"

"Understand, they thought him somewhat the fool," said the Old Father. There was unmistakable sadness in his voice, although McHenry wasn't entirely certain for whom the sadness was intended. "But they felt he was ill used by the crew of the *Enterprise.* However, they also saw opportunity presenting itself: opportunity in the form of Apollo's assignation with the mortal woman, Carolyn, who was your ancestor. They saw you as a potential bridge to the status and power they once enjoyed. I endeavored to talk them out of it, but they would not listen to reason.

"I knew then what I had to do, in order to stave off potential disaster. I knew, however, I could not do it alone. After all these millennia, even I am not what I once was. I needed an ally . . . and the only reasonable ally was someone whom the others felt antipathy for, and he for they. Someone who had no love lost between himself and his associates. Wisely or unwisely, I chose my son."

"Let me guess: He has lots of names as well."

The Old Father nodded. "Anubis, among the Egyptians. The Greeks called him Ares, the Norse knew him as Loki. Aborigine people called him the Coyote god. Ultimately, his forte was trickery, so really, who better?"

"I thought Anubis was the Egyptian god of death."

"It's much the same. Consider those who lie in agony, waiting for the release of death, yet it does not come. Meanwhile newborn infants lie asleep in their beds, just beginning their lives, and they are snuffed out for no apparent reason. Dictators and tyrants lead long, happy lives, while peacemakers and lovers of all who live are cut down in their prime. There is no greater perpetrator of morbid jests than death."

"I'm living proof of that . . . maybe," said McHenry ruefully. "And in exchange for helping you, he was spared the indignity of being stuck away in some between dimension."

"Exactly so. So I, with the aid of my trickster son, started gathering them up, one by one, shunting them away into another dimension, where they could cause no trouble. Artemis was the last of them . . . and, damn my sentimentality, I was not able to complete the task I had set out to do." He shook his head, clearly disgusted with himself. "She begged me, she pleaded. She swore to me that she had learned from observing her departed brother the foolishness of trying to thrust oneself into the affairs of mortals."

"And so you spared her," McHenry said tonelessly.

"Aye. I did."

"I don't blame you," he said. "She can be very persuasive when she needs to be."

"So I let her and Anubis wander free . . . certain in my foolish confidence that I, ever vigilant, would be able to keep the rest of the beings contained. There is nothing so foolish as the pride of an old fool," he added. "Although really, I should have known. When one has a son whose reputation is based upon trickery, what else can one expect but betrayal?"

"So Artemis pleaded her way out of exile. Hunh." McHenry actually laughed at that. It was the first thing he'd found amusing about any of this insanity. "Boy. If Artemis had been penned up, my life would be very, very different. I'd be alive like a normal person, for starters. My parents wouldn't have been driven insane by her presence in my life. . . ."

"I am sorry, lad, for my misjudgment which brought her down upon you," said the Old Father. "Unfortunately, I know that means very little."

"No . . . no, actually, it does mean something," said McHenry, choosing to be philosophical about the matter. "Especially when you consider that, for centuries, peoples' lives have been messed up by random calamities. At such times, they've always begged deities for enlightenment as to why these things happened. But they're never really given any concrete answer. This may be the first time that a deity has actually stepped up and said, 'My mistake. Sorry for the inconvenience.' It's appreciated. It doesn't change anything, but it is appreciated." McHenry pondered the situation a moment more and then asked, "How did he do it? Or I should say, how did *they* do it?"

"How did they release the other Beings?" When McHenry nodded, the Old Father grunted in response. "Those damnable gateways."

"The *gateways?*" McHenry remembered them all too well. Portals through time, through space, even—it was believed—into other dimensions. They had begun popping up all over the galaxy, like weeds, manipulated by an alien race as part of a galactic power play. One of the blasted gateways had even swallowed Calhoun and Shelby, necessitating their rescue from an ice world that had nearly been the death of them.

The Old Father simply nodded. "It did not occur to me that my wayward son would become bored with the absence of his sparring partners. Nor did it occur to me that Artemis, so humble in her pleadings to me to be spared, so truthful in nature, would be deceitful enough to seduce Anubis over to the idea of releasing the others and turning my punishment back upon me."

"Wait a minute," McHenry said, a thought occurring to him. "Anubis . . . Loki . . . whatever you call him . . . is he a giant?"

"Not a colossus, certainly. But by the standards of your race—of most races—he stands far taller and wider than could remotely be considered the norm." The Old Father looked slightly askance at him. "Why do you ask?"

"Well, during the gateways incident," said McHenry, "according to Captain Calhoun's write-up on the subject, the words 'Giant Lied' were etched in the snow on that ice world I mentioned before, by a dying member of one of the races caught up in the whole affair. Did that giant refer to Anubis?"

"Very likely."

"What did he lie about?"

The Old Father shrugged. It seemed such an odd gesture for a god to make. "Specifically? I could not say. My ravens keep me apprised of much, but it is a vast cosmos to try and keep track of everything."

"I thought gods were omniscient, all-knowing."

"Don't believe everything you read. In any event, although the details of Anubis's 'lies' to this individual are lost, I have no doubt that he deceived the poor creature into taking actions that suited Anubis's goals. Very likely he was instrumental in finding a way to utilize the gateway that released the other Beings into the world."

"At which point they came looking for you."

"And put me here," said the Old Father sadly, but with the air of one who thought the outcome to be inevitable.

"So . . ." It was quite possibly the question that McHenry most dreaded asking. "So . . . what do we do now?"

"Now," said the Old Father with one eyebrow raised. "Now we count on my son."

"On your son? On Anubis? Excuse me if I wasn't paying attention, but . . . wasn't he the one who put you into this situation in the first place?"

The Old Father shook his grayed head. "Not him. My other, far younger, half-mortal son. Oh, he does not have much in the way of abilities . . . not anymore, not since the passing of his mother . . . but at least he can perceive us, and possibly obtain help for us."

"What? What are you . . ."

And then, of course he understood.

"Moke," he said.

The Old Father made a sour face. "I despise that name, I should make quite clear. His mother named him that. Hardly an appropriate name, particularly for one who so obviously took after his father. What with his storm-related abilities and such. Me . . . I would have named him Thor."

TRIDENT

i.

SHELBY KNEW SHE SHOULDN'T feel a chill when Ambassador Spock materialized on the transporter pad. Nevertheless, she couldn't help it. She had encountered him before, but she found that her basic reaction to being in his presence was exactly the same. The man was, literally, a living legend. She had studied his exploits in Academy texts. How could one be undaunted in encountering such an individual?

When the shimmering of the transporter beams ended, she squared her shoulders and stepped forward. "Welcome aboard, Ambassador," she said formally, and then correcting herself, said, "Ambassa*dors*." For standing directly behind Spock were Si Cwan and Kalinda, both looking none the worse for wear. Si Cwan's face was an inscrutable mask that surpassed Spock's for sheer unreadability, but if Shelby was going to guess at his mental state, it would be total chagrin.

Spock, meantime, inclined his head slightly and stepped down.

"May I present my executive officer, Commander Katerina Mueller. And I believe you already know Lieutenants Arex and M'Ress."

"Indeed," said Spock. "Lieutenants Shiboline M'Ress and Arex Na Eth, it would appear that the years have been far kinder to the two of you than to me."

M'Ress looked as if she were fighting to avoid having an emotional breakdown, so clearly happy was she to reencounter this figure from her past. "Don't underestimate yourself, Mr. Spock. You look wonderful. A sight for sore eyes."

He frowned slightly. "If your eyes are sore, Lieutenant, might I suggest a simple medicinal wash easily available in sickbay."

She smiled. "Thank you, sir. I'll get right on that."

"We've arranged quarters for you, Ambassador Spock," said Mueller. "And your guest quarters are as you left them, Ambassadors Cwan and Kalinda."

"Most considerate," said Spock. "I think it would be best, however, if we proceed directly to the nearest briefing room so we may discuss the circumstances that have brought me here."

Mueller looked blankly at Shelby. "Briefing room?"

"Conference lounge," Arex said softly. "That's what they call them now."

"Of course," said Spock. "I should have recalled. One of the disadvantages of age. That which is far distant is the most clear. The conference lounge, then, by all means."

Shelby nodded and led the way as the small group

emerged into the corridor. As they walked along, Shelby noticed the distinct change in the attitude of the *Trident* crew. Naturally they continued to conduct themselves as professionals; she would have expected nothing less. Still, there were all manner of double takes, lingering gazes, whispered conferences among crew members who walked past the *Trident*'s new guests.

She couldn't really blame them. It wasn't often that living history walked the corridors of the *Trident*.

Spock, meantime, seemed oblivious—the operative word most likely being "seemed"—of the stir he was creating. Instead he was having an animated discussion with M'Ress and Arex. "Your presence here is most unexpected. Did the two of you fall out of your own time together?"

"Totally separate circumstances, sir," said M'Ress. "I came through a sort of time portal as a result of an ill-fated landing party . . ."

"Which they call 'away teams' now, by the way, just to avoid further confusion," Arex said. "And I was on a shuttle that fell through a wormhole."

"I see," said Spock. "And you both wound up in this time, serving together. It gives one cause to ponder."

"Ponder what, Ambassador?" asked Mueller.

"The true nature of the universe, Commander." He indicated M'Ress and Arex with a nod of his head. "The odds of the two of you, former shipmates, being hurled into the future to this particular time period, and serving together once more, are minuscule at best. One is almost inclined to perceive a divine plan."

"A divine plan?" Mueller said skeptically. "Ambassador, I would think you, of all people, with your extensive science background, would be the ultimate supporter of rational matters in all things."

"In my life, Commander, I have seen sufficient things to determine that the line between the rational and the irrational is not as strongly demarcated as you might think."

"Meaning—?"

He cast her a sidelong glance. "I would have thought my meaning was clear enough," he said, as they approached the turbolift. "I—as have all of you—have seen beings of such might that your ancestors considered them gods. I have seen beings who long ago surpassed the need for physical incarnation. There is a being named Q—with whom I have had some rather lively debates—who wields power bordering on the omnipotent. I had a half-brother who sought out what he believed to be God, and turned out to be anything but. That which some would term a Supreme Being may simply be an entity which we have neither encountered nor defined in terms that we could understand. To dismiss such a notion out of hand simply because we have not witnessed it firsthand would be highly illogical."

They stepped into the turbolift and the doors closed behind them. "Deck three," said Shelby, and as the lift moved off, she said, "I never looked at it in quite that way, Ambassador. Would you call yourself an agnostic?"

"I would call myself a Vulcan," replied Spock. "I leave humans to apply other labels to me . . . a pastime at which they have, historically, excelled."

ii.

Si Cwan was waiting for some sort of snide remark from Shelby. A contemptuous glance, a mocking sentiment. None was forthcoming. From the moment that they met in the transporter room to their sojourn to the conference lounge, Shelby—and Mueller, for that matter—were nothing but professional. In fact, Si Cwan was rather surprised when Mueller suggested a private dinner to him in a low voice for later that evening.

He received a further surprise when the turbolift opened on deck three, and a familiar, white-furred presence was standing there waiting to step in. "Ambassador Cwan!"

"Ensign Janos," replied Si Cwan. "Aren't you on the wrong ship?"

"There's been some mixing of the crews," Shelby told him. "The *Excalibur* had some . . . difficulties. She's laid up in drydock, so we took on some of her crew."

"Yes, I . . . heard about that," Si Cwan said.

"Terrible business," said Janos in his cultured voice. "Simply terrible. I trust it will all be sorted out sooner rather than later, and retribution will be distributed all around."

"One can only hope," Kalinda spoke up.

Janos stepped aside, allowing everyone else to emerge from the turbolift before he stepped aboard. Si Cwan thought he might have imagined it, but he could have sworn he saw Janos's furred hand brush against M'Ress's as they stepped past each other, and she smiling to herself as a result. It was so fleeting a moment that it was hard to tell.

"Captain," Mueller said, "if we're going straight into conference, it might be best if Lieutenant Commander Gleau were present as well."

This time Si Cwan was certain it was no fanciful notion on his part: He saw M'Ress stiffen slightly at the mention of Gleau's name. He wondered why that would be, but wasn't entirely certain that it was any of his business.

Shelby, meantime, nodded. "Yes, I think you're right, XO."

Mueller promptly tapped her combadge and summoned Gleau from the bridge as the small group walked into the conference lounge. Gleau arrived less than a minute later, and Si Cwan watched M'Ress carefully to see how she reacted. But there was no visible response from the Caitian aside from a slight inclination of her head in acknowledgment of Gleau's presence. Still, Si Cwan sensed that something was most definitely wrong, and was beginning to think that rather than content himself that it was none of his affair he might instead want to consider ways to *make* it his.

As if aware that something was up, Gleau looked at Si Cwan with an air of suspicion. But obviously Si Cwan wasn't doing anything that Gleau could respond to, and so the Selelvian contented himself to take a seat after formally greeting the Vulcan ambassador.

Spock remained standing as he spoke, striking quite the impressive figure in his large, ridged traveling robes. "I am here," he began without preamble, "at Starfleet's request. Under ordinary circumstances, Captain, they would have communicated with you via normal subspace transmissions. These are not, however, ordinary circumstances. Indeed, extreme caution is being dictated, since we do not yet fully comprehend the full scope of the situation presenting itself."

"Meaning we don't know what's happening yet," commented Mueller.

Spock looked at her with raised eyebrow. "I believe I just said that."

"Yes, of course. Go ahead, Ambassador," said Shelby, firing a mildly annoyed look at Mueller which amused the hell out of Si Cwan.

"As you know, individuals presenting themselves as 'the Beings' came to the planet Danter and have struck a bargain with the natives. In exchange for being worshipped, they will provide a substance they call 'ambrosia' to the Danteri. This substance, when ingested, is alleged to elevate the physical well-being of the consumers to previously unheard-of levels."

"I can attest to that personally," Si Cwan said immediately.

"You've eaten it?" asked Mueller.

"No. I did, however, get myself tossed around by someone who had. Someone whom I would have been able to break in half without much difficulty before that. Whatever their claims are that this stuff can do, I suspect it's barely scratching the surface."

"I don't understand," Gleau spoke up. "Did you say they will provide this stuff in exchange for . . . being *worshipped?*"

"That is correct."

"That's exceedingly strange."

"Perhaps," agreed Spock, "but not out of the question as far as their psychopathology goes. I have encountered such creatures before, you see. That is why Starfleet brought me in from Romulus, asking me to delay my work on unification between the Vulcans and Romulans, and focus instead on this rather pressing question."

"You did?" Shelby turned to M'Ress. "Have you as well, Lieutenant? Or you, Arex? You served with the Ambassador . . ."

"It was before their time, Captain. The encounter involved an individual purporting to be Apollo, on Stardate . . ." He paused half a moment, recalling information. ". . . 3468.1. In the vicinity of planet Pollux IV, the *Enterprise* was accosted and held immobile in space through a rather unique method."

"Did it involve a giant hand?" asked Shelby. "Because, if so, that's what happened to Captain Calhoun as well."

Spock blinked slightly. "Apparently it was not as unique as I had thought."

"Obviously Apollo's kind isn't all that interested in coming up with new tricks," said Arex.

"You stay with what works," Mueller said with a shrug.

"In any event," continued Spock, "Apollo's obsession likewise involved being worshipped."

"Why?" asked Shelby. "Why such interest in being worshipped? It sounds like . . ."

"Ego run amok?" suggested Kalinda. "Because I've had some small experience with that." When Si Cwan stared at her in surprise, Kalinda immediately added, "I wasn't referring to you, Cwan."

"I should hope not," he said archly.

Spock continued to stand precisely where he was, but Si Cwan noticed that he had steepled his fingers and appeared quite thoughtful. "Apollo's interest in worshippers seemed to stem primarily from a sort of nostalgia. He appeared to prefer humans when they were more pliable . . . more impressed by the various feats he could perform which—to more primitive minds—appeared to be magic."

"It had to do with control, then?" asked Shelby.

"Possibly," said Spock. "I myself did not have the opportunity to interact with Apollo to any degree when the captain and the landing party went to the planet's surface."

"I would have thought," said Gleau, "that as science officer, you would have been first to the transporter pad to go down and interact with such a new and fascinating life-form."

There was an air of challenge to Gleau's tone that did not strike Si Cwan as especially respectful. Nor did he think it seemed that way to Shelby or the others, judging by the annoyed look that Shelby and her second-in-command gave him.

Spock, however, was naturally unperturbed. "Indeed. Were it an option, I would have been most anxious to interact with the newfound 'god.' Unfortunately, he was disinclined to invite me to his world."

"On what basis?" asked Mueller.

"Apparently," said Spock without a trace of irony, "I reminded him of Pan, and Pan always bored him."

"Pan?" said Gleau. "That doesn't make much sense."

Spock raised an eyebrow. "Does it not?"

"What do you mean, Lieutenant Commander?" asked Shelby.

"Well," and Gleau turned in his chair, facing Shelby with a relaxed attitude. "I've done a bit of studying of

Terran myth. Pan was a god of nature, of music and ribaldry and comic adventures. No offense intended to Ambassador Spock, but he doesn't exactly strike me as the comic adventuring type."

"Pan also traditionally had pointed ears," Shelby said. "That may well be where the familiarity arose from."

"Plus I remember Mr. Spock played some sort of Vulcan musical instrument," said Arex.

"Lyre," Spock said.

Arex blinked and looked confused. "Oh. I'm sorry. My mistake. I wasn't intentionally trying to deceive—"

"The Vulcan lyre. Or harp, as it is also called." He looked at Shelby with mild curiosity. "Do *all* your meetings tend to wander in this manner?"

"Sometimes," she admitted.

"You may wish to consider restoring the term 'briefing room.' 'Conference lounge' implies a leisurely pace is to be taken. 'Briefing room' is far more to the point."

"I'll take that under advisement, Ambassador," she said dryly.

"That would be wise," said Spock, and without blinking returned to the point. "Had I interacted with or questioned Apollo myself, I might have been able to determine if there were any priorities beyond a salving of his ego and a desire for control over what he deemed to be mere mortals. I was not given that opportunity. As it is, there are hypotheses. But there are always hypotheses. Without definitive fact, it would be pointless to speculate about them.

"Nevertheless, given my presence during the *Enterprise* encounter, I am as near to an expert as Starfleet has available, aside from Montgomery Scott. Of the two of us, given my status as ambassador, it was decided I would be best suited on this mission."

"And what mission is that?" asked Shelby.

Spock began to walk the perimeter of the conference room in slow, unhurried strides. "The Danteri have slowly begun to inform chosen races of the existence of ambrosia and their involvement with the Beings. It is believed by Starfleet that they are doing so in order to build a power base with the Beings at its core. Such a development could seriously affect the current, rather delicate, balance of power within the Federation. It is Starfleet's directive that the *Trident* bring me to Danter—and remain on station—so that I may converse with the Beings and determine the full extent of exactly what they have in mind."

"And which way does the Federation fall on this?" asked Si Cwan.

The Vulcan turned and looked at Si Cwan. "In what respect?"

"I believe," Kalinda said, "my brother is asking whether the Federation is interested in keeping the Beings at arm's length . . . or interested in getting their hands on the ambrosia so they, too, can have this beloved 'golden age' the Beings claim to want to bring to us all."

Si Cwan nodded in confirmation.

"That decision," Spock said, "will stem, to some degree, from my recommendation . . . although mine will not be the only voice to be heard in the matter."

"Then hear mine," Si Cwan said immediately. "They are dangerous. I've experienced them close up. They altered the mind-set of an entire world in a relatively brief period of time. I can't believe that sort of influence is remotely healthy."

"Frankly, with all respect, I can't believe I'm hearing this," Mueller said. She had gotten to her feet, and the scar on her face was turning bright pink. It reminded Si Cwan of Calhoun's own scar, which tended toward similar discoloration when he became upset. "These Beings, in pursuit of bringing about their supposed golden age, nearly annihilated the *Excalibur!* Or has that been forgotten?"

"The Federation is well aware of the assault upon the *Excalibur,*" Spock said. "My understanding is that it was a hotly debated topic at Starfleet Headquarters. Ultimately, however, they are looking at the bigger picture."

"The *bigger picture!?*"

"Sit down, XO," said Shelby.

Mueller whirled to faced her. "The *Excalibur,* Captain. That's your husband's ship. I'd think that should matter to you. Or are *you* only concerned about the bigger picture as well?"

Suddenly the atmosphere in the room became very cold, although the temperature remained the same. Si Cwan thought he saw a flash of contrition in Mueller's eyes, as if she realized she had gone too far.

Shelby's face could have been carved from teak.

"Sit. Down. XO."

Mueller sat, the scar burning even more brightly pink against her face.

"And that," Spock abruptly spoke up, "is another reason it was felt I would be the best suited to be involved. Emotions have a tendency to run high in connection with the Beings. That is not a consideration for me." He passed forward a data chip to Shelby. "The full details and official Starfleet orders are contained on this, Captain. It is not expected that you were to take solely my word on this matter."

"Thank you, Ambassador," she said. She rose from the table. "I will review this immediately, and then we'll make ready for the trip to Danter. Naturally the full facilities of the *Trident* will be at your disposal. Anything else?" She glanced around the room. Si Cwan noticed that her gaze seemed to skip right over Mueller. "Arex, M'Ress, if you'd be so kind as to escort Ambassador Spock to his quarters. That's all, then. Dismissed."

Everyone rose, with Shelby leading the way. That mildly surprised Si Cwan. He would have thought that Shelby would hang back, desire to speak to Mueller. Obviously she was too annoyed, and wanted to have the opportunity to calm down.

Si Cwan quickly caught up with Shelby in the corridor outside the conference lounge. "Captain, two things?"

She turned, her hands on her hips, clearly making an effort to be patient. "Yes, Ambassador?"

"First, I very much appreciate, in regards to my personal situation, the lack of—what's the best way to put it . . . ?"

"I-told-you-so's?" Despite her clearly distressed air, she said it with a sense of humor.

"Yes. That," admitted Si Cwan.

Kalinda, speaking from just behind him, piped up, "Cwan was extremely concerned about what you were going to say."

"I wouldn't say 'extremely concerned,'" he corrected her.

"Ambassador," said Shelby, "I try not to kick people

when their pride is down. I advised against your going to Danter because I was concerned about your welfare. When we heard about what happened there, I had no idea what happened to you and Kalinda, but I wasn't holding out much hope. The bottom line is, you're back and you're alive, and that's all that matters. Although I suppose I should be flattered that my opinion means that much to you. What's the second thing?"

"Yes. The second thing. I am aware that Commander Mueller spoke out of turn just now. I would consider it a personal favor, however, if you were not too—"

"Don't overstep yourself, Ambassador," Shelby interrupted. She didn't sound angry, but there was a definite edge to her voice. "Anything else? No? All right then," she continued without waiting for him to respond, and then she turned and headed off down the corridor.

The Thallonians watched him go, and Kalinda said softly, "You should have stayed out of it."

"Your retroactive advice is always appreciated, little sister," replied Si Cwan. "Have you considered . . . ?"

Suddenly there was a thump that sounded from within the conference lounge, and Si Cwan thought he heard raised voices. He exchanged a brief, bewildered look with Kalinda, and then started quickly toward the lounge, Kalinda right behind him. Before he could get there, however, the door slid open and Gleau emerged. He looked slightly stunned, but when he saw the others approaching, he immediately pulled himself together. He gave a nonchalant nod and quickly headed off in the opposite direction.

Then Mueller came out, smoothing out her uniform shirt. "Ambassador," she said briskly. "Good to have you back. Are you free for dinner tonight?"

"I . . . suppose, yes."

"My quarters. Twenty-two hundred hours. You remember the way?"

"Yes, I—"

"Good." Her back ramrod-straight, she walked briskly away in the opposite direction from Gleau.

Si Cwan and Kalinda stared at one another. "You know what I've noticed about these Starfleet vessels?" asked Kalinda. "I always feel like I'm coming in on the middle of someone else's scenes."

iii.

As the conference lounge emptied out, Kat Mueller realized that she and Gleau were going to be the last ones out. "Lieutenant Commander Gleau," she said softly, standing right next to him. "A moment of your time, if you please."

He looked at her questioningly as the conference lounge door slid shut behind the departing form of Spock. He had been standing, but now eased himself into the nearest chair. "What can I do for you, Commander? If you're looking for advice . . . ?"

"Advice?" There was confusion in her cobalt blue eyes. "On what?"

"Well, on your little mishap with the captain just now." He smiled in a manner that Mueller believed he felt extraordinarily ingratiating. "I've been known to have a way with people, and I might be able to give you some hints . . ."

"I studied your psych profile records," she said abruptly, her eyes hardening.

She was pleased to see that Gleau was thrown off by her switch in topics. "Pardon?"

"Your psych profiles. From when you first joined Starfleet. All incoming cadets are required to undergo psych profiles and, as part of that, a study for any potential talents that would be considered 'paranormal abilities.' "

"Paranormal meaning those things that humans are incapable of doing," said Gleau with a smug air. "Amazing. You know, in your Earth's history, you all once thought that your world was the center of the galaxy. It's curious how so many of Starfleet policies continue to be derived from that philosophy."

"Yes, curious as hell. That's not the point, Gleau. The point is, such profiles are standard issue . . . except you didn't undergo them."

"Didn't I?" He cocked an eyebrow. "It was so long ago, I don't recall."

"You received a special exemption for anything except the most minimal, surface scanning," she said. She had gotten up and had come around to where Gleau was sitting. She rested a hand on his shoulder as if she were being friendly with him. "The specific reason given was that Selelvians had a long cultural tradition of believing that intrusions into the mind were the height of personal violation. The argument was that it would be a violation of the Prime Directive to force such procedures on you. The request came down directly from Federation representatives to exempt you from more detailed scans, and Starfleet deferred to the UFP." Her hand squeezed tighter on his shoulder. "Remember now?"

"It's starting to come back to me, and by the way, you're hurting my shoulder." He kept his voice low and even, but Mueller was reasonably sure she heard a touch of fright in it. Good.

"So tell me, Gleau," said Mueller. "Did Selelvian representatives use 'the Knack' on any Federation representatives to sway them over to their concerns? You know . . . that handy little Selelvian technique of convincing people to do what they'd like?"

"Commander," and he laughed uncomfortably, "I've genuinely no clue what you're—"

"Or did you seek cover for yourself because you have other talents, in addition to the Knack, that you don't want anyone to find out about."

He paused. "Such as?"

"Such as being able to insert yourself right into somebody's mind. To haunt them in their dreams."

He blew air through his lips in annoyance. "What has M'Ress been telling you now?"

"I never mentioned her."

"You don't have to. It's painfully obvious what this is about: more harassment. If you'll excuse me . . ."

"I don't think I will."

"I don't think I'm giving you a choice, Commander," he said, and he got up from his chair and shoved her hand away.

Without hesitation, Mueller spun him around and shoved him down on the conference lounge table. The tabletop shook as his back slammed into it and he gaped up at Mueller, all of his posturing and self-satisfaction having magically evaporated.

Mueller stared deep into his eyes, because she was confident of one thing above all else, and that was that she was an excellent judge of character. She assessed everything that was going through his mind, looked for a hint of what was truly going on with him, and became convinced in a heartbeat that what the Caitian had told her—what she had, at first, dismissed out of hand—was, in fact, true. An innocent man would have had anger in his eyes. But what she was seeing was fear and, above all, guilt. Her gaze dissected him and found that what was left was the equivalent of a child with his hand caught in the cookie jar.

"If I find out that you've been threatening Lieutenant M'Ress—or anyone—or if anything happens to her, or if I happen to have a bad dream about you . . . you're finished. Are you clear on that, Gleau? I will finish you personally."

"Are you *threatening* me?" he gasped out.

"Yes. Absolutely. Are we clear on it?"

He looked as if he was about to make some sort of defensive, arrogant retort, and so to be preemptive about it, Mueller raised him up slightly and then slammed him back down again.

"All right! All right!"

"Good. Then we have an understanding."

She released him then and stepped back. Quickly he sat up, out of breath, watching her with glazed eyes like a trapped animal. Then, losing no time, he bolted from the conference lounge.

Mueller came right after him and then saw Si Cwan and Kalinda standing there. Her mind raced, allowing for possible future developments, and she came to the conclusion that the Thallonian ambassador might be of help.

"Ambassador," she said, smoothing her uniform top to achieve some semblance of polish. "Good to have you back. Are you free for dinner tonight?"

He looked bewildered, as if he had expected her to say something else entirely. "I . . . suppose, yes."

"My quarters. Twenty-two hundred hours. You remember the way?"

"Yes, I—"

"Good." She turned on her heel and walked off, wondering what she had just gotten herself into.

EXCALIBUR

i.

MACKENZIE CALHOUN LEANED FORWARD, resting his elbows on his desk, and stared thoughtfully at Zak Kebron. "Are you quite sure of this, Mr. Kebron?"

"Positive, Captain," Kebron said firmly.

The Brikar security chief was idly scratching at the base of his nonexistent neck. Calhoun noticed that more large flakes of his hide seemed to be coming off. "Are you having a problem, Mr. Kebron?"

"Problem?"

He gestured. "With your skin. Significant chunks of it appear to be breaking away."

"It's seasonal," Kebron said.

"We're on a starship, Mr. Kebron. We don't get seasons."

"That's true."

Which seemed to be more than enough of an answer to satisfy Kebron, even though it naturally made no sense whatsoever to Calhoun. Calhoun exchanged a glance with Commander Burgoyne, who had been standing there listening to the exchange. Burgoyne shrugged hir slim shoulders ever so slightly, but gave no reaction beyond that. Obviously it made little sense to hir as well, but both knew Kebron well enough to be certain that further questions along such lines would be useless.

So instead Calhoun turned his attention back to what Kebron had wanted to inform him of. "So the *Trident* is being sent to Danter?"

Kebron nodded. At least, he gave what approximated a nod for a Brikar, namely bending slightly at the waist as if he were bowing in deference.

"And the Beings appear to be gathering there in force?" asked Burgoyne. "As part of some sort of new, grand plan by the Danteri to form an alliance of Being worshippers?"

Again Kebron nodded/bowed.

"Well, this is certainly an interesting turn of events," said Calhoun, tilting back in his chair. "Zak . . . are you positive?"

"I answered that."

"Yes, I know. I'd like to know the source, though. Because Captain Shelby has not informed me of this."

"No reason she should, Captain," Burgoyne pointed out. "No more so than any other starship would keep every other ship up-to-date about its activities. If she received word directly from Starfleet, she's under no obligation to file a flight plan with you."

"You're saying it's none of my business."

"No. You're saying that." S/he paused and then added, "I'm just thinking it."

Calhoun looked back to Kebron. "Source, Mr. Kebron?"

"Ensign Janos," Kebron said after a moment's hesitation. "Felt I should know."

"Hmmm," said Calhoun. "Well, he's certainly a dependable enough man . . . or being, I'm never entirely sure what to think of him as, actually." He scratched his smooth chin thoughtfully, missing the beard that he had shaved clean by popular request. With nothing of substance to do in drydock, the crew had amused itself during copious downtime by taking polls. The only thing the crew of the *Excalibur* seemed to agree on, nearly to one hundred percent accord, was that he should lose the beard. Calhoun had acquiesced, and a party had been held in his honor. It had been a damned good party and he couldn't remember the last time he'd gotten quite as drunk. But he was still nostalgic for the whiskers. "How did he find out?"

"He keeps his ear to the ground," said Kebron.

Burgoyne nodded. "That would certainly explain his odd posture."

"All right," Calhoun said. "Thank you for bringing this to my attention, Mr. Kebron."

Kebron was not one for words or sentiment. He tended to speak directly when he chose to speak at all, and he was not much for expressing sentiments of any sort. The matter-of-fact dismissal in Calhoun's tone would normally be more than enough excuse for Kebron to depart, since face-to-face discussions and conferences were not his favorite thing. So Calhoun was duly surprised when Kebron moved toward him and rested his massive hands on the edge of Calhoun's desk. In

Calhoun's imagination, the entire ship actually tipped slightly in Kebron's direction due to the shift in weight.

"When I first started serving under you, Captain, I had very little patience with you," Kebron said. "Frankly, I didn't think much of you."

Burgoyne and Calhoun exchange bewildered looks. "I think, for form's sake, one generally prefaces a comment like that with 'Permission to speak freely,' " Calhoun observed. "I invariably grant it, but it's the thought that counts."

As if Calhoun hadn't even spoken, Kebron continued, "That's changed over time. I've come to believe you to be a just individual. What those . . . creatures," and he said the word with more loathing and contained fury than either of them had ever heard from him, "did to this ship . . . it must not be countenanced. We must find them. We must make them pay. You will make them pay for what they did to us, won't you, Captain." It was not exactly a line drawn in the sand, defying Calhoun to ignore the sentiment under pain of personal retribution. But neither was it posed as a question. Kebron wanted to know right then, right there.

Calhoun's instinct, based upon protocol alone, was to inform Kebron that he had stepped way over the bounds of personal conduct. Even though Calhoun was extremely elastic in how he allowed his subordinates to address him, there were still rules and limits, and Zak Kebron had clearly exceeded them. He could dress him down, confine him to quarters, put him on report, even stick him in the brig if he was so inclined. Although, truthfully, the spectacle of security guards trying to haul Kebron to the brig if the powerful Brikar was disinclined to cooperate was not a particularly appealing image.

But Calhoun saw the fervency, the anger in Kebron's eyes. The truth was, Calhoun had always thought that one of Kebron's few weaknesses was the utter dispassion he brought to all his duties. His blasé nature often made it seem as if he didn't care whether he did his job or not, although he invariably did it better than anyone else could. So Calhoun was reluctant to do anything that might extinguish these first buds of genuine passion for his work that might be blooming in Kebron.

As a consequence, Calhoun opted to walk a fine line. "On the record, Mr. Kebron," said Calhoun, although it wasn't as if he was actually keeping a record of the meeting, "I am not enthused with the manner in which you just addressed me. Another captain would have busted you back to ensign because of it. So keep that in mind. Off the record," and slowly he nodded, "we'll get the bastards. No one does that to my crew and my ship. No one. Not even the gods themselves. In this case, whom the gods themselves tried to destroy, they didn't just make mad; they made fighting mad."

"Good," said Kebron with that approximation of a nod, and then he turned and walked out of the ready room.

"Where the hell did that come from?" Burgoyne demanded the moment Kebron was out of the ready room.

"I don't know. He was never one for fervent discourse." He tapped his fingers idly on the desk. "Talk to Soleta. She's known him the longest. Perhaps she can shed some light on this. Oh . . ." he added, with a smile. "Dr. Selar informed me of Soleta's little stunt in sickbay. Officially, I'm required to disapprove of her actions. Unofficially, please convey to her my sentiment that her attempted mind-meld with McHenry took a lot of guts, and I admire her for it. According to Selar, Soleta actually managed to . . . come into contact with him somehow. That single action has given us the first real cause for hope since this entire, hideous affair began. Tell her . . . I appreciate it. But you didn't hear it from me."

"Yes, sir," said Burgoyne, obviously amused. Then s/he grew serious again. "About Kebron . . . about what you said to him . . . about the gods making us fighting mad?"

Calhoun rose, smoothing his shirt. "I remember what I said, Burgy." His sword from his days as a Xenexian warlord was hanging, as always, from its place of honor on the wall. He took it down, removed a soft cloth from his desk, and proceeded to polish the gleaming blade. "We've been laid up for weeks, Burgy. Last thing I heard was three days to finish everything up."

"Yes, sir."

"Is that ironclad?"

"Pardon?" asked Burgoyne.

"Whatever needs to be done, can it be done in transit? On the way to, say, Danter."

Burgoyne was clearly considering all that needed to be attended to. Then, thoughtfully, s/he nodded. "It's possible, Captain. I wouldn't advise it."

"I wasn't looking for advice, Burgy. Just a simple yes or no."

"Yes," Burgoyne said briskly.

"Good. Inform Chief Mitchell down in engineering to fire up the engines. We're taking her out for a spin."

"For a spin, sir?" said Burgoyne with a look of caution in hir face. "Or for vengeance?"

Calhoun was halfway around the desk when Burgoyne spoke, but he paused and leaned against the side. "You disapprove?" he asked, folding his arms.

"It is not for me to approve or disapprove."

"You disagree."

"Captain, I had a firsthand view of the threat the Beings pose," said Burgoyne reasonably. "Believe me, if they had one great heart, I would rip it out and personally devour it."

"Your sentiments are appreciated, if not your cuisine choices."

"But," continued Burgoyne, "I believe there may be issues at work here that you haven't considered . . . not the least of which is that *Trident* may see this as an encroachment."

"I'm aware of that, Burgy," said Calhoun with a mildly regretful sigh.

"And that doesn't concern you?"

"Yes. It concerns me. But Burgy . . . I didn't trust the Danteri from the get-go. They subjugated my people. They always have other motives. And the Beings were malevolent rather than beneficent. McHenry saw right through them."

"McHenry said they were not to be trusted, and only then was the assault started," Burgoyne reminded him.

"What are you saying? That the attack was *McHenry's* fault?"

"No. It likely would have come sooner or later anyway. But his sentiments likely triggered it. I'm simply saying, Captain," s/he continued quickly when s/he saw the increasing clouding of Calhoun's face. "I'm simply saying that Captain Shelby, considering her lack of per-

sonal animus with the Beings, might be the ideal choice
of officer to be on the scene at Danter."

"You're right, Burgy. She might be." Then his face
hardened. "But she might not. And I'm not interested in
playing the odds. Not when my presence can double
them in our favor. Now . . . let's get this boat under way."

ii.

Robin Lefler was seated at her ops station, moving her
hands slowly over the totally rebuilt surface of the controls. There was no trace of the damage that had been
done during the attack. It was almost as if the assault by
the Beings were imaginary. If the evidence was gone, it
was just that much easier to sweep the reality away into
the farthest recesses of recollection.

Well, that was why she had wanted to get rid of the
holoimage of her mother, wasn't it? As selfish as that had
been? By banishing that . . . that *thing* from existence, it
would be that much easier for Robin to avoid thinking
about her. Just toss her from her mind, erase any feelings
of hurt or love or . . . or anything. Just be nice and bliss-
fully numb over the loss of the one individual in her life
whom she had never known quite how to relate to.

On the screen in front of her was the steady image of
Starbase 27 as they continued their leisurely orbit
around it. Her gaze wandered from the rather boring
view over toward the conn station. Fully repaired,
gleaming and new, it nevertheless looked pitifully
empty. In addition to McHenry, two backup navigation
officers had been killed during the attack of the Beings.

Naturally there were crewmen who could fill in in a pinch, but Starfleet had dispatched two new officers to cover the day and night shifts. They were expected to arrive within the next three days.

Devereaux was finishing some work at the tactical station, as Zak Kebron stood near and glowered down at him. It was obviously distracting the hell out of Devereaux, but he lacked the nerve to say anything about it. She couldn't entirely blame him; Kebron could be a daunting figure when he wanted to be. Or even when he didn't want to be.

Then Devereaux looked up as the door to the captain's ready room slid open. "Captain on the bridge," he barked out.

The rest of the crew had long since given up sending odd looks Devereaux's way. There were indeed some Starfleet captains who preferred the ceremonial announcement whenever the top-ranked commanding officer set foot on the bridge. But Calhoun's priorities did not lie in that direction. The first time Devereaux had bellowed the proclamation, Calhoun had told him quite politely that it wasn't necessary. That everyone in the place had eyes and could see him just fine.

Devereaux, equally politely, had told him that—the way he was raised in a family that had followed a tradition of Starfleet service for two centuries—there was simply no option. He had sworn to Calhoun that he would try to restrain himself. Sometimes he managed to refrain from saying it at all, and other times he said it softly. Every so often, though, he just had to let it out. Calhoun simply shrugged it off. Lefler had even begun to suspect that—on some level—the captain kind of liked it. At the very least, he seemed to get a kick out of the way everyone looked at Devereaux.

Instead of heading to the captain's chair, Calhoun stopped a few feet from the exit of the ready room and said, "Mr. Devereaux . . . three hours ago you told me your work on the computer core would be completed. Because I'm a generous sort of fellow, I've given you three hours and two minutes. Where do we stand?"

"We stand completed, Captain," said Devereaux briskly. "The entire system has been stripped down, flushed out, buffed up, and is ready to go. And without so much as the loss of a single operating system for so much as a minute."

"There are fewer great satisfactions than that of self," Calhoun replied solemnly.

For her part, Robin felt a distinct sinking sensation. She felt . . . unclean. Ungrateful. Hell, she had to be candid with herself: Even though she knew there was no basis in fact to feel that way, it was as if she had somehow condemned her mother to death with her own hand.

"All right then," said Calhoun after a moment. "Impress me, Mr. Devereaux."

"Computer," Devereaux called.

Without a moment's hesitation, the computer voice filtered through the bridge. "Working."

The voice was jolting for Robin. She'd never fully realized, now that Morgan was gone, just how much the computer voice—even under normal circumstances—sounded like her. She'd noted a resemblance in the past, but now . . . now it felt as if the same woman was speaking.

Devereaux looked to Calhoun expectantly. Calhoun

merely shrugged, waiting. So Devereaux said, "Computer: List all ships currently active in Starfleet registry."

"Specify order: Alphabetically by ship name, in order of date of registry, or numerically by registration number."

Devereaux started to respond, but Calhoun cut in and said quietly, "Computer, you choose."

The computer proceeded to rattle off with crisp, cool, and monotone efficiency every starship, transport, troop ship . . . everything that had a Starfleet registration number. It listed them alphabetically, beginning with the *Adelphi.* By the time it got to the *Ellison,* Calhoun had obviously heard enough and made a throat-cutting gesture.

But there was something going on that Lefler couldn't quite understand. She saw a look of quiet contemplation on Calhoun, as if he was comprehending something that was simply not obvious to Robin Lefler at all.

"Computer, begin running diagnostic checks on all systems. Report when completed." He turned to Calhoun and said, "Satisfied, Captain?" But even Devereaux seemed a bit puzzled by something.

Then Lefler realized what it was, or at least she thought she did. It was exceedingly odd that the computer had responded at all when Calhoun had given it a choice of what order to list the vessels. It really should have said "Unable to comply" or "Specification required." Still, it was entirely possible that there was simply some sort of default program or setting.

"Computer," Calhoun said suddenly, "access personnel file," and his gaze swiveled over to Robin, "Lieutenant Robin Lefler."

"Accessing," the computer said without hesitation.

Lefler frowned, not understanding at all what the purpose of this was.

"Captain . . . ?" said Devereaux, also clearly bewildered.

Calhoun ignored him. "Computer . . . read out the entirety of Robin Lefler's personal medical history. All details. Then her psych profile. All details. As a matter of fact," he continued, "access her personal log. Read that out, too. Begin with that."

Robin's cheeks flushed bright red. *"Captain!"* she said in shock.

"Captain Calhoun, I must protest," said Devereaux. "There's many other ways to test computer efficiency!"

"Captain, I respectfully agree," Soleta said, casting a look toward Robin. "This is a most intrusive . . ."

But Burgoyne turned and said, "Soleta . . . it's all right." She looked visibly surprised for a moment in response, but said nothing further.

In the meantime, curiously, the computer had not carried out its ordered function. "Computer," Calhoun said, and he strolled toward the center of the bridge, arms draped casually behind his back. "Execute orders."

"Medical records accessible only to chief medical officer. Personal recorded material is under confidential seal," the computer said after a moment's more hesitation. "Access denied."

A sigh of relief escaped from Robin, but Calhoun didn't appear fazed. "Computer, I am employing command override priority One Zero Zero Zero One. Execute my orders. Let's all hear Robin Lefler's most personal, intimate thoughts."

Robin braced herself.

The computer was silent.

"Computer," said Calhoun with a warning tone. "Don't make me come in there. Execute my orders, override priority One Zer—"

"You bastard," the computer said.

There was startled gasps from throughout the bridge, but Calhoun simply laughed.

"Captain!" an alarmed Devereaux squeaked out. "I . . . I didn't instruct it to—!"

"Mr. Devereaux," Calhoun sighed, walking over to tactical and resting a hand on Devereaux's shoulder, *"you* may know computers. But *I* know people. And one person I knew—Morgan Lefler—was not someone who was of a sort to go gently into that good night. Morgan! Front and center. That is an order, and this one I definitely *am* expecting to be obeyed."

The computer screen wavered, and then the image seemed to dissolve into bits and pieces, billions of dots floating on the monitor for a heartbeat before snapping back together and reassembling into a familiar, and somewhat annoyed, visage. Robin jumped back in her seat, her jaw dropping, as her mother looked out at them from the screen.

"With all respect, Captain, you are *some* piece of work," she said in obvious annoyance.

"This is *impossible!"* Devereaux cried out.

"And yet, here we all are," said an amused Calhoun.

"I could have stayed hidden within the computer indefinitely," Morgan said. Behind her was a background that was an exact replica of the bridge of the *Excalibur.* She had obviously conjured it at a whim. It was so realistic that Robin half thought she would be able to turn

170

around and see her mother standing directly behind her shoulder. "Kept things running without a hitch. You'd never have known."

"Morgan, you masked your presence from me for about two minutes," Calhoun pointed out. "I don't think long term would really have been an option, do you?"

"Captain, you don't understand," Devereaux said, his voice practically trembling with frustration. "I'm one of the top people from Daystrom! No one alive could have been more thorough than I was. What we're seeing here, this is . . . this can't be occurring. There's no *way* the personality of Morgan Lefler would have been able to withstand the rebooting of the computer."

"I can see your point, Devereaux," said Calhoun, sounding quite reasonable. "But I look at it from a different point of view. The way I see it, we haven't yet developed the equipment that can overcome the sheer force of willpower, human or otherwise. Early man knew beyond question the world was flat and sailing too far would send you off the edge . . . yet some explorers found it to be different. Heisenberg would have told you that, by his uncertainty principles, a matter transporter cannot possibly exist . . . yet it does. Einstein would easily explain why faster-than-light travel is an absurdity . . . yet here we are.

"In this case, despite all reasonable beliefs to the contrary," and he looked at the face on the screen, "I was certain from the outset that no technology or procedures, as sophisticated and thorough as they were, would be able to obliterate the personality of Morgan Primus Lefler. Turns out I was right."

"And if you'd been wrong?" demanded Morgan.

"Would you have let my daughter's most personal concerns become aired publicly?"

"I knew I wasn't wrong," Calhoun replied, and it was clear from the way he said it that any further pressing of the question would be a waste of time.

"So . . . what now?" asked Robin.

"Morgan," Calhoun said, "it's my surmise that, short of blowing up the *Excalibur*—again—you're more or less here to stay."

"More or less," Morgan allowed, and then she glanced cautiously at Robin. "Provided . . . that's acceptable to you, Robin."

Robin let out a breath of relief that sounded surprisingly to her like a laugh. "That's . . . perfectly acceptable, Mother. It wasn't the same without you."

"Morgan . . . I think you knew immediately that I was testing you," said Calhoun, and now he sounded very serious. "On that basis, I wasn't really expecting you to obey me . . . as you were likely aware. That is *not,* however, an acceptable option for the future. Do you understand that? I don't care that you have a mind of your own. Henceforth, I tell you to do something, you do it. You refuse to carry out an order again, and I *will* scuttle this vessel, without hesitation. Is that clear?"

"Clear, Captain," Morgan said quite formally.

"Good. Can you take over the conn station?"

"Of course."

"What?" Robin was on her feet, and the others appeared startled as well. "Captain . . . ?"

"We're heading out, and I'm not inclined to sit around and wait for Starfleet to get personnel here. We'll swing back for them or rendezvous at a future date," Calhoun said briskly. "Mr. Devereaux, you'll return to Starbase 27 at once. We're pushing off in ten minutes."

"Course, Captain?" inquired Morgan. With no change in her expression to indicate any effort on her part, the conn and navigation station came awake from standby position, humming to life and illuminating.

"Danter. Best possible speed."

"Danter, Captain?" inquired Robin.

"That's right, Lieutenant. Danter." He smiled grimly. "We're heading there for round two. And this time, I'm hoping for an ungodly ending."

TRIDENT

i.

KAT MUELLER, NAKED, MOVED SLOWLY in the dimness of the room, the lights at half so as not to awaken Si Cwan, who was stretched out on the bed. The dinner that she had invited him to eat remained unconsumed on a table nearby. Fortunately enough, it was a cold chicken dish to start with. Kat had surmised ahead of time that they might find other activities to occupy them beside food.

A thin coat of sweat covered her body, as she brought her arm up and around in a slow, circular pattern. Then it went down, her other arm came up in a gentle sweep, and then very, very slowly, she thrust forward her right hand in a tiger claw grip. As slowly as she was moving, each muscle strained against itself. She had been moving through the routine for five minutes, and it was superb isometric exercise for her.

She balanced perfectly on one leg as she drew the

other up, keeping her toes pointed, and she snapped out a precision kick.

Then she heard movement from the bed, and sheets rustle. A moment later, Si Cwan was standing next to her, just behind her, looking in the full-length mirror in which she was watching her reflection. Naked alongside her, he proceeded to imitate her moves perfectly, falling into the smooth, easy rhythm she had achieved.

They said nothing to one another. It was as if they were the only two beings alive in the entirety of the universe. Mueller came to the surprising realization that she liked having Si Cwan around. It was surprising because Mueller was the sort of person who generally didn't like having anyone around, so she couldn't quite comprehend why it was she felt different about Cwan. Perhaps it was because he was more like her than anyone she'd ever been involved with, with the possible exception of Mackenzie Calhoun. And in Calhoun's case, the unfortunate truth was that they were too much alike. As a result, they would never really have worked well as a long-term couple.

Another fifteen minutes passed in the silent routine before Mueller finally exhaled a long, steady breath, and Si Cwan followed suit.

"That was stimulating," she said. Si Cwan simply nodded.

They showered together, scrubbing each other down. There was nothing especially sensual about it, although she certainly did appreciate the hardness of his muscles and sleekness of his body. And she was quite sure that he had the same opinion about her body because, of course, who wouldn't.

Even as they bathed, her mind was elsewhere. Most

particularly, she was thinking about Shelby. The captain had said nothing to her since their confrontation in the conference lounge. That disturbed her. The truth was, in retrospect, Mueller probably had gone too far in her comments about Calhoun. Naturally the woman cared about her husband. She really was out of line. But it wasn't in Mueller's nature to seek out Shelby and apologize or seek her forgiveness. If Shelby *told* her to apologize, she would do so willingly, even gratefully. Initiating the discussion, though . . . that, to Mueller, came across too much like groveling. She had far too much German pride for that.

Shelby hadn't come to her, though, and that bothered Mueller. As Mueller and Si Cwan dressed in silence, Kat felt as if the disagreement was festering, and that it might even start to bore its way into the captain–executive officer relationship. She knew that wouldn't be a good thing, that it could be detrimental to the entirety of the way affairs were conducted on the *Trident*.

"What are we doing here?" Si Cwan asked abruptly.

Talk about conducting affairs. "We're finishing putting on our clothes," she said matter-of-factly.

"You know that's not what I'm referring to, Commander."

"Commander?" She laughed coarsely. "Are you always that formal with women you sleep with?"

"Only when they're keeping me at arm's length."

Mueller's uniform top was still hanging open. She faced him and pressed her bare torso up against his. "There. Not arm's length. Satisfied?"

"What's going on here, Kat?"

She looked up at him, and even in the dimness of the

room, the annoyance in her eyes was certainly visible. "You said 'Robin.' You called me 'Robin.' "

"I did not!" Si Cwan protested. "I just called you 'Kat'!"

"Not now. Earlier. During."

"That's absurd. I . . . didn't do such a . . . I would never . . ." He frowned and seemed to deflate. "I did?"

She nodded. "Loud and clear. 'Robin.' Lefler, I assume?"

"Oh gods. I'm sorry." He turned away from her, sitting on the edge of the bed. "She's . . . been on my mind, lately. Something Kalinda said . . ."

"You know what, Cwan?" She fastened closed her uniform shirt, and shrugged. "Let's just leave it. It's all right. I shouldn't even have mentioned it."

"It's not all right. I—"

"Cwan, you're not getting it. I said we leave it. So we leave it. This," and she gestured around the room, indicating in one sweep of her arm all the activity that had passed there, "this is what it is. I'm really not interested in anything beyond that anyway. I'm content to be two ships passing in the night, especially if you feel your harbor is elsewhere."

"Kat . . ."

"You can be of help to me, though." There were so many things she wanted to say, but she managed to keep her voice even and dispassionate. She did so from long practice, and had never been more glad of it. "I may have a problem. Could be my imagination . . . could be not."

"What sort of problem?"

In quick, broad strokes, she described to him the encounter she'd had with Lieutenant Commander Gleau.

Si Cwan took it all in, nodding and listening, asking a question here and there, but otherwise silent.

"So you don't know for sure," Si Cwan said finally, "whether he really did threaten Lieutenant M'Ress."

"No. I don't. Frankly, my first inclination was to dismiss her worries out of hand. But since then . . ." She tapped her solar plexus. "My gut tells me what she said is true."

"A conjecture," said Cwan after a moment's thought. "Let's say, for argument's sake, he did threaten her. It's possible it was an empty threat, one that he never intended to carry out. Perhaps he did so in order to gain some sort of . . . of 'revenge' for having to sign the oath of chastity enforced upon him, which he would most certainly blame her for. It was, after all, her initial complaints about his using the Knack upon her to have his way with her that set all that into motion in the first place."

"Let's say you're right," said Mueller. She had seated herself near the table and was idly munching on a breadstick. Cwan came over and joined her, sitting opposite her. She waved the breadstick at him as she spoke. "Are you claiming, then, that what he did was acceptable on some level . . . ?"

"No, of course not," replied Si Cwan. "I am saying, however, that it might not be the life-and-death scenario that you believe it to be."

She bit off a piece of the breadstick. The crust was hard and made very loud noises as she crunched down on it. She chewed it quickly and swallowed, and then said, "Perhaps you're right."

"Perhaps I am."

"However," she continued, "in the event that you're

wrong . . . if something should happen to me—something violent or mysterious—I want you to know that Gleau might very well be behind it. And if that's the case, I would be most obliged if you could find it within you to rip his head off his shoulders."

"Violent or mysterious?" He looked appalled. "Are you saying you believe this Gleau to be a direct threat to you?"

"I don't know what to believe, to be honest, except that one should never downplay possible actions that others may take. If Gleau thinks I'm a potential threat, and he thinks he can dispose of me without being caught doing so . . ."

"How would that be possible?"

"Who knows what he's capable of?" she asked reasonably. "If he does have some sort of mind powers that we're unfamiliar with, who knows what sort of suggestions he could plant in my head. What if he managed to convince me that it would be a superb idea to put a phaser in my mouth and pull the trigger? We don't know. We can't know until after it happens . . . and if it does happen, I wanted you to be aware to be on the lookout for it."

"And you haven't told Captain Shelby any of this?"

"It's my job to tell the captain what I know. Not what I suspect but can't verify."

"It seems to me your job is whatever you decide it to be, and if you wanted to tell Shelby, you could."

"Cwan," she said, "you have to understand that I have a very suspicious nature. If I told Captain Shelby every time I was suspicious about something, I'd be coming to her constantly about all manner of things, to the point where I would be useless as an advisor. And ninety percent of the time, those suspicions turn out to be baseless, or else the basis for matters that are so inconsequential as to not be worth the captain's time. I will not inform the captain of something that does not yet warrant her attention."

"It seems to me that you're allowing your pride to get in the way," he told her.

"Perhaps," she agreed. "But it's my pride. And my way."

"I can see that." He looked at her askance. "Would you like me simply to dispose of this Gleau for you?"

She blinked. "Pardon?"

"I can do that, if you'd like. Quickly, cleanly, efficiently. None will connect it to you, or even me."

"Don't be insane, Cwan. You can't just unilaterally decide who lives and who dies . . ."

"I can and I have, on several occasions," Si Cwan replied.

"Back when you were a Thallonian noble, perhaps . . ."

"I still am a Thallonian noble," said Si Cwan with assurance. "The fact that the Thallonian empire is gone is beside the point."

"See, I would have thought that *was* the point."

"No. Nobility comes from here," and he tapped his heart. "In my heart, in my pedigree and training, I am a noble still. And as such, I will do what needs to be done if I feel it needs doing."

"Well, don't," she said flatly. "Don't kill Lieutenant Commander Gleau. That's not what I want."

"You want me to avenge your death rather than preempt it."

"I didn't say that."

"No," he replied, sounding quite reasonable about it.

180

"I did. You said everything but that. I merely put it all together."

She didn't have a ready answer for that because she knew, on some level, that he was absolutely right.

ii.

Captain Shelby looked up as executive officer Kat Mueller strode into the ready room. She knew Mueller's body language all too well. Her shoulders were squared, her jaw set. She was either looking for, or anticipating, a fight.

"Captain," she said briskly, "I believe we need to talk."

"Do we."

Shelby's calm demeanor seemed to throw Mueller slightly off balance. Mueller cleared her throat after a moment, her hands tightly behind her back, and said, "We had a disagreement several days ago in the conference lounge . . ."

"Did we?"

Mueller frowned, staring at Shelby with a distinctly suspicious air. "Captain, are you being coy with me for some reason?"

"I don't believe so. I'm curious as to what you think we disagreed about?"

"Regarding your husband . . ."

"He's the captain of the *Excalibur*. I think we pretty much concur on that."

"*Captain!*" said Mueller in obvious exasperation.

Shelby got up from behind her desk and strolled to the viewing window. She looked out toward the stars as if she could see the *Excalibur* somewhere out among them. "Look, XO, you implied that my concern over my husband was secondary to my concern over Starfleet orders. The hard fact is, there's some small element of truth in that. As long as I'm captain of this vessel, my allegiance has to be to what Starfleet wants, and what's best for the needs of this ship and her crew."

Her eyes narrowed. "But that doesn't mean I don't care. It doesn't ever mean that if something happened to Mac because of my inaction or inability to help, it wouldn't crush my heart . . . probably beyond its ability ever to recover. And as long as you never imply anything other than that, we'll have no further problems. Is that clear?"

Mueller looked as if she was going to say something else entirely, but then her features softened and she simply said, "Yes, Captain."

"Good. Say anything like that again, and I'll fire you."

"You're joking," said Mueller. "You would relieve me of duty?"

"No, I would fire you, as in, out a photon torpedo tube."

"Ah." There were the slightest hints of a smile at the edge of Mueller's mouth. "Understood."

"Is there anything else you wanted to discuss with me?" asked Shelby.

She thought for an instant that there was something on Mueller's mind. But if there was, Mueller obviously chose to refrain from sharing it, because she simply shook her head and said, "No, Captain."

At that moment, Takahashi informed Shelby that they were drawing within hailing range of Danter, and she and Mueller immediately headed out onto the bridge.

Shelby wasn't remotely certain what to expect upon their first contact with Danter. Considering that they had sent Si Cwan and Kalinda speeding on their way with surface-to-space blasts, there was no reason to assume they might not be treated in a similar manner. So it was with distinct trepidation that she sent a preliminary hail down to Danter when the ship settled into orbit around the planet. She also made certain that Si Cwan was standing next to her when she got a response back, and that Ambassador Spock was there as well . . . although he was off to one side, not endeavoring to pull attention to himself. He seemed most intrigued with the bridge, inspecting it carefully. Shelby had a feeling that, if asked, Spock could easily draw a perfect reproduction of the bridge from memory.

When the image appeared on the screen, she didn't recognize him at first, nor did Si Cwan. What she saw was a Danteri with a young, robust look to him, round face, pleasant, modulated tone. In fact, he practically seemed to glow with good health. He spread wide his hands and said, "Greetings, my friends. Greetings from Danter. It is good to see you again, Captain Shelby. And before anything else is said, this must be said first: Lord Cwan, I see you there. Can you ever forgive me for our inhospitable treatment of you?"

Si Cwan stepped forward, bewilderment etched on his face, and then it cleared only to be replaced by even more confusion. *"Lodec?"* he managed to say.

At first she thought he had to be in error, but then she realized that, no, it was the senate speaker of Danter, all right. But this was not the aged Danteri whom she had met some time ago. Actually, it *was,* but he was barely recognizable as himself.

"I . . . I don't understand," said Si Cwan, nor did

Shelby. "Lodec, you . . . you look so very different . . . is it you?" He looked at Shelby. "Is it him?"

Takahashi was already running a quick double check through his ops board. "He's our boy, all right," drawled Hash. "His voiceprint matches with the record of his previous communiqués. Match is ninety-nine percent, which is as close as we ever get with that method of ID. You want better, you're gonna haveta go for genetic, but as they say, this is close enough for jazz."

"They say that? Who says that?" asked a confused Si Cwan. "No one I know says that. And who is 'Jazz'?"

"It is understandable you would be so astonished," said Lodec easily. "These are astonishing times. That is what we tried to convey to you, Ambassador . . . and failed utterly in doing so."

"I'd call attempted murder a bit more than simply failing to get a point across," Shelby said, sitting upright in her chair, her arms folded, her gaze leveled upon Lodec's image. "Si Cwan and Kalinda nearly died in space. They would have, if not for a lucky happenstance."

"There is no such thing as lucky," Lodec informed her, his voice rising and falling in an odd sort of singsong. "There is only the will of the gods. They walk among us, you know. They love us, and we love them."

"Sounds charming," Si Cwan commented sarcastically.

"We admit, there were some difficulties as we became adjusted to the power of the ambrosia, and comprehending our new place in life's great plan," continued Lodec as if Si Cwan hadn't spoken. For all Shelby knew, he hadn't even heard Cwan say anything. "But we understand now. There is no longer any need for hostility.

Come. See for yourselves. You will walk among us unmolested."

"And what of the Beings?" asked Shelby. "Are they here?"

"Yes. Of course," said Lodec. His smile was so wide it looked as if it could meet around the back of his head. "They walk among us and speak to us of so many things. And we have our prayer meetings, and we worship the greatness that is the Beings. They, in turn, give us ambrosia and guidance, and are helping us to build a great empire that will—in time—spread from one farthest star to the other."

"How very special for you," Mueller spoke up.

"Come. Meet them. Encounter them. See the vast improvements over how things are done now, as opposed to how they once were handled. Your safe passage is guaranteed."

"As was ours, until you tried to kill us," Si Cwan pointed out.

Lodec's smile couldn't be disrupted. "My dear Si Cwan," he said, "perhaps I have not made myself clear. The Beings are here. The residents of the *Trident* have seen the results of the Beings' wrath firsthand. Their might is no less now than it was then; greater, in fact. If the Beings had hostile intent . . . do you think for a moment that your vessel would still be in orbit?"

This caused an uncomfortable silence as the bridge crew glanced around at one another. Visions of the battered *Excalibur* came to Shelby's mind, and there was no reason to think that it wasn't foremost in everyone else's concerns as well.

"You do not answer," Lodec continued after a moment. "That's perfectly all right. You don't answer because we all know what the response would be. Come to the paradise that is now Danter. See for yourselves the life we lead . . . and the life that is viewed with such suspicion by your Federation."

"Captain," Spock said softly, "it will be problematic for me to carry out my intended objectives if I am to remain in orbit for the entirety of our time here."

Shelby nodded, taking this in, and then turned her attention back to the screen. "Very well. An away team will be sent planetside. Their findings will be instrumental in informing Federation decisions in regards to the offers of these 'Beings.' "

"Captain, if I may," asked Spock, and she nodded to him to go ahead. "Speaker . . . are we to understand that the Beings are still interested in providing ambrosia to whomever desires it?"

"All manner of possibilities exist, Ambassador," Lodec assured him. "Come and let us discuss matters, like civilized creatures."

"A team will be along shortly. Shelby out." She nodded once to Hash, who promptly shut off the com link. Lodec's smiling visage vanished from the screen, to be replaced with an image of the planet rotating below.

"I do not trust them," Si Cwan said immediately.

"Logic would indicate, Ambassador," Spock told him, "that your concern is colored by the fact that they endeavored to kill you."

Hash laughed in a way that bordered on the sarcastic. "And why *ever* would he allow his concern to be colored by that?"

"I don't believe anyone asked you, Mr. Takahashi,"
Mueller said sharply, and then turned to Shelby. "Captain . . . I hope you're not considering heading up this
away team."

"It had crossed my mind, XO."

'With all respect, Captain," said Mueller, the emphasis on "respect" so meticulous that Shelby couldn't possibly have taken offense unless she had a chip on her
shoulder the size of a moon, "the situation, unstable as it
is, is not one that our commanding officer should be
thrusting herself into."

"Even though the Beings could conceivably reach up
from the planet's surface and swat us at any time?" asked
Shelby. "An argument could be made that no one is safe."

"I'm convinced," Hash piped up. "Let's get the hell
out of here."

Shelby ignored him, which was usually the best practice to follow when Hash was employing what he fancied to be his rapier wit. "Recommendations, XO?"

"Away team consisting of myself, Ambassadors
Spock and Cwan, and Lieutenant Arex."

"What about Captain Calhoun?" Mick Gold spoke up
from conn.

Shelby turned and frowned. "I'm not entirely sure how
Captain Calhoun is relevant to the conversation, Gold."

"He's only relevant in the sense that he's here."

All eyes were suddenly on the monitor screen as, sure
enough, dropping out of warp was the *Starship Excalibur.*

"I was unaware the *Excalibur* had been assigned to
this mission," Spock said.

"That's because they haven't been," Shelby said
tightly. She thought she heard a soft chuckle come from

Mueller's direction, but when she looked at her second-in-command, Kat's face was purely deadpan. "Hash. Raise them."

An instant later, Calhoun's face appeared on the screen. She noticed he'd shaved. Figured. She'd just gotten used to the beard. "Captain," she said in as formal a tone as she could muster. "We weren't expecting to see you here."

"Yes. I know. My understanding is that Starfleet is endeavoring to be circumspect in its broadcasting of orders these days."

Her eyes narrowed. "Are you saying Starfleet ordered you to rendezvous with us at Danter?"

"I'm afraid I can't say at the present time," Calhoun informed her.

I'll kill him, thought Shelby even as she kept a smile plastered on her face. "I think it best we get together, Captain, so we can make certain our orders aren't in conflict with one another."

"Excellent idea, Captain," replied Calhoun. "Your place or mine?"

"Yours. I'll be right over." Shelby turned to Mueller. "Would there be a great deal of paperwork involved if we simply opened fire on the *Excalibur* and blew her out of space?"

"I believe Starfleet would frown upon it, Captain."

"Damn," muttered Shelby.

"Captain," Spock observed, "it would appear to me that you have some little antipathy for the *Excalibur* in general . . . or her captain in specific."

"He's my husband."

"Ah," said Spock. He paused, and then said, "In my

day, captains were generally considered to be married to their ships."

"Those were good days," said Shelby and headed for the turbolift.

And she heard Spock say, "Indeed," as the lift doors slid shut behind her.

EXCALIBUR

i.

MOKE WAS BECOMING ACCUSTOMED to having the ghosts around.

He had given up trying to comprehend them. He didn't know why they were there, or what they wanted. He was a flexible child, and so had decided that his new lot in life was to have shades of departed crew members or mysterious one-eyed men following him around.

He didn't see them all the time, and that was partly how he knew they weren't just in his mind. After all, if they were, then he would have been seeing them twenty-four hours a day, seven days a week. They would have had no reason to be anywhere else. But because he only perceived them from time to time, he concluded that they had other things they had to attend to. What sort of things, he couldn't begin to imagine. Ghost things. Shades of the departed things. Things he probably wouldn't really want to know about, if given his preferences.

The shade of McHenry had conveyed to him the importance of silence. Moke had done as he was bid, for several reasons. First, he had convinced himself that the secrecy was part of the ability to see them. If he started blabbing it, they would go away. He didn't want to take that risk, because—much to his surprise, considering how disconcerted he'd felt in their initial encounters— he liked seeing them. He had become fond of being one of the only people on the ship who could see these rather odd ghosts wandering the corridors.

The only other being, to Moke's knowledge, who was able to see them was Xyon. He wasn't sure at exactly what point the child became aware of what he was seeing. Moke simply noticed one day that Xyon was staring straight at the one-eyed man, and was even waving one of his chubby little fists at him.

Moke was no doctor, no man of medicine. He had no clue why he and Xyon were able to perceive these shades whom everyone else on the *Excalibur* was walking right past, or even through. Perhaps it was a fundamental innocence on Xyon's part which made him particularly susceptible to such images. Or maybe something in the genetic structure of his half-breed heritage enabled him to see past reality to the unreality.

Maybe he was just damned lucky.

Either way, the old one-eyed man waved back to him, which prompted Xyon to giggle and coo and bat at the empty air.

Still, Moke was beginning to feel as if his withholding of information over what he was perceiving might have some sort of negative impact on everything his adoptive father and the crew of the *Excalibur* were experiencing. This was particularly the case when Soleta sat down with him in his quarters and gently began asking questions for which he did not have easy answers.

She kept coming back to statements that Moke had made which indicated that he had seen McHenry wandering around the ship in disembodied form. She wanted to know more about that, wanted to comprehend exactly what it was that Moke was seeing and how it could be that he was seeing it.

But Moke was very aware that both McHenry and the one-eyed man didn't want their presence or connection to Moke discussed. And when Soleta made casual mention of "the others," referring to the other godlike beings, Moke suddenly began to suspect just why the need for secrecy was so important to them. Obviously McHenry and the one-eyed man were concerned that these other "beings" might be listening in somehow to whatever Moke was saying. That for some reason, the Beings didn't know that McHenry had broken free of the confines of his body, and might not even know that the old bearded man was walking around unseen on the ship. But if Moke talked about it, and they were "listening" somehow, then the secret would be out and there might be all kinds of trouble.

Moke was not anxious for trouble. It wasn't all that long ago that the Beings had attacked Moke's spacegoing home and Moke had been quite, quite certain that he was going to die that day. He wasn't anxious for a repeat.

Besides, McHenry continued to make his wishes known. When Soleta faced Moke and said, quietly but firmly, "Moke . . . are you able to see McHenry? Are

you seeing him now?," McHenry was standing just behind her and wildly gesticulating and shaking his head.

Moke, without even realizing he was doing it, shook
his head in imitation of McHenry.

"Have you seen any other . . . individuals?" she
asked. When Moke again shook his head, she came as
close to exasperation as she usually allowed herself.
"Then why have you led me to believe that you did?"

"I guess I wanted to believe I saw them. Maybe I
thought I could help if I did, or it would make people
feel better," he offered. He didn't think it sounded very
convincing, and Soleta didn't especially look as if she
accepted what he was saying. Nevertheless, she didn't
push it much beyond that.

His reluctance to be forthcoming, however, began to
prey upon him. Finally he decided to speak with the one
individual on whom he could always count: Calhoun.
He figured that if he phrased his concerns in a vague
enough manner, he might be able to get useful answers
without giving away more than he should.

Standing in the middle of his quarters, Moke said,
"Computer. Where is Captain Calhoun?"

There was a pause. That surprised him. Moke didn't
have all that much call to interact directly with the ship's
computer system, but even he knew that response was
always instantaneous.

He was even more surprised when the computer
replied, "Why are you asking?"

"I . . ." He blinked, trying to parse out what was going
on. "I just . . . wanted to know."

"Why?"

Moke put his hands on his hips, looking slightly defiant. "I don't think you're supposed to be able to ask me things like that! Just tell me where he is?"

"Captain Calhoun is in conference lounge two."

"Okay," said Moke, and he started to head for the door.

He stopped in his tracks, however, as the computer said, "If you're planning to go see him there, I wouldn't advise it."

He knew that the computer shouldn't be interested in advising him on anything. But that was less important to him than the reasons for the computer's concern. "Why not?"

"This would not be a good time."

"Why?"

"Cover your ears."

Moke couldn't remember when he'd felt more bewildered over something that should have just been a normal interaction with standard equipment. "Cover my ears?"

"Yes."

"With what?"

It almost sounded like the computer was sighing in exasperation. "With your hands, boy."

"Oh." Feeling a bit sheepish, he obeyed.

A moment later, the room was flooded with several voices. Moke thought Mac's was one of them, but it was hard to be sure, because they were all shouting at one another, and it was clear that everyone was very irritated. Even though his hands were already over his ears, he pressed them together tighter, wincing at the oral barrage as he did so.

Mercifully, it was shut off within seconds.

Moke was stunned. "What . . . was that? Who was Mac fighting with?"

"It wasn't a fight. It was a discussion," the computer informed him. "A very loud discussion . . . with some profanity mixed in. Adults do that on occasion."

"So do kids! And the adults yell at us when we do! So who yells at the adults when they do it?"

"Other adults."

"I don't understand," Moke said in exasperation.

"Don't worry. When you grow up—"

"I'll understand then?"

"No," the computer informed him. "Adults don't understand much more than children do. They just don't understand it at a higher volume."

ii.

"I don't understand, Mac!"

"I'm not *looking* to you to understand, Eppy!"

"Well, you certainly got what you're *not* looking for!"

It was just the two of them in the conference lounge, which was why Shelby wasn't holding back in the least. If other crew members were there, she would have forced herself to be far more reserved. As it was, she didn't hesitate in giving vent to the frustration she was feeling at that moment.

She knew Calhoun was as irritated with her as she was with him. The infuriating aspect of the man, though, was that he wasn't showing it. He simply sat there with his fingers steepled like some sort of damned Buddha statue. Although he was speaking as loudly as she was, it seemed motivated less by anger than simply by the desire to make himself heard over her.

She paced the room, running her fingers through her hair and fighting the impulse to start tearing it out at the roots . . . and the further impulse to rip out Calhoun's hair instead. "Mac, the *Trident* is the ship that's supposed to be here. Not the *Excal*."

"I was given no orders that told me to stay away from this world."

"Oh, for crying out loud, Mac, what're you? Nine years old? You have to have everything spelled out for you as to what you can and cannot do, and if it's not specifically forbidden, then you figure it's fair game?"

"Curious thing: On some worlds, I would be considered nine years old, when one allows for the amount of time it takes for the planet to complete its orbit around the—"

Shelby stopped pacing and leaned forward, resting her knuckles on the table, her face only a few inches from Calhoun's. "Don't get cute, Mac."

"Cute works if you're nine years old."

Her voice tight, she said, "Turn this ship around and get out of here."

Something in the air changed when she said that. She felt as if, for the first time since they'd entered the room and confronted one another over the *Excalibur*'s unexpected arrival, she had truly gotten Calhoun's attention. And she wasn't entirely certain that was a good thing.

"Don't try to give me orders, Elizabeth," said Calhoun icily, his eyes like flint. "The *Excal* is here because we need to be here."

"Right, of course. You need to be here. Because you're so convinced that the *Trident* can't get the job done."

"Not everything that goes on in the galaxy is about

you, Elizabeth," Calhoun said, repeating her first name formally as if to drive home to her how far away his mind-set was from the usual, affectionate "Eppy." It was odd. She had loathed the nickname, then grown to tolerate it, and now actually was a bit upset that he wasn't using it. "My showing up here isn't intended as a commentary on my belief as to whether or not you can handle a difficult situation."

"Well, that's great to hear, Mackenzie," she replied, choosing to be as formal as he was being. "Particularly when one considers that my ship saved your ass weeks ago. So whose ability to handle difficult situations is being brought into question?"

The moment she had finished saying it, Shelby suddenly wished she could take it back. But the last thing she was going to do was back down or show weakness, because certainly Calhoun would never respect her if she did that.

Then again, seeing the look in his eyes made her think that maybe he wasn't going to respect her, no matter what. He was too angry. He looked like a volcano fighting its own eruption.

"I see," he said, knocking the ambient temperature in the room down by another ten degrees. "Well, then: How fortunate that we showed up here. That way, should we get into trouble, you'll be able to get us out of it again."

"Mac, you're being ridiculous . . ."

And he was on his feet, and Shelby took a step back. For the first time in her entire life, she was genuinely afraid of Mackenzie Calhoun. She did not, for a heartbeat, think he was going to attack her physically or try to do her harm. Nevertheless, she saw what the residents of his native Xenex had seen . . . and, even more specifically, what the oppressive Danteri had seen when the warlord juggernaut known as M'k'n'zy of Calhoun would charge into battle against them. And when he spoke, his voice sounded like distant rumbling thunder.

"This is not about you . . . or me . . . or our ships," Calhoun said. "I have a man in sickbay who's in some sort of stasis that none of us completely understands. I have a crew that was battered by a group of creatures that, again, none of us understands. And those creatures, those 'Beings' who did that to us, have chosen to take as their center of operations a world populated by the most notorious race ever to set foot on my homeworld. The potential for disaster here is gargantuan. Furthermore, if any of these Beings are capable of undoing the damage they've done, or somehow restoring McHenry to normal, then I owe it to the people they've killed and the people they've hurt to force them to do it."

"How do you intend to 'force' a race of entities who appear to be, to all intents and purposes, invincible."

"I'll find a way. That's what all good Starfleet captains do, so I'm told. They find ways. Unless you think me incapable of that, as well."

It was a loaded question and one that could easily lead to another half hour of arguing. But Shelby realized that such a means of passing thirty minutes would be counterproductive. "No," she said neutrally. "No, I don't think you incapable of that." She licked her lips, since they suddenly felt bone dry. Then she took a deep breath and let it out unsteadily. "All right. Look. At the very least, we don't need to be duplicating each other's efforts. We certainly don't want to give the Danteri the impression that we're working at cross-purposes. If they think there's divisiveness between us, that may well tempt them to try and exploit it."

Slowly he nodded. "Yes. That's probably true."

She was relieved to hear him say that. It meant he wasn't so completely over-the-top furious that he was blocking out everything she might be saying. "I've already selected an away team to head down, consisting of Mueller, Ambassadors Spock and Cwan, and Lieutenant Arex. Why not send several of your people in conjunction with our away team, instead of beaming down a separate group."

"All right. I'll go down with Soleta and Kebron."

"Mac, I wouldn't advise that you put yourself on the away team."

"Because I don't trust the Danteri? Because I can't approach the situation with dispassion?"

"Yes."

"You're probably right."

"But you're going anyway."

"You're probably right."

She sighed and shook her head. "It's your decision, Calhoun. Do as you wish. We'll send over the coordinates for the transporter rendezvous and coordinate the beam-down."

He simply nodded, acknowledging the plan. Feeling she had nothing else to say, Shelby turned and headed for the door. As she headed out, Calhoun suddenly said, "Captain."

She turned to face him. "Yes?"

"Nothing," he said after a moment. "I just . . ."

"You just what?"

"I wanted to see if you would turn around to look at me or just stop and talk to me with your back turned."

She sighed heavily at that, then walked out the door. When he called her name again, she didn't stop walking.

iii.

It was some hours later when Moke finally got up the nerve to address the very odd computer once more.

Moke hadn't been sitting around contemplating in horror the notion of talking to the computer again. He'd been busy with Xyon, who had been his usual rambunctious self. Xyon had been looking around at empty air in a most aggressive fashion, and Moke had the feeling that Xyon was trying to catch sight of the "ghostly" inhabitants of the *Excalibur.* Moke was quite certain that they were keeping themselves scarce.

He couldn't help but wonder if it had something to do with the planet they'd come to. He'd been able to overhear enough scattered conversations to put two and two together and realize that more of these strange "Beings" were present on the world below. So it might well have been that McHenry and the one-eyed man were either hiding, or else doing everything they could to shield their presence from those whom they wanted to avoid. Either way, they sure weren't around.

Still, Moke was starting to feel it was definitely time to seek out Mackenzie Calhoun and tell him what had been going on. After all, what if McHenry and the one-eyed man were, in fact, gone for good? Certainly, then, no harm would be done by letting Calhoun know about their presence.

He and Xyon were in the holodeck, Xyon romping around on a holo-created beachfront. The green ocean came rolling in and washed up over his toes, and he giggled in childish glee, as Moke abruptly called out, "Computer."

And then he jumped back several feet in shock as a woman materialized in front of him. He shook his head in bewilderment and then said, "Wait . . . I know you. You're Robin's mother, aren't you?"

"That's correct. Well . . . I was. Actually . . . I suppose I still am."

"Why are you here?"

"I'm in the computer now. I'm part of it."

"Oh." He wasn't sure what to say to that. "Does it hurt?"

"No," she assured him. Then she just stood there, smiling, her head slightly tilted in a polite and attentive manner.

"Why are you just . . . standing there?" he asked.

"You summoned me. I'm waiting for you to—"

"Oh! Oh, right!" He thumped his forehead with the base of his palm in chagrin. "Right, of course. Sorry. Uhm . . . do you know where Captain Calhoun is? Is he still in the shouting meeting?"

"Captain Calhoun is no longer on board the ship."

"He's not? Are you sure?"

"I'm a computer, Moke. Being sure is more or less all I do now."

"Oh. Okay. Well . . . where is he?"

"Captain Calhoun has gone down to Danter as part of

an away team, along with Lieutenants Soleta and Ke-bron."

"When will he be back?"

"I don't know."

"Hah!" he said challengingly. "You said being sure was all you did."

"All right," said Morgan, sounding rather reasonable. "He will be back precisely 0.00003 seconds after being beamed back aboard the ship."

He looked at her suspiciously. "That's not much of an answer."

"Perhaps. It is, however, one I am sure of." She took a step toward him, which startled him slightly. For some reason he'd just assumed she was rooted to one spot. "This is the second time you have desired to converse with him. Is there a matter of some urgency you wish to discuss? I can make it known to him upon his return."

"All right. Tell him that Mark McHenry and a strange, bearded one-eyed guy are walking around the ship, except they're invisible and can walk through things, like ghosts, and only Xyon and I can see them."

"Hmmm." She processed that information. The way in which she stored it was an endlessly complex procedure that only an expert in computer systems would have been able to explain. Visually, she simply looked thoughtful for a moment. "Very well. I will convey that to him. That is a most unusual message."

"I guess." Feeling much better, and satisfied that he had done his duty, Moke went to play with Xyon in the rolling waters as the computer image of Morgan blinked out of sight.

DANTER

i.

SI CWAN HADN'T HAD THE FAINTEST IDEA of what to expect, but whatever that lack of expectations might have been, it certainly hadn't included what he ultimately encountered on the surface of Danter.

Kalinda had wanted to go with him to the planet's surface, but Cwan had been quite firm in forbidding it. "If something happens to me," he had said to her, "you will be the last remaining member of Thallonian nobility. Danter is too unpredictable. We can't take the chance of something happening to both of us." Kalinda had understood his reasoning, but nevertheless was frustrated by it and wasn't the least bit happy about it.

When he beamed down to a central plaza, along with Ambassador Spock, XO Mueller, and Lieutenant Arex, he wasn't all that surprised to see that Mackenzie Calhoun, Soleta, and Zak Kebron had already materialized. Calhoun offered a ragged smile upon seeing Si Cwan.

"I hear you've had some adventures since departing us, Ambassador," he said.

"And your life has been no less an adventure." But then his attention was caught by Zak Kebron, and he looked the Brikar up and down. "Kebron, are you quite all right? You look . . . odd."

Kebron just stared at him stonily.

Cwan knew perfectly well that Zak Kebron was not his biggest fan. He wasn't going to pretend that he was all that solicitous or caring about Kebron's welfare. Still, the Brikar had his uses in a combat situation, and since Cwan was still leery of Danteri reception, he wanted to know that Kebron would be up to snuff if a battle arose. It was the strangest thing. It looked like pieces of Kebron's thick hide were actually peeling off. Kebron was obviously aware of it; he brushed away a few small pieces while endeavoring to look nonchalant about it. Turning his back to Kebron, he sidled over to Calhoun and said in a low voice, "Seriously . . . is Kebron in ill health?"

"Hard to tell with him," said Calhoun.

Except by that point, Si Cwan wasn't actually listening to what Calhoun was saying. Instead he was looking around the central plaza, and he noticed from the corner of his eye that Arex was having the same reaction.

"What's wrong, Lieutenant?" asked Mueller, noticing the way her security chief was gazing around in bewilderment. It would have been hard to miss it. Arex's head had stretched out on its distended neck, and he was surveying their surroundings with the attitude of someone who thought he might have wound up in the wrong place.

"It . . . wasn't like this," Arex said. And Si Cwan knew exactly what he was referring to.

When they'd come to the planet's surface last time, and indeed beamed down to pretty much this exact space, it had been an away team consisting of Si Cwan and Kalinda, Captain Shelby, and Arex. Then, as now, there had been various tall, majestic buildings. In fact, everything had smacked of being overdone, as if the Danteri were collectively interested in trotting out the glory that was the Danteri race to anyone who happened by their world.

But a number of those buildings, including places that he knew for a fact had housed senate offices, were gone. And they'd been replaced by structures that were decidedly simple and boxy in their design, but no less ornate. They were decorated with statues and mosaics, and they were busy.

Quite busy.

Various Danteri were going in and out of the buildings—about half a dozen in all—and they seemed to be all business as they did so. People who were entering were carrying branches, or garlands, or small livestock, and those who were leaving were empty-handed. But all of them carried with them beatific smiles upon their faces. He had never seen so many people looking so damned happy. Their general bronze skin color seemed to glow with health and life.

There was a steady, pungent burning smell in the air, and at one point Si Cwan was certain he heard a small animal cry out.

"These . . . these things weren't here . . . were they?" Arex looked to Si Cwan for confirmation.

"No," Si Cwan assured him. "They weren't. And it wasn't all that long ago that Kalinda and I were driven from this place. Which means they must have built these structures incredibly quickly. But . . . what—?"

It was Ambassador Spock who replied. "Temples, Ambassador Cwan," the Vulcan said quietly, in that gravelly but unperturbable tone of his. "They have built temples. These structures are not dissimilar from the structure upon which Apollo resided when we encountered these godlike beings during my tenure on the *Enterprise.*"

"Are you sure?" asked Calhoun.

"Always," Spock told him in an offhand manner, as if the notion that he could ever be anything else was so ludicrous that it hardly warranted being addressed. "I did not see the structure in person, but I was able to discern its specifics clearly enough when we were firing ship's phasers at it."

"So at the instruction of the Beings," Soleta said, taking readings of the temples with her tricorder, "the Danteri have built temples to them. For worship?"

"One would conclude so," said Spock.

Another animal cried out, and then the cry was abruptly truncated. The members of the away team looked at each other with barely disguised distaste. "So . . . those animals . . ." said Si Cwan.

Spock nodded in confirmation. "Sacrifices."

"Charming," said Mueller. She was looking at the steady stream of supplicants. "I suppose, Captain Calhoun, it would be considered poor form to shoot them."

"Personally, I'd give you a commendation," Calhoun told her. "Unfortunately, I think it would be frowned upon, yes."

"My friends! My dear friends!"

Si Cwan was certain he recognized the voice instantly, and sure enough, there he came: Lodec, the senate speaker, his arms thrown wide in greeting, and his skin scintillating with the same glow of health that everyone else in the damned area seemed to possess. The hem of his long, blue and white garment swished around on the floor as Lodec approached him, looking as if he were greeting old and beloved companions.

Then he stopped in his tracks, his hands clasped almost delicately in front of him. He sighed heavily, as if exhaling the weight of the world. "Oh. Oh, yes. But you very likely don't consider me your dear friend, do you. At least several of you. You . . . Captain Mackenzie Calhoun."

He approached Calhoun, who stood there with his face clouding like an incoming storm. "You, who still blame me for the death of your father."

"That's probably because you killed him," replied Calhoun, his tone flat.

"Under orders from my superior, at a time of war. But you must believe me now, Mackenzie . . . I would sooner have my right arm cut off—again—than bring harm to another living thing."

"Really. Testing that resolve might prove educational."

Inwardly, Si Cwan winced. He was quite aware that Captain Shelby wasn't sanguine over Calhoun's presence upon this world. He was positive that his antipathy for the Danteri would make his functioning there problematic. At the same time, though, he could very much understand it. It wasn't as if there were any love lost between Si Cwan and the Danteri in general, and Lodec in particular.

As if sensing what was going through Cwan's mind, Lodec turned and beamed that chillingly calm smile at

Si Cwan, apparently deciding to ignore Calhoun's last gibe. "And Ambassador. What can I possibly say . . . what words of apology can conceivably be offered . . . to make clear just how stricken I am over our ghastly treatment of you."

There was a great deal that Si Cwan wanted to say at that moment . . . most of it hostile. Plus, some vivid imaginings regarding sustained pummeling were likewise crossing his mind. But he quickly decided that it might just further provoke Calhoun to rash action, and the Thallonian didn't want to feel responsible for that.

"There is nothing you can say," Si Cwan told him evenly, "so perhaps it would be best . . . to say nothing."

Lodec bobbed his head. He actually seemed grateful, which further perplexed Si Cwan, because he hadn't thought he was being especially generous in his response.

"Very wise, Ambassador," he said. Then he turned and regarded the others. "And you would be Commander Mueller . . . Lieutenant Arex, I believe it was . . ." He looked blankly at the two Vulcans and the Brikar. When his eye caught Zak's, he looked up, and up a bit more. "My. You're a considerable individual."

Zak glowered at him.

"This is Lieutenant Soleta, my science officer," Calhoun said, "and my security chief, Lieutenant Kebron, and this," and he paused with what seemed to Cwan to be some dramatic significance, "is Ambassador Spock."

Even Lodec appeared impressed. "The legendary Spock?"

"Yes," said Spock, matter-of-factly. Si Cwan suppressed a small smile. None could ever accuse the Vulcan of lack of hubris. Then again, "hubris" might be the wrong word. It meant, after all, "exaggerated pride," and Spock's accomplishments were such that there was no reason for exaggeration. The truth was impressive enough.

"I am here," Spock continued, "representing the interests of the United Federation of Planets."

"Because of the ambrosia."

"That is correct."

"The ambrosia is the food of the gods." He smiled reverently. "The Beings provide it to us in exchange for our love and devotion. They give us so much, and all that is truly required from us is our appreciation. It is a remarkable bargain, is it not?"

"Remarkable," Soleta echoed, exchanging a glance with Spock.

"And permit me to guess," said Lodec. Amusement twinkled in his eyes. "You are here to obtain a sample of the ambrosia."

Calhoun looked as if he were about to respond, but Mueller spoke up before he could do so. "That is one consideration," she said. "But my orders were simply to observe the impact that the presence of the Beings has had upon you."

"Why, they have had a benevolent impact," Lodec said, as if any other notion was too absurd to contemplate. "How could any reasonable person think otherwise."

"Considering," Spock said, "that the Beings assaulted and nearly destroyed a Federation starship . . . and that the earliest known Being, one 'Apollo,' held my shipmates hostage a century ago . . . and that one of them aided you in terrorizing Ambassador Cwan and his sister . . . one would logically have to conclude the Beings are sending mixed messages insofar as benevolence is concerned."

To Cwan's surprise, Lodec laughed softly at that. "My, you do have a way of turning a phrase, Ambassador. Very well, point taken. But things have changed, you have to see that."

"We intend to see what needs to be seen," Calhoun told him sharply.

For a moment, Lodec studied Calhoun, and then he just shrugged neutrally. "Then you shall do so in as unimpeded a fashion as possible. You are free to do what you will. Go anywhere you wish, see anything you wish. We've nothing to hide here. None of my people will hinder you."

"And the Beings? Where are they?" asked Calhoun.

"Oh," and Lodec gestured in a vague manner, still smiling. "They are around. They move in mysterious ways."

"Summon them."

For the first time, Lodec looked perturbed. "That . . . is not within my ability. I would accommodate you if I could, but I swear I cannot. The Beings come and go as they will. If they choose to appear, they do so. But we do not control them."

"No, no . . . you just adore them," said Calhoun. He was now much closer to Lodec, and Si Cwan could see that the scar which Calhoun perpetually carried upon his face was flushing a slightly brighter crimson . . . a sure sign that the starship captain was becoming angry. "I want Artemis. I have an injured man because of her. A man who might very well be on the brink of death . . . or worse. I believe she's the only one who can do anything about it. And she had better, or . . ."

"Or what?" Lodec sounded gently reproving. "What do you think you could possibly do that will deter her in some way? Artemis is what she is. They all are what they are. If you," and he glanced at Spock, "have any hope of working out some manner of cooperation with the Beings, or if you have a desire to obtain ambrosia, then it's far preferable that you respect them as we do."

"By building temples to them?" asked Arex. "By sacrificing helpless animals to them?"

"Yes," Lodec said, as if it was the most natural thing in the world.

And Si Cwan realized that, to Lodec, it very likely was.

ii.

The away team had split into three groups, heading off in different directions in an almost arbitrary fashion. The notion was, after all, that they were upon a fact-finding mission. So they went their separate ways to find facts. Since they were all in easy communication with one another, there didn't seem to be a problem.

Nevertheless, Calhoun insisted that each of them check in with him every half hour. He had no intention of losing touch with any of his people. And Mueller, for her part, kept in constant touch with the *Trident,* and the *Trident* with the *Excalibur.* No one was taking any chances.

Mueller and Arex walked from residence to residence in the city, stopping and talking with passersby, or knocking on doors and speaking to whomever inside would talk to them. Mueller was impressed by the forthright way in which the people spoke to two offworld strangers.

Her study of the typical Danteri mind-set indicated that they should have treated them in a high-handed, arrogant manner. But that definitely was not what she and Arex were encountering. Instead the Danteri greeted them warmly, welcomed them into their homes, spoke to them of their hopes, dreams, and aspirations.

And, of course, they spoke of the Beings.

"We were lost without them."

"They have focused us."

"They are greatness personified."

"The Beings are the source of all things wise and wonderful."

These and many other comments were uttered with the sort of unshakable conviction that Mueller only ever saw in the truly dedicated . . . or the truly demented. Nor was it always easy to tell the difference.

After several hours of hearing the same thing over and over again, Mueller and Arex stopped in the center of a lush park and sat on a bench. More correctly, Mueller sat. The bench wasn't designed in such a way that the three-legged Arex could make himself comfortable, so he chose to stand.

"I have never seen this many happy people in my life," Mueller said. "Have you?"

"Yes," said Arex serenely. "My people. But we're a singularly cheerful race."

Mueller half-smiled and shook her head. "Thank you for the clarification, Lieutenant." Then the smiled faded as she considered the array of chipper individuals they'd met. "Tell me, Lieutenant . . . even amongst your 'singularly cheerful race,' are you all happy in the exact same manner? About the exact same thing?"

"No. And I see what you mean and where you're going with the thought," he said. "It's an impressive uniformity of mind."

" 'Impressive' would not be the word I'd use. 'Frightening,' perhaps. It's almost as if they've started functioning as a hive mind. They're like the Borg, except they're not trying to assimilate us."

"Aren't they?" said Arex. "Perhaps the ambrosia is the means of assimilation."

She opened her mouth to speak, and then closed it and nodded.

They were silent for a moment, and then Arex moved in a slow circle around Mueller. "What do you think of the M'Ress and Gleau situation?"

"What?" She blinked in confusion. "Where did *that* come from?"

"I thought this might be a good opportunity to discuss it, away from the ship." His head extended a bit further from his body. "I assume you know what I'm referring to. . . ."

"Of course I know. But why are you asking me?"

"Because," Arex said slowly, "I have reason to believe that you and the good lieutenant commander exchanged some harsh words."

"And how," inquired Mueller, her voice taking on an icy edge, "would you know that?"

"I'm head of security, Commander, and a starship—for all its size—is still little more than a small town in space." He shrugged, which was a truly odd gesture for someone with three arms. "People overhear things, people tell other people things, and sooner or later most people know each other's business. And if the security chief doesn't know, he's not much of a security chief."

"And yet, here I am feeling not especially secure."

"I notice," said Arex, "that you're also not answering the question."

"Here's a concept, Lieutenant," Mueller replied, rising from the bench and standing with her sharp, angled chin pointed in an imperious manner at Arex. "I'm your superior officer. I am not required to answer any questions that I'm disinclined to answer."

"I wasn't disputing that." He drew closer to her, tilting his head and studying her with a gaze that seemed to bore right through her head. "But here's something else that is beyond dispute. M'Ress is a dear, dear friend. And it's my firm belief that Gleau is out to harm her. I suspect it's your belief as well. But I'm not going to allow it to happen. So I was curious as to whether you were going to allow it."

There was far more to what he was saying than the mere words. Mueller was not the least intimidated by the intensity of his stare. Instead, her interest was piqued. "A dear, dear friend? How dear a friend?" There was a distinct air of challenge in her voice.

She was pleased to see that Arex seemed a bit taken aback by the way she addressed him. "What do you mean by that?"

"What do *you* mean?" A slow smile spread across her sharp-edged features. "My God . . . are you in love with her?"

Arex promptly retracted his head, his neck sinking as if it were deflating. "That is a pointless subject to—"

"You *are*."

"It is pointless to discuss it," he said, and he turned his face away. "Our . . . species . . . would not be compatible. Whatever I might feel for her intellectually, even emotionally, is rendered moot by certain physical realities."

"And she doesn't know."

He turned back to her. "And you must never tell her."

"Are you issuing me an order, Lieutenant?" There was an almost condescending challenge in her voice. "I don't do well with subordinates ordering me about."

"It's not an order. It's . . . an emphatic request."

"I see." Her lips twitched, and she said nothing for a time. Arex waited, as if he knew that she would talk eventually. Slowly she lowered herself back onto the bench, lost in thought.

"Do you," she asked finally, "believe Gleau presents a threat?"

"I have already said I do," Arex said promptly, as if he knew she would ask. "My question is, do you believe it?"

"I don't know," she admitted. "I feel as if something is off . . . but it's nothing actionable."

"Did you threaten him?"

She shifted on the bench. "We had . . . strong words."

"He won't stand for it," said Arex. "He will do something to retaliate."

"Such as?"

"Such as . . . I don't know what. But that, I believe, is part of my job. To not wait around to find out what sort of threat someone poses."

"And what would you do, to be preemptive?"

"Whatever was necessary."

"To be blunt, Lieutenant," Mueller said, "that sounds as much like a threat as anything that Gleau has said."

Arex considered that. "Good," he finally decided.

iii.

Soleta, Spock, and Si Cwan—the "S" squad, as Si Cwan had dubbed them, getting absolutely no humorous response from the Vulcans (and not really expecting any)—approached one of the temples. They walked right past the lengthy line of people waiting to file through and perform—what? Prayers? Rituals? Slaughter? All of them at once?

They had not gone directly to the temple. Instead they had first spent time at a meeting of the Danteri senate, and Si Cwan had been quite frankly astounded by what they had witnessed.

"Committees working in unison," he told Spock and Soleta as they left after several hours of observing, shaking his head in incredulity even as he recounted it. "Votes being passed unanimously. All points of view being represented and considered before one firm direction is decided upon."

"Not, I take it, what you were accustomed to during your stay here?" inquired Soleta.

"It was impossible to accomplish anything while I was here," Si Cwan told her. "Every project, every proposal was awash with selfish considerations, tied to irrelevant concerns, and caught up in week upon week of endless discussion. It seemed that the world was governed more through back-room gamesmanship and betrayal than anything approaching uniformity of spirit and will. Now it's as if . . ."

"They're all drugged?" suggested Soleta.

It gave Si Cwan pause, and then slowly he nodded. "You're saying . . ."

"The ambrosia."

"An intriguing hypothesis," said Spock, "and not remotely outside the parameters of possibility."

As they approached the ring of temples that adorned the part of town casually referred to as "Worship Circle," the people waiting in line didn't seem to care that the three offworlders appeared to be cutting in front of them. In fact, they stepped back and indicated that the trio should feel free to do what they wished.

"Not precisely the renowned Danteri aggression of which I have heard tell," Spock commented as they walked past, "and providing of only further support for the lieutenant's ambrosia hypothesis." Then he glanced at Si Cwan. "Curious the twists and turns of fate, is it not, Ambassador?"

"I'm not sure what you're referring to, Ambassador," replied Cwan. "And for that matter, I wouldn't have thought Vulcans to be big believers in 'fate.' "

"I do not speak of 'fate' as predestination, but merely a convenient term to apply to life's vagaries which we can retroactively perceive," Spock said in his singularly smooth cadences. "As to what I am referring: The last time the three of us were together, Soleta and I were endeavoring to escape imprisonment on Thallon, and you were our captor."

Cwan smiled at that. "Yes. Yes, I remember."

"Yet now we are thrown together as colleagues."

"It is rather amusing, isn't it."

"Speaking as someone who would likely have died in prison if left to Thallonian tender mercies," said Soleta rather dourly, "you'll forgive me if I don't join in the general air of nostalgia."

"You are forgiven," Spock said with no hint of sarcasm.

They entered the temple. As Si Cwan looked around, he decided that "temple" might be too strong a word. "Shrine" was probably more accurate.

A small altar had been erected and a Danteri family—father, mother, two sons—were kneeling in front of it, their hands clasped before them in supplication. They weren't in the process of sacrificing any small living creatures, which Si Cwan was a bit relieved about. What instead caught his attention were the crude paintings on the wall opposite them, on the far side of the altar.

It was an ebony-skinned being with the head of a fearsome dog.

"That's Anubis," Si Cwan said softly. "In the picture."

"Anubis. The Egyptian god of passage to death," Spock said.

"Whatever he was . . . that's the bastard who damned near killed me," Si Cwan told him.

"Indeed," said Spock, looking back at the pictures. "Fascinating. And what prevented him from doing so."

"Kalinda managed to—"

One of the supplicants, the father, turned abruptly and, putting his finger to his lips, spat out an annoyed *"Shhh!"*

Si Cwan was reasonably certain that he could break the father's arms and legs without exerting much strength. But he restrained himself, and was rather pleased that he was able to do so. In a voice barely above a whisper, he said,

"Kalinda managed to get her hands on his weapon . . . that," and he pointed at the short scythelike blade that Anubis could be seen holding in his hand. "And she threatened him with it. He didn't seem especially anxious to attack her while she held it."

"Indeed," said Spock, cocking an eyebrow curiously. "That could be of extreme significance."

"Or it could be that he simply had no desire to destroy a lesser being."

The voice had come from behind them. The father of the worshipping group, irritated at the newcomer making no effort to keep his voice down, turned his scowl toward the person who had just spoken. Upon seeing the speaker, however, the father's eyes went wide and he immediately prostrated himself upon the ground, practically groveling. His family took one look where he'd been looking and did likewise.

The newcomer was clad in Egyptian garb, with winglike ornaments that ran the length of either arm, festooned with a mixture of black and white feathers. His face was quite handsome, and his eyes were a deep, glistening yellow. He had a slender nose and angular face, and his skin was a healthy olive brown. Something similar to a crown was perched atop his head.

"Greetings, Soleta," he said.

"Thoth." She glanced at Spock and Si Cwan. "Gentlemen . . . this is Thoth. Egyptian god of writing, mathematics, law . . ."

"And truth," he reminded her softly. "Let us not forget truth."

Si Cwan saw a subtle shift in Soleta's expression, as if something had been brought up that made her most uncomfortable. Thoth, for his part, was looking at the supplicants groveling upon the floor. He reached out with one sandaled foot and prodded the father in the side. "Rise. Your prayers have been heard, and they will be answered. Anubis has assured me of such. Now you may depart. And tell others to remain outside for a brief time, if you'd be so kind."

They hastily exited, bowing and scraping as they did so. Thoth watched them go, his mouth drawn in a thin line, looking as if he felt sorry for them. Then he turned back to Soleta and the faint disdain radiantly became a smile. "It is good to see you again, Soleta."

"A friend of yours?" asked a skeptical Si Cwan.

" 'Friend' might be overstating it. Thoth, this is Ambassadors Si Cwan and Spock."

Thoth barely acknowledged Si Cwan's presence, his attention instead focused upon the stately Vulcan ambassador. "I know you of old, I believe," he said.

"We have not met."

"No. But Apollo made the acquaintance of you, and what he knew, we all know. A tragic figure, Apollo was."

"Perhaps between his assaults upon us and his kidnapping of our officers, we were not in the proper position to appreciate the tragedy of his situation," Spock replied.

Thoth eyed him a moment and then said, "Hunh. And I take it that you, on some level, object to this world, despite its serenity."

" 'Object' is too strong a word. 'Have reservations' would be the more proper sentiment. You see, Thoth, I have had some little experience with worlds signing away their growth, development, and independence in exchange either for protection by false deities . . . or else for spores or some other element that seems to present a paradise, but for a hidden price."

"And you see us as false deities with a hidden price. How tragic, Ambassador. And how little you know of us." He looked back to Soleta. "Our time together was cut short, Soleta. There are other things that need to be said."

"Then you can say them here," Si Cwan told him.

"Yes. I can," agreed Thoth with an amiability that nevertheless hinted at someone who was not only accustomed to getting his way, but powerful enough to make certain he did. "However, I think it best for all concerned if they are said elsewhere."

"Apollo followed much the same pattern," Spock reminded him. "A neutral observer might take note that his story ended, as you say, tragically."

Thoth's smile widened, although the outward amusement wasn't reflected in his eyes. "Why, Ambassador . . . are you warning me? Threatening me?"

"No. Merely noting that those who do not listen to history are doomed to repeat it."

"Perhaps. But that has little bearing to one who actually *is* history. Besides . . . you called us secretive. Far be it from me not to live up to expectations. Soleta . . . let us go and discuss matters."

Si Cwan was about to say something, to protest, but it made no difference. One moment, Soleta and Thoth were there, and the next—with a sound like a popping soap bubble—they were both gone.

iv.

In the main receiving room of his spacious residence, Lodec rose from his couch and spread wide his arms as Calhoun and Kebron strode in, having just been announced by one of Lodec's servants.

"My friends, it is good to see you again," he said in such a way that he really, truly made it sound like he was pleased to see them. "May I get you something to eat or drink?"

"That won't be necessary," said Calhoun evenly.

"Sit. Sit, please."

He gestured toward a large, comfortable-looking chair. Calhoun's impulse was to stay exactly where he was, but he yielded to the trappings of polite society and seated himself. Lodec sat opposite him.

"I was true to my word," he said. "Were you at all impeded in your inspection of Danter? Is it not all that I said, and more besides?"

"It's very peaceful," said Calhoun. "I'd hardly recognize it."

"Indeed. To be candid, Captain," and he leaned forward a bit as if speaking with an intimate and old friend, "I think upon what we once were, and I am appalled. But look at all that we have accomplished! And if the galaxy were united in the cause . . ."

"We remain unclear as to what that 'cause' might be."

"Why . . . to worship the Beings, of course," said Lodec, for whom it apparently seemed the most obvious concept in the world. "To benefit from their radiance, to . . ."

"I want a sample of this ambrosia," Calhoun said. "Something I can take back to my ship, to study, to . . ."

Lodec politely shook his head. He looked almost grief-stricken as he said, "My apologies, Captain, but . . . I am afraid that's not possible. You are neither ready nor—and I regret I must say it—deserving."

"I see. And you are?" he asked humorlessly.

"Well, obviously."

"Obvious to you, perhaps," said Calhoun, his voice tightening. "Now I'll tell you what's obvious to me. It's obvious that you're going to provide me with this 'ambroisa' so I can make a thorough report to Starfleet. Furthermore, I want Artemis, and whatever difficulties might be involved in that are of no interest to me."

In a way, Calhoun was hearing his own voice from a distance. He heard the flatness of it, the mercilessness. Even to his own ear, he sounded as if he were spoiling for a fight. For a moment, the concerns of Shelby came back to him. She had been so convinced that the history between Calhoun and the Danteri in general, and between he and Lodec in particular, was going to make it impossible for him to do his job in a dispassionate manner.

He hadn't cared what she'd said. He hadn't listened to her. Now the cold, detached part of his brain which never left him—the one that served to analyze a situation in an unemotional way no matter how dire the circumstance, and had thus enabled him to survive any number of to-the-death battles—was telling him that Shelby might very well have been right.

Unfortunately, he was making the conscious decision not to heed what she'd said. There was no point in second-guessing himself. He was here, and this had to be dealt with. And the fact that he could still see himself in his mind's eye, lunging forward, wrapping his hands around Lodec's throat and squeezing and squeezing . . .

He took a deep breath and shook it off, and suddenly the hairs on his neck were standing on end.

Calhoun had an almost infallible inner warning sense. He really didn't know how he had come by it. All he knew was that it had saved his life on any number of occasions, and this might very well be one of them.

He pivoted and Kebron, seeing that his commanding officer had suddenly come to full alert, likewise turned to see what it was that had alarmed Calhoun.

The creature that greeted their eyes was as big, if not bigger, than Zak Kebron. His skin was darkest black, so much like the depths of space that Calhoun might have expected to see stars floating against it. His head looked like that of some great beast.

Calhoun was utterly taken aback, but he did not let the fact that he was startled show. Furthermore, although he had not had an opportunity to discuss Si Cwan's "adventures" with him in detail, Shelby had been good enough to forward him her logs and accounts of what the Thallonian had told her and he'd read them over quickly before beaming down to Danter. So he had at least some idea of who and what he was facing.

"Anubis, I take it," Calhoun said evenly.

"Very good, Captain!" Lodec said, looking quite pleased, as if Calhoun was a clever student who had just produced some marvelously timely answer.

"And is your plan to try and treat Lieutenant Kebron and myself with the same distinctive lack of hospitality that you provided Si Cwan and his sister? To try and manhandle us, toss us about?"

"Please. Try," said Kebron. Calhoun noticed Kebron's fist tightening, and a slight snapping sound coming from it. Apparently Kebron was cracking his knuckles.

"I already told you, Captain," Lodec said with a heavy sigh. "Although, in the grand scheme of things, it hasn't been all that long since Si Cwan's abrupt departure from our world, much has changed in—"

"Death," Anubis said abruptly, interrupting Lodec as though what he had to say was of no consequence. He was pointing a taloned finger at Calhoun.

"Are you threatening me?" Calhoun asked calmly.

It was hard to tell if Anubis was smiling, or even capable of doing so, for his thin canine lips were drawn tightly back against his teeth. He lowered his hand and growled in a deep, hoarse manner, "We have much in common, you and I. In a way, we are brothers."

"Striking family resemblance," deadpanned Kebron.

Calhoun fired him a look, then turned back to Anubis. "We have nothing in common. You know what I'm seeking. I want a sample of ambrosia, and I want Artemis. Unless you're willing to provide either of those, we have nothing to talk about."

"We have much to talk about," Anubis replied.

He began to stride toward Calhoun, and Kebron promptly interposed himself, providing a looming living barrier between the advancing "god" and the *Excalibur* captain.

Anubis didn't appear to give Kebron any more priority than he had Lodec. He seemed to be considering only Calhoun and himself to be the only two individuals in the room. It was flattering in a way. A sick, perverse way, but a way. Nevertheless, he came to a halt a foot or so short of Kebron, although it was difficulty to tell whether he was doing so because he thought Kebron posed a threat.

"We are very much alike," Anubis said. His pointed teeth clicked together when his long snout moved in speech. "We have made death an art. We embrace it. We guide our opponents to the other side knowing, as we do so, that how we die defines how we live. If we greet death with bravery, we are brave. If we meet it sniveling, we are cowards. The measure of a man is taken in his last breath. We both understand that in a way that others cannot possibly."

"What I understand is that you're beginning to annoy the hell out of me," Calhoun said. He suddenly wished he had his sword with him. He had a phaser on his hip, and Kebron who was as strong as any ten men guarding his back, but nevertheless the blade he'd wielded as a Xenexian warlord would have provided him a greater measure of security. "What I understand is that your kind nearly destroyed my ship and killed members of my crew."

"These are non-issues," said Anubis.

"To you, perhaps," said Calhoun, bristling. "To me they are very real issues indeed."

"You can learn so much more than you know now," Anubis told him.

"That's nice to hear. But I've no intention of learning it from you."

"Perhaps you will, despite yourself."

Suddenly he made a swift motion toward Calhoun.

Zak Kebron, far speedier than anyone unfamiliar with him would have thought, matched the move and was directly in the path of Anubis. Kebron usually disdained to use weapons of any kind. He considered his own body all the weapon he required, and besides, his gargantuan fingers did not fit easily around the trigger mechanism of a phaser.

Anubis's hand whipped out and around, and he was holding his short scythe. The curved blade swept right through Kebron's guard, slicing across his chest. Kebron staggered and the blade was a blur, cutting right and left across Kebron at will. Blood welled up from Kebron's chest, blood with the same color and consistency of tar.

Another low growl escaped Anubis' lips. It was a growl that was matched only by the sound coming from Calhoun's own mouth as he charged forward. Anubis switched his attention from Kebron to Calhoun and brought his scythe whipping around.

Kebron was not accustomed to dodging, and certainly wasn't built for it. His tough hide was normally all the protection he required. Not this time, however. Calhoun suspected that, had any of the cuts been even an eighth of an inch deeper, Kebron's organs would be splattering out onto the floor. He wasn't certain whether it was remarkable luck on Zak's part or supreme control on the part of Anubis. Nor was he intending to wait to figure it out.

"You will learn respect," Anubis said quietly. "Even one who is such a purveyor of death that he could be my brother, will still learn respect."

Calhoun tapped his combadge. "Calhoun to *Excalibur*. Two to—"

And then Kebron, with a roar, charged Anubis.

Anubis appeared briefly taken aback, and then he swung his scythe once more. Kebron buckled at the knee and took the point of the scythe in his shoulder. It buried itself in there and Anubis tried to yank it out. But it was in too deep.

The Egyptian "god" was clearly startled, and then Kebron thrust one of his massive hands forward, catching Anubis just under the jaw. Anubis lost his grip on his scythe as he was literally lifted off his feet, and he crashed to the ground several yards away.

Kebron grabbed at the scythe and then, with a grunt, pulled it clear. More of his dark blood massed at his shoulder, but he didn't seem to notice or care. "I'm guessing, without this, you're helpless," he rumbled.

That was when Anubis' eyes began to glow red. He reached behind his back and suddenly there was another scythe in his hand. "You guessed wrong."

And suddenly Lodec was in between them, his arms spread to either side. *"No!"* he cried out, and to Calhoun's surprise, turned to Anubis. "Please, great one," he implored, "I have promised these individuals safe passage! I have spoken to them of how matters have changed! I would not presume to question your righteous wrath, but this action is most unfortunate in terms of ongoing relationships with Calhoun and his associates! I beg you not to do this thing!"

Calhoun's hand hovered over the combadge, prepared at a moment's notice to call for emergency beam-up. It was against his nature to run, but he had a wounded man who required immediate attention. Besides, the way

Anubis was staring at Lodec, it seemed as if the god was just as content to annihilate his follower as he was Calhoun and Kebron.

But then the glow subsided from Anubis' eyes. Although he glowered in Kebron's direction, he was addressing Lodec when he said, "Very well. Out of deference to you and yours, I shall not pursue this matter further."

"*You* won't pursue?" snapped back Calhoun. "After everything that you and your fellow Beings have done, what gives you the impression that *I* won't pursue it?"

"For one thing," Anubis said, his teeth still clicking together, "I would like to think that you are not that stupid. But if you are eager to prove me wrong, by all means . . . please do." He shifted his gaze back to Lodec and said, "They require manners. It would be most wise for them if they acquired them by the next time we met." He turned on his bare foot and strode out of the room.

"Drag him back in here, Captain," Kebron said defiantly.

"Why would I want to do that?"

"So I can collapse on him." And with that, Kebron fell forward, like an avalanche.

"Kebron!" shouted Calhoun, dropping to Kebron's side. Lodec was making fluttering apologizing noises that Calhoun ignored as he tapped his combadge once more. "Calhoun to *Excalibur*. Two for emergency beamup. Then start rounding up the others and get them the hell off this world."

"Aye, sir," came the response from the combadge. He recognized the voice instantly. It was Morgan.

"Captain, this is most unfortunate!" Lodec called out. "I assure you, I—"

"Save your assurances and bank one of mine," said Calhoun. "If Kebron dies, I'll tear this place apart with my bare hands."

Even as his hands ran along Kebron's thick hide, he was stunned to have a huge piece of it come off in his hands. It was a chunk at least a foot wide, and beneath the skin was roughly the same color, albeit a bit lighter.

And over the continued pleadings for understanding from Lodec, the captain and security chief of the *Excalibur* were beamed off the surface of Danter.

EXCALIBUR

i.

THE GHOSTLY, intangible image of Mark McHenry and the elderly man who called himself Woden or Aman-Re or possibly Santa Claus stood outside the sickbay and watched dispassionately as Zak Kebron was hauled in on an antigrav gurney that was just barely powerful enough to support his weight. The doctors grunted as they hauled him into the sickbay, and McHenry saw the horrific gaping wound in his shoulder and the scythe protruding.

"What the hell is that thing?" he demanded, pointing at the curved blade that Calhoun was holding as he followed Kebron in.

"A scythe," said the old man calmly. "It is the symbol of Anubis."

"Yeah, well you know what I'm starting to think would be my best symbol? A good kick in the ass for whoever gets in my way." McHenry began to pace. "I'm tired of standing around like Banquo's ghost while life goes on all around me, and I'm helpless to participate. I . . ."

"No," the old father interrupted him. "You don't understand."

"Well, that's possibly because you haven't explained it. What exactly am I supposed to be understanding?"

The Old Father turned to him, and there was determination glistening in his eye. "The Beings took a considerable setback in their battle with the *Excalibur.*"

"A setback? They practically annihilated the ship."

"Nevertheless, they suffered a great weakening as a result. But now they are preparing to fight back again. It means their confidence is beginning to grow once more. That scythe is a channel for Anubis . . . or Loki, as he is also known. It is not, however, active at the moment. He likely has another."

"All right," McHenry said slowly, "if this is the part where you're explaining things, then I'm not keeping up with you."

A brief smile played across his immaterial lips. "Let me put it to you this way. The Beings do not have infinite resources, despite how things may appear. They have been monitoring us all this time, 'concerned' over what we might do that could interfere with their plans. You may not have been aware of it, but I very much have been. To some degree, I have been shielding you from them. Keep in mind, the predicament in which you presently find yourself resulted from an unguarded moment between yourself and Captain Calhoun, when you conveyed to him your opinion that Artemis and her associates were not to be trusted. Their ability to monitor communications is to be underestimated at great personal risk, even in our current condition. It seems, however, that now their attentions are drawn to other matters. That, and they are starting to become suffused with an air of confidence that could, in the long run, prove very costly to them."

"Meaning what? What happens now?"

"What happens now," said the Old Father, "is that we endeavor to communicate with Captain Calhoun. We step out from the shadows and move toward the daylight. Our time is swiftly approaching."

"Our time. You mean I'm finally going to have a chance to live again?" asked McHenry, his hopes rising.

"You? No. No, chances are you'll wind up completely obliterated."

"Oh." McHenry considered that and said, "Our time stinks."

ii.

Dr. Selar was never one to let frustration show, but Calhoun thought that this was about as close as she had ever let herself get to it.

"The bleeding is not stopping," she said, standing several feet away from the examination table where Kebron lay stretched out. It was not actually one table. He was laid out sideways, his upper torso lying upon the table, the rest of him supported by two antigrav gurneys.

"I have managed to slow it," she continued, "but the epidermis is refusing to regrow despite the applications."

"Is it because Kebron's skin is unique on this ship?"

"I have the Brikar specifics in my medical logs,"

replied Selar, her arms folded in front of her. "I have set the specifications of the regrow tools correctly. It is not, therefore, comprehensible as to why—"

Suddenly there was a loud rending sound.

Kebron's eyes had snapped open. He was starting to sit up.

His skin began to rip straight down his chest, and the med techs were running in from every direction, trying to stop him. A spray hypo was pressed against his arm but he batted it away, along with the med tech, who went flying across sickbay to crash into a far wall.

"Kebron!" shouted Calhoun. He wasn't at all sure that Kebron could hear him, or was even aware of his surroundings, but he couldn't simply stand there and let a delirious Brikar destroy the sickbay. "Kebron, stand down! That's an order!"

Kebron had lurched to his feet, and he turned and stared at Calhoun without actually seeming to comprehend who was standing before him. With a low growl, he staggered toward the captain, his arms raised over his head, hands curled into fists, each of which was larger than Calhoun's head.

Without backing down in the slightest, Calhoun said evenly, "I said that was an order, Lieutenant. Stand the hell down. *Now.*"

Kebron wavered for a long moment . . . and then, slowly, lowered his arms.

"I didn't like you at first, you know," he said. "Long ago."

"Nobody likes me at first, Lieutenant. Call it a gift. Are you all right?"

Zak Kebron once again didn't appear to be paying attention. Instead he was pulling at his skin as if it was a full-body irritant. There were more tearing sounds, and then Kebron pulled at the back of his neck as if he were hauling a sweater over his head. With one final, ear-splitting rending noise, he pulled the entirety of his thick hide up and over, yanking it out from under his uniform.

There were startled gasps from even the most hardened of med techs. Selar, of course, simply arched an eyebrow. "Fascinating," she said.

Kebron held the tattered hide in front of himself, like Peter Pan dangling his shadow. "Yes, it is, isn't it." His own skin—the one that was currently covering his body—was glistening and shiny, almost like a newborn's. It was basically the same color, but a bit lighter. "Is there somewhere," he said, "that I can dispose of this? Unless of course, Doctor, you're interested in studying it. Or perhaps, Captain, you'd care to mount it on your wall. Claim you bagged a Brikar."

Calhoun noticed immediately that there was something completely different about Kebron's voice. Instead of the typical gruff surliness, he sounded calm. Almost pleasant. Whereas before every word was given up almost unwillingly, now he seemed almost . . . chatty.

"I shall attend to it, Lieutenant," said Selar. She gestured for several of the med techs to take the torn skin from Kebron, which they did with a combination of fascination and mild revulsion. Selar, meantime, was running a medical tricorder over his shoulder. "The bleeding has definitely stopped," she announced. "I cannot explain it."

"And yet I have a feeling that Lieutenant Kebron can," said Calhoun. "Personally, I'd love to hear it."

"I grew up," said Kebron.

Calhoun stared at him. "Grew up? What do you mean, grew up? I don't . . ."

"He was an adolescent," Selar said abruptly.

"What?"

"The doctor is correct, Captain," said Kebron. "We Brikar age and develop far differently than you. I have been what you would term a 'teenager' for approximately forty of your years. Since well before I attended the Academy."

"That would explain his general attitude," Selar said. "His reticence, his surliness and air of superiority . . ."

"Well, to be fair, Doctor, in many things I simply *am* superior," said Kebron. "It was, however, time for me to move forward in my physiological and emotional development. And now I have."

"Just like that?" asked Calhoun.

"Yes, Captain. Why? Would you prefer that it be as prolonged as possible?"

"No, not at all. But . . ."

"This is certainly the preferable way to attend to it, don't you agree? Now then," he continued, "that scythe you're holding. The one that Anubis used against me to such devastating effect. We may want to have it thoroughly analyzed to see if it might present some sort of clue as to how to combat these so-called gods. Don't you agree, Captain?"

"Yes," said Calhoun hollowly.

"Very well. If you wish, I shall bring it forthwith to science labs. They can get started on it, and Lieutenant

Soleta can coordinate with them upon her return. Is that satisfactory, Captain?"

"That . . . would be fine."

"Excellent. Good day to you all, then," said Kebron. Calhoun noticed that, as opposed to his usual swaggering, lumbering walk, he now had an almost graceful movement to him.

He became aware that Selar was now standing next to him. Her normally inscrutable face looked as puzzled as his own was.

"Is it just me," said Calhoun, "or was the taciturn, surly Kebron easier to take?"

"It is not just you," Selar said.

"I think I'm beginning to understand why humans are the most common species on starships. Fewer bizarre and unexpected metamorphoses."

"True. On the other hand, many of them do have a passion for baseball."

Calhoun shuddered. But then, all business, he tapped his combadge. "Calhoun to Burgoyne."

"Burgoyne here," came back the voice of the ship's second-in-command. "Is everything all right, Captain? The transporter room said that Kebron was injured. What's his status?"

"Kebron is fine. Well . . . relatively speaking, at any rate," he amended as he exchanged looks with Selar. "Burgy, contact the away team, and alert Captain Shelby as well. The Beings are on Danter, all right, and at least one of them is out to cause serious problems."

"Aye, sir. Should we beam them all back immediately?"

Calhoun's first instinct was indeed to bring all members of the away team back to the relative safety of the

Excalibur. But then he reasoned that he had no idea what sort of situation the others might be in. They could be having very different experiences than what he and Kebron had encountered. And really, how were they to pursue any sort of fact-finding mission if they ran from the very place where the facts were going to be made available to them?

"No," he said after a moment, the speed of his response belying the thought he'd gone to in order to reach it. "But alert them as to the situation. It's earlier than scheduled for the check-in time, but they need to know what's happening, and to watch their backs. We're talking extremely capable people. If I just unilaterally take them off Danter, it would effectively be saying that I didn't trust them to do their jobs."

"But do you?" asked Selar quietly.

He fired a glance at her. Meantime Burgoyne's voice came over the combadge. "Pardon, sir? I didn't catch what Selar said . . . ?"

"It's nothing, Burgy," Calhoun said pointedly. "Just let them know what's happening. Calhoun out."

Selar looked as though she was waiting for him to say something else. Deliberately choosing not to do so, Calhoun turned and walked out of sickbay.

He was halfway to the bridge when it was reported to him that, moments earlier, Lieutenant Soleta had disappeared.

SOMEWHERE

SOLETA LOOKED AROUND in bewilderment and, feeling disoriented, reflexively put her arms out to either side to ward off an anticipated fall. She staggered, went down to one knee, but then quickly pulled herself together and stood once more. Then she looked around to get a better handle on her whereabouts.

She was standing on a plateau that appeared to be, as near as she could tell, the top of a mountain. But it was impossible to determine how high, for below her clouds ringed the towering peak on which she stood.

Turning in place, all she could see in all directions was a miasma of darkness. Yet the darkness itself appeared to be moving, like caliginous shifting sands flowing through a wildly distorted hourglass.

She heard a distant rushing of air. She thought that perhaps she was in some sort of huge vortex. Then it occurred to her to pull out her tricorder, and she immediately tried to get readings of where she was and what she was seeing. Unfortunately, she wasn't able to discern any conclusive findings. There were definite high energy flux readings, but she couldn't determine anything beyond that. What kind of energy, or what its source was. Nothing.

"Hello?" she called out tentatively, and felt the fool for doing so. What sort of thing was that to say in this strange circumstance. *Helloooooo*. Very unscientific and most unproductive.

Beside, she knew exactly who it was that had subjected her to this, so why not come straight to it?

"Thoth," she said. She spoke firmly and in her best no-nonsense voice. "Thoth. I am not amused by this. I demand that you return me to Danter immediately."

"Why?"

The voice came from directly at her right shoulder, and she was so startled she almost backed up off the edge of the towering plateau. Snake-quick, Thoth reached out a hand and snagged her by the forearm, steadying her. "Careful," he said.

She pulled her arm away from him, being careful not to do it so violently that she threw herself off-balance. "I am always careful," she assured him archly.

He stared at her, a smile playing across his lips. *"Always?"* he asked.

"Yes. And whatever this place is, I insist you take me from it at once and return the two of us to Danter."

Instead of instantly complying, he circled her slowly, never taking his eyes from her. This gave him the look of nothing so much as a large hawk circling its prey. "The casual observer might note," he said, his voice never wavering from its quiet, patient tone, "that you are dissembling slightly. You have been known to take chances on more than one occasion, and act outside the rules. Is that not true?"

"I have no idea to what you are referring," Soleta said. But she very much disliked the way he was looking at her.

"You forget yourself," he said, and it might have been her imagination, but it almost seemed that the very air around her surged with power as he spoke slightly louder. "You forget to whom you are speaking. I am a god of truth, Soleta."

"No. You are an alien Being who has assumed the form of a god of truth."

"The two cannot be separated. I am what I am. And you are what you are. Half Vulcan, half Romulan. That puts you outside the parameters of your beloved Starfleet, does it not?"

Soleta glared at him. "This is the second time you have brought up that aspect of my lineage. I did not ask for, nor did I create, the circumstances of my birth. I see no reason that I should be penalized for it."

"And causing the death of dozens of Romulans? Should you not be penalized for that as well?"

Soleta's blood, normally cold, ran colder. She was certain that her face had suddenly become ashen. She turned away from him, except there he was, right in front of her again, and she spun in another direction and there he was again. "Stop. Doing. That," she said icily.

"There are only two individuals in all this galaxy to whom you cannot lie, Soleta. One is yourself. The other is me."

"And what have I done," she asked, her voice drenched in sarcasm, "to warrant such attention?

Why have you singled me out for his harassment?"

"Is it harassment to perceive a potential for greatness within someone and want to try and help them achieve it?" he said.

"If it involves absconding with them to some sort of transdimensional nowhere, then I would be thinking yes, it is."

He took her by the shoulders, and his voice was soft and even a bit alluring. "From time to time," he said with gentle insistence, "my people would come upon mortals who possessed tremendous potential. They would take them and impart the godhead to them, and the result would be some of the greatest heroes in all mortal history."

" 'Impart the godhead.' That," she said slowly, "would be a euphemism for 'have sex with,' am I correct?"

"More or less."

She pushed his hands off her shoulders. "Then it will have to be 'less' in my case."

"Oh, I know your case," he assured her. "I know your case all too well. Your soul is heavy, Soleta. You carry the burden of overwhelming guilt upon you. Not surprising, really. You know yourself to be a child spawned of a violent act, inflicted by a member of a vicious race upon your mother, and yet part of you actually feels drawn to that race. It makes you question everything about yourself. Your own trustworthiness, your dedication to the organization you presently serve, the—"

"Shut up!"

All her equanimity and Vulcan training evaporated in that instance of overwhelming anger, and she lashed out at him, clamping her hand down upon his bare shoulder in the Vulcan nerve pinch.

It had no effect upon him, other than to provoke a mocking smile. Abruptly he grabbed her, wrapping his arms around her and pulling him toward her in a violent kiss. For half a heartbeat she actually felt herself melting against him, and then she rallied and shoved him away, her chest heaving with contained fury. "Do not touch me," she said fiercely, "or I shall find a way to kill you. Believe me. I will."

He smiled. "You were the proper choice. That is becoming even more clear to me." Then he stepped back from her and put his hands out and open in front of him. "Very well. I give you my word as a higher Being that I will not force myself upon you . . . even though you realize that I could. I could do so and make you think it was your idea. That, however, would not be seemly for a god of wisdom and truth. And knowledge. It is knowledge that you seek. And I shall provide you with that knowledge. Not only that, but I shall provide you with what is your greatest desire."

"And what would that be?" Her voice was laced with scorn, but she had to admit to some mild curiosity.

"Peace."

"Peace? My greatest desire is peace?"

"Yes. Peace from the raging torment that gives your soul no rest. You deserve such peace, Soleta. You deserve not to feel perpetually torn by the dual aspects of your nature, and the guilt over activities in the past. You did not mean to kill those Romulans. . . ."

"I know that."

"You were tricked," he said, and he was approaching her once more, his arms at his side, swaying in a relaxed manner. This time, however, she did not back away.

"Tricked by the Romulan you knew to be your biological father. You foolishly believed that if it was possible to find redemption in such a creature, that it could lead to your own redemption as well. If he had hidden depths of righteousness, then you might be more of a righteous female than you credited yourself. Instead he turned out to be a traitor, to you and to his people. And since that time, your own concerns over your trustworthiness have haunted you. Tell me, Soleta . . . how loud are the screams of the Romulans in your dreams when you dwell upon the deaths you caused?"

She wanted to make some sort of snide reply. She wanted to tell him it was none of his damned business. She even wanted to run away. Instead, she heard herself admit the truth: "Very loud. And every night. Every night . . . I hear their screams." Her voice was thick with that most insidious of traits, emotion, but she wasn't dwelling on that. Instead all the sleepless nights she had spent, from that day to this, were surging within her. "When the building blew up, thanks to the bomb I set off through my father's trickery. I should have known . . . should have realized . . ."

"But you could not have."

"But I should have."

"Would you like to ease that suffering? Your soulsickness? If only for a while?"

She shook her head, even as she said, "Yes."

He raised his hand, and there was something in it. It appeared to be glowing. Overcome by curiosity, she leaned forward to get a better look at it.

It was the oddest thing she had ever seen. It seemed to be some sort of gelatinous mass, but it was shimmering gold. It was attached to a small branch, giving it the appearance of something that had been plucked from a tree or a bush. It throbbed and pulsed, almost as if it was alive, as it lay there in his palm. He reached over with his other hand and lifted it up. By all rights, it looked as if it should just fall apart, losing all its cohesion. Yet it stayed together, giving it the curious look of something that was both solid and liquid at the same time, like mercury.

And she felt a warmth radiating from it. That was the eeriest thing of all.

"What is it?" she asked.

"You already know."

The strange thing was, she did. "Ambrosia."

"Yes."

Automatically, operating entirely on reflex, she brought her tricorder around and scanned it. The readings surprised her. It registered as a simple collection of proteins. There was nothing remotely toxic about it, nothing to explain the feeling of . . . of total peace she derived just from looking at it.

"That sensation you feel," he said as if reading her mind—which certainly seemed to be within the parameters of his abilities—"is a sensation of your wounds being cleansed by an inner light."

"Ah. Is *that* what that feels like."

"You attempt to jest, but you know in your heart that I am right. It washes over you, as nurturing as a gentle surf. As much as you may deny it, truly you welcome it. You know that to be the case."

"Let us say . . ." She stopped and cleared her throat, because it suddenly felt clogged. "Let us say that it is true. Not that it is, but just for sake of argument . . ."

"Very well," he said, sounding generous. "For sake of argument."

"Then what would you suggest. That I consume this unknown substance?"

"That is exactly correct. Consume as much or as little of it as you desire."

"You must truly think I am deranged."

"No. I truly think you are desperate. It is said that most creatures live lives of quiet desperation, but your desperation is not quiet at all. It cries out to me for surcease, and I can provide it if you will let me."

"Why would I want to do that."

"Because," he said, and he seemed genuinely sad, "the truth is . . . you've nothing to lose."

She so very, very much wanted to disagree with the assessment. She wanted to take the ambrosia and throw it in his face. She wanted to further break her Vulcan training and laugh at him, or shout at him, or in some way loudly proclaim that he didn't have the faintest idea of what the hell he was talking about. Yet she found herself picking up the ambrosia just the same, and looking at it, and seeing in it a salvation she hadn't even thought possible.

And then she was raising it to her lips, even as her mind screamed at her that this was totally insane, and he must be doing it to her somehow, must be inside her and manipulating her in ways previously thought impossible, but somehow none of it seemed to matter because the temptation to still the voices that cried out within her was just too overwhelming, and besides, it was in the name of science. What scientist worth her salt wasn't willing to take a chance, to lay herself on the line at some point in her life, in the spirit of discovery?

She bit into the ambrosia, and her first thought was disappointment, because the taste was nothing special, faintly honeylike. Nor did it seem to be having any effect on her at all. She chewed it a couple of times and swallowed, and still there was nothing untoward about it. After all that. After that incredible "sales pitch," after all that buildup, she felt no different. . . .

Then she noticed that there was some sort of warmth starting to build in her chest. It was like a small ball of heat, coming together in her solar plexus, and then it started to radiate outward. Her hands and feet were tingling, and she was beginning to get light-headed. She gasped and staggered, and then she felt as if something was lifting her up. It was as he had said before, about waves and water, and she felt caught up in a surf, riding a crest of a massive wave that was carrying her higher and higher. She laughed and cried and shrieked all at once, and the voices of the Romulans, of her inner doubts, of everything that had gnawed at her and eaten away at her was gone for the first time in ages. There was just her, there was Soleta, and she was happy with being Soleta, and more, she was happy with Thoth for giving her this, happy with the Beings for existing, for providing her with this miraculous substance, and she knew that she would do anything, just anything that was required in order to make sure that she would never, ever have to stop feeling this way again.

And somewhere in the far reaches of her consciousness, she knew that Thoth was laughing, but that was all right, because so was she. . . .

TRIDENT/EXCALIBUR

i.

SHELBY COULDN'T QUITE BELIEVE that she had heard Mick Gold properly. "The *Tholians?* Are you sure?"

He nodded grimly, half-turning in his chair at ops. "No question. I recognize the energy signature of their ships a mile off. It's them."

"Perfect." Seated in her command chair on the bridge, Shelby was starting to wonder if there was anything about this day that could remotely go right. "Raise the *Excal* for me."

"They're hailing us, Captain."

"Figures. Put them on screen."

Moments later the concerned face of Burgoyne appeared on the screen. "I will give you the courtesy, Captain, of assuming that you've come to the same conclusion as we?"

"That the Tholians will be here at any moment?"

248

S/he nodded. "An imminent Tholian arrival is never good news."

"Believe me, Burgy, I know that all too well," she said grimly. "I suggest a three-way conversation with the Tholians as soon as they arrive."

"Agreed. I'll follow your lead, if it's all the same to you, since you are the ranking officer."

"I appreciate the vote of confidence. Where's Mac?"

"He just beamed down to the surface. Soleta's gone missing and he's going down to confront Lodec about it."

She felt her blood rushing to her temples, which was not an uncommon sensation for her. "He's doing *what?*"

"Going down to confront Lodec over Soleta's disappearance."

"What type of security team does he have with him."

"None."

"What?" She hated that her voice had just cracked and the decibel level had been practically earsplitting, but it was too late for that now. "How could he—?"

"He said that if this Anubis dispatched Kebron so easily, then a multitude of human guards wouldn't accomplish anything except to make him look as if he was so afraid of the Beings that he required security backup."

"But he *does* require security backup, to provide him—"

"To provide him what, exactly, Captain?" asked Burgoyne, sounding rather reasonable about it. "How likely is it that another security squad would fare better than Kebron? It was Captain Calhoun's belief that the only thing that could possibly win the day was a show of total confidence. Bringing a security squad to 'hide behind,' his words, would simply send the message that he was afraid of the Beings."

"They damned near tore your vessel apart, Burgy," Shelby reminded hir. "If you're not afraid of them to some degree, you won't survive." She shook her head in disbelief. "Mac going down there to face a god single-handedly. That's . . . that's so . . ." Then she just shook her head in weary acceptance. "That's predictably typical, actually. Can you raise him?"

"We were about to try and do so when you contacted us," Burgoyne's voice came back, sounding a bit cheerful that Shelby wasn't going to continue carping about Calhoun's command decisions. "I felt that, at the very least, he should be kept aware of the situa—"

Suddenly Burgoyne stopped and looked sharply to hir right.

"Burgy? What's wrong?" asked Shelby with concern.

"I . . . thought I saw, for just a second . . ." But then s/he shook hir head. "Sorry. Must have been my imagination."

Shelby leaned forward in her command chair, her brow furrowed. "What did you think you saw, Burgy?"

"I . . . thought I saw McHenry standing near by the conn station, big as life. Wishful thinking, I suppose."

"Yes. I suppose," said Shelby sympathetically. She was familiar with the phenomenon. The tendency to believe that a lost crewmate is standing there, big as life. It was similar to someone who had been deprived of a limb having sensations of a phantom arm or leg.

Burgoyne shook it off and then, all business, said, "I'll inform the captain. And then . . . we'll see what happens."

"Yes," Shelby agreed. "We surely will."

ii.

"S/he saw me. I'm sure of it," said McHenry.

He circled Burgoyne on the bridge of the *Excalibur,* trying to regain hir attention. He was certain that, just for a heartbeat, the Hermat had seen him. But now there was no further response. Instead Burgoyne was busy finishing a conversation with Shelby, and then endeavoring to raise Captain Calhoun on the planet's surface.

The Old Father stood nearby, arms folded, watching McHenry's gyrations with what seemed to be a distant sadness. "This one is rather unusual. It sees the world in a slightly different way than others. More animalistic."

"S/he's not an 'it.' S/he's a . . . a s/he," said McHenry. For some reason he felt slightly defensive.

"I see. Still, for his . . . her . . . its . . . ?"

"Hir."

". . . hir . . . attributes . . . that shouldn't be sufficient, in and of itself, for hir to perceive you. Is there some other link . . ." Then he paused and a slow smile spread across his face. "Were you and this individual . . . intimate . . . at some point? Yes, yes, I see by the look of chagrin. You were indeed. Were you at the time of your . . . mishap?"

"No," said McHenry quietly. Even though Burgoyne was less than a foot away, s/he seemed ever so much farther. "No. That was over quite some time ago. S/he was interested in someone else. I was more of a . . . a diversion, really." Then, just as quickly, he shook off the somber mood. "But I don't understand. I've been in hir sight line before this. Why now? Why is s/he perceiving me now, even if only for a moment?"

"Because," said the Old Father with grim satisfaction, "you're getting stronger. There are forces, energies, available to you. You do not consciously know how to tap into them, but nevertheless you are gradually developing the ability to manipulate them."

"S/he's not seeing me now." He waved his hand in front of Burgoyne. S/he stared right through him.

"Because s/he does not believe you are here. S/he has dismissed the notion from hir mind. If hir mind is closed to you, then s/he will not see you."

"My God, how many rules does this . . . this whole thing have?" he asked in frustration.

"Only one, actually," the Old Father told him. "One that was best articulated by a human being named Descartes many centuries ago. *Cogito, ergo sum.*"

"I think, therefore I am?"

The Old Father nodded.

"Believe it or not," said McHenry dryly, "that isn't as helpful as you obviously think it is. These energies . . . do the Beings manipulate them as well?"

The Old Father again nodded slowly. "Yes. With far greater sophistication and skill than you, but yes."

McHenry laughed, but there was a bitter tinge to it. "That's just perfect, isn't it. Artemis wanted me to become like you people. I said no. So what happens? I have my 'mishap,' as you call it, and I wind up becoming like you anyway."

"No. Not like us. You have far too much conscience. The Beings care only for themselves. But your growing strength is one of the things I've been waiting for."

"And what else?" McHenry suddenly felt a surge of anger. "What else have you been waiting for? How many layers are there to this? What haven't you been telling me? How do I know that you aren't working with them somehow? Maybe . . . maybe you're just part of some master plan to keep me distracted or in check, to stop me from—"

"From what?" asked the Old Father, eyebrow cocked in curiosity. "Left to your own devices, what would you do? Precisely? If I'm holding you back from some action that you'd rather pursue, then let me be the first to tell you to go to it. Best of luck to you. I'll wait here."

Stuck for some sort of concrete strategy to pursue, McHenry rallied as best he could. He circled the bridge once more as he spoke, this time walking carelessly through crewmen at their stations. "Why *are* we waiting here?" he demanded. "Captain Calhoun is on the surface. The Beings are on the surface. What the hell are we doing in the *Excalibur?* Can't we just go down there, and—"

"Yes. We can," said the Old Father brusquely, suddenly seeming less avuncular than he had before. "Directly into the source of power of the Beings. Perhaps we elude the perceptions of your crewmates, but the Beings will detect the both of us immediately . . . and put an end to you."

"Not to you?"

The Old Father shrugged. "They can try. They would not succeed. You, on the other hand, are far more vulnerable, and they would make short work of you. Or else they might actually convince you to join them. Honestly, I'm not certain which would be the worse fate."

"So we continue to just wait?"

"And you build power, yes."

"Until . . . ?"

"Well . . . until that, for one thing."

The elder guard was pointing at the viewscreen, and McHenry turned to see what he was indicating.

There was a glowing, triangular-shaped vessel approaching. McHenry could see the ripple in space which indicated where it had just dropped out of warp space.

It was at that moment he realized that the ripple effect shouldn't have been visible to him. For normal human sight, it was visible for perhaps half a heartbeat before a ship settled into normal space. But McHenry could still perceive the energy surges and space-fabric disruption long seconds after the ship had already dropped into "real" space. It underscored for him the steadily deteriorating impact that faster-than-light travel had slowly had upon the environment of space. It also made him realize that his senses were expanding in ways he hadn't been aware of, or even thought possible.

He didn't know whether to be pleased about it or frightened, and settled for both.

His pacing around the bridge brought him to a halt near Burgoyne. He stretched out a hand and allowed it to "rest" upon Burgoyne's shoulder, then "stroke" hir face, knowing that Burgy didn't feel it. He wondered if, at night, in the recesses of hir sleep, hir innermost private dreaming, Burgy ever gave any passing thought to their time together.

McHenry had stepped aside willingly and immediately upon understanding that Burgy's attentions had lain elsewhere. For a moment, he wondered if somehow his life might have turned out differently if he hadn't been such a good sport about it. Very quickly, though, he set aside the notion. There was no point in dwelling on it. What was done was done. Burgoyne had truly wanted Selar, despite overwhelming differences in their personalities and odds to the contrary. And no power had been able to come between them.

Except . . .

Well . . . McHenry had power, didn't he. He just hadn't used it.

And wouldn't it have been interesting . . . if he had?

And as he mused on such things, the Old Father regarded him with a very worried air.

DANTER

CALHOUN ARRIVED outside the Danteri Senate several minutes before Ambassadors Spock and Si Cwan, but didn't enter immediately as he was busy attending to a rather worrisome communication from the *Excalibur.* From within the Senate house he could hear the voices of the various senators discussing and debating this, that, or some other damned thing. The specifics were of far less interest to him that what he was hearing from his ship.

"The Tholians?" he said worriedly in response to Burgoyne's voice over his combadge. "Well, that's exactly what this situation needed. Estimated time of arrival?"

"Five minutes, Captain. Shall we beam you up?"

It was certainly his first impulse.

But then he began to do something that he very rarely, if ever, did: He started to second-guess himself.

It wasn't as if he was leaving Burgoyne hanging for

an extraordinary amount of time. In point of fact, the entire decision process occupied fleeting seconds. And what it dwelt upon was Captain Elizabeth Shelby.

The truth was that Calhoun was still smarting over the way he'd handled the *Excalibur*'s rescue by the *Trident*. It had less to do with Shelby than it did with his own infernal pride. He doubted he'd have felt any better about the situation if it had been Jean-Luc Picard himself to the rescue. Nevertheless, he was sure that Shelby had taken his frustration as some sort of commentary on the fact that it was his own wife who had come riding to his rescue. That the true sting came with being beholden to her. That somehow, in his way of looking at the universe, she wasn't worthy to be the one to bail him out.

He didn't feel that way. At least . . . he wanted to believe he didn't feel that way.

And certainly matters had been exacerbated when he'd shown up at Danter. Her ire over his abrupt appearance had been quite obvious. Once again she took it as an implicit statement that she wasn't up to certain challenges on her own. That she needed Calhoun watching her back. As far as she was concerned, Calhoun had made the careful and considered judgment that he was more qualified to handle the Danteri than she was.

Again . . . he wanted to believe he didn't feel that way.

So now another matter had arisen. The Tholians, notoriously belligerent, certainly up to no good, had come upon the scene. Both the *Trident* and the *Excalibur* were potentially at risk and Shelby, as ranking officer on the scene, would be the one to make the key decisions as to how to proceed.

Unless Calhoun returned. In which case he would be senior officer, and Shelby would be required by Starfleet protocol to take her cues from him.

It would make eminent sense for him to return to the *Excalibur* and take charge. And the chances were that Shelby would certainly see it that way. Not even think twice about it.

Then again, there was always the possibility that she might take it as yet another tacit commentary on her capabilities.

Certainly that wasn't his problem. If she had such issues, then they were hers, not his. Except there was the possibility that he had contributed to them.

And besides, this was his wife. Although she might well raise a protest to the very idea, in Calhoun's mind that still entitled her to special considerations.

There was no way that Burgoyne would have suspected that all of that had gone through Calhoun's mind in the brief instants of silence. And then Calhoun said, "Tell Captain Shelby that I trust her to handle the situation. Calhoun out."

There. Just like that, Calhoun had made abundantly clear that he had every confidence in Shelby's command skills. He was, after all, trusting the welfare of his vessel to her.

"What situation, Captain?"

Calhoun knew perfectly well that Si Cwan had been approaching him from behind. Even distracted as he was, very little happened anywhere in proximity to him that Calhoun was unaware of. He turned to see both Cwan and also Ambassador Spock a few yards away.

As quickly as he could, Calhoun outlined what he'd

just learned. Si Cwan simply shrugged, having little to no experience with the Tholians. Ambassador Spock, on the other hand, commented, "I am not entirely surprised. There are very few predicaments that the Tholians cannot exacerbate if they put their minds to it."

"You're familiar with them?" asked Calhoun.

Spock inclined his head slightly, signaling the affirmative. "When one reaches my age, Captain, one is hard-pressed to find anything with which I do not have at least some degree of familiarity."

"And what happened when you encountered them?"

"They endeavored to snare the *Enterprise* in what was, conceivably, the most inefficient device ever utilized to attempt capture of a ship: a large energy web that required both an inordinate amount of time to construct and also the target vessel to remain in one spot during that entire time."

"And the *Enterprise* cooperated with those conditions?" asked Calhoun.

"It was necessary for us to remain on station in order to retrieve our captain from a dimensional rip."

"Sounds interesting."

"I would have thought 'tedious' to be the more accurate summation," Spock replied.

"So there's no problem then," said Si Cwan. "All the ships need to do is keep moving, and there shouldn't be a problem."

"Not necessarily. In the time since we encountered them, their weaponry has improved."

"So has ours," Calhoun assured him, all business. "Now would you mind telling me what you two are doing here?"

"Is it not obvious?" asked Spock.

Calhoun smiled raggedly. "In retrospect, I suppose it is. You were the ones who reported that Soleta was missing. I told you I was going to come here to the senate, to confront these bastards over Soleta's disappearance, and also the business with Kebron. To say we're getting mixed messages regarding the Beings is to understate it. I'm tired of being told how benevolent they are and then having my people ill-treated by them."

"I have to say I agree, Captain," Si Cwan said readily, "but if my weeks of experience here on Danter are any guidance, you'll be extremely lucky even to get a word in edgewise with the Danteri senate. Gods know I tried on a number of occasions. They were certainly polite enough when they wanted me to come here initially, but they showed their true selves soon enough. Every single action I tried to take, every initiative I introduced to help bring the new Thallonian Empire to fruition, became hopelessly bogged down in committees, politics, and individual interests."

"I regret to inform you, Ambassador," said Spock, "that you will find that to be the case quite frequently in virtually any governing system other than a dictatorship."

Si Cwan stared at him a moment. "If that was intended to disparage the worth of dictatorships, Ambassador, then I regret to inform you that you've failed utterly."

Spock merely raised a skeptical eyebrow. Then he turned back to Calhoun. "Do you have a plan as to how to proceed, Captain?"

"I was considering going in there and hitting people until they give me what I want."

"Ah. The Kirk Maneuver."

Calhoun looked at Spock askance for a moment, not

entirely sure whether that was intended as a compliment or a joke, and then pivoted on his heel and headed into the senate building. After a brief pause, Si Cwan and Spock followed him in.

Calhoun walked past the various statues and mosaics depicting great moments in Danteri history. He knew them all too well, having been to Danter on previous excursions. Excursions that had left him with a very bitter taste in his mouth.

Suddenly he stopped so abruptly that, had Si Cwan had slower reflexes, he would have collided with him. *"Grozit,"* murmured Calhoun.

"Captain, what's wr—?" asked Si Cwan, and then he looked around and saw it as well.

All the depictions of the proud history of Danter were gone. In their place were mosaics of various of the Beings. They were drenched in glittering represented sunlight, and in each of the renderings, there were people on their knees, gesticulating and bowing to the Beings as they looked down benevolently at their worshippers. Calhoun spotted the rendering of Artemis instantly, and there was Anubis, and there were others as well that he didn't immediately know.

Si Cwan realized it too. "What happened to the frescoes? The pictures of Danteri history."

"History has changed."

It was Soleta who had spoken.

She stood there, calmly and coolly, her hands casually in front of her and her fingers interlaced.

And she was smiling.

That was naturally the thing that struck Calhoun almost instantly. His Vulcan science officer was smiling.

It wasn't a broad grin or any such thing, but there was a definite smile of pleasure.

"Lieutenant . . . are you all right?" Calhoun said, taking a step toward her. "And what do you mean 'history has changed.' Are you saying there's some sort of temporal shift . . . ?"

She laughed. Calhoun had never heard her laugh. It was an odd sound, like something that had rusted over and was only now being oiled into use. "No. No, Captain. This isn't like when you slingshot us back through time. I simply meant that things are different around here now. We saw some of that before, didn't we, Ambassador Spock?"

"We did," Spock said in his gravelly voice. "That was, however, before you were kidnapped. Such an action would seem to indicate an environment that is less than hospitable."

"I wasn't kidnapped, Spock," replied Soleta. "To be kidnapped, you have to be transported against your will."

"I think we all know the definition of kidnapped, Lieutenant," said Calhoun. "The question is, where did you go? What did—?"

"Captain, with all respect, those questions can wait. I want to show you something." Without waiting for Calhoun to reply, she turned and walked toward the inner chambers of the senate. Calhoun glanced at the others, shrugged, and followed her.

Moments later they were standing in the observation gallery of the senate. It was not at all the way Calhoun remembered it . . . or, for that matter, the way Si Cwan recalled it either. The Thallonian was shaking his head in what was obvious disbelief.

"What do you see, Si Cwan?" inquired Soleta, leaning forward on the railing, her smile only growing.

"Well," Si Cwan said slowly, "as opposed to my previous stay on Danter, when a typical senate meeting was marked with arguments, hostility, crosstalk, and very little sense of anything being accomplished . . . what I'm seeing here is quite the opposite. Discussion about various topics seems to be proceeding in a reasoned, calm manner. People are . . . well, they're smiling . . . and . . ."

"It goes deeper than that, Ambassador." She seemed to be warming to the topic. "The spirit of the senate these days is one of total cooperation. Various projects designed to help the needy—projects which once would have stalled in endless committees—are gliding through. Resources are being allocated where they're truly needed, instead of being hijacked by whomever has the most political coin to spend. What you're seeing here is the ideal government, operating in perfect unity . . ."

"Like the Borg?" said Calhoun.

She shook her head, that unassailable smile still fixedly in place. "Not at all. The Borg endeavor to use the concept of unity to obliterate races. The Danter simply use unity in order to build up their own strength of character."

"And the unity," Spock said slowly, "comes from concerted worship of the Beings."

"Yes."

"And they, in turn, give you ambrosia," said Calhoun, making no effort to hide his mounting anger. "Like drug dealers endeavoring to get poor fools hooked into a habit . . ."

She raised an eyebrow as she asked, with no heat, "Are you calling me a poor fool, Captain?"

"You've eaten the ambrosia."

"Of course."

Indeed *of course.* Calhoun wasn't stupid. He had more or less figured out exactly what had happened. "Lieutenant," he informed her, "you are to report back to the *Excalibur* immediately. Dr. Selar will—"

She shook her head, never looking anything less than polite and attentive. "I'm afraid that won't be necessary, Captain. There's nothing Dr. Selar needs to do for me. I'm quite well. Better, in fact, than I've ever been in my life. Than anyone has ever been in their life."

"Lieutenant . . ."

"Captain," she interrupted. When she spoke her voice was slightly singsong, almost loving. "You have no idea how much confusion I've lived my life in. I can't really convey it to you, but trust me, it was a lot. And now . . . everything is fine. Everything is peaceful. The voices and noises in my head have stopped. Different aspects of my life make sudden sense now. And I have the Beings to thank for it, and their ambrosia. Look around you, Captain," and she indicated the entirety of the senate chamber with its many senators working in smooth tandem and harmony. "This is the race that conquered Xenex. Who oppressed your people for so many years. They could never do anything like that now. They are interested purely in benevolent acts, in helping themselves and others."

"They're interested in serving and worshipping the Beings," replied Calhoun.

Soleta's shoulders moved in a half-shrug. "That's certainly true enough. But everything comes with a price."

"And tell me, Lieutenant . . . what would happen if

the Beings instructed the Danteri not to be so benevolent," he asked, his voice becoming frosty. "If they dispatched them upon a holy war in order to serve their needs and desires."

"They would never do that."

"You don't know that," Si Cwan spoke up.

And suddenly Calhoun felt the hair on the back of his neck prickling, a typical indication that things were suddenly about to take a downward spiral. Sure enough, there were bursts of light from all around them seconds later. Calhoun didn't know where to turn first, but reflexively his hand went for his phaser and it was in his outstretched hand. It didn't provide him with all that much sense of security, but at least it was something.

A Being flared into existence next to Soleta, and Calhoun immediately recognized him from the descriptions he'd heard as Thoth. But to one side of him was Anubis, and to the other side, Artemis. They were smiling at him in the archly superior manner that only creatures who believe they hold all the cards can have. Unfortunately, Calhoun was hard-pressed to think that they didn't hold all the cards.

"She does know that," Thoth said quietly. "And, candidly, it's rather discourteous that any of you would question her understanding of matters that you know nothing about."

"I know you've given her something that's controlling her mind," said Calhoun.

"Controlling? No." In what looked appallingly like a gesture of tenderness, he brushed a strand of hair from her face. "No, the ambrosia has simply eased away some of the more frustrating and distracting concerns that have cluttered her mind. Far from controlling, she is now free to think clearly for the first time in her life."

"And by a fascinating coincidence," said Spock, "once she is thinking clearly, all she is able to think of is you?"

Thoth looked at Spock suspiciously. Then he glanced at the others as if seeking confirmation. "You know who this one reminds me of . . . ?"

"Pan," Spock said with a slight sigh.

The Beings actually appeared surprised. "You've met him?"

"I have never had the pleasure."

"Captain, you really don't have to worry about me," Soleta assured him.

"At the moment, I'm less worried about you than I am about the objects of your worship," said Calhoun. "I've had people injured and killed because of you creatures. Did you think I'd just forget about that?"

"We hadn't actually given it any thought at all," Artemis said. "That's always been the problem with you mortals. You operate under the impression that what you say or do means anything to such as we."

"And yet," said Spock, "you crave worship."

"We crave nothing," Anubis spoke up, with that voice that sounded as if it was coming from beyond the grave. "We seek only gratitude in exchange for our generosity."

Thoth draped an arm around Soleta's shoulders. She looked up at him with an expression of such puppylike devotion and adoration that it nearly turned Calhoun's stomach. Every impulse screamed within him to attack this creature and its associates, but he wasn't exactly in love with the odds.

"In response to your other stated concern," Thoth

said, "you need not worry yourself. Holy wars generally start when mortals take it upon themselves to try and determine where the interests of the gods lie and act on their own accord. Invariably such endeavors are far more attuned to the desires of the mortals than any matters that are of concern to the gods. We are more than capable of attending to our own needs."

"As we are about to demonstrate," Artemis said with a smile.

"What are you talking about?" said Si Cwan.

At that moment the steady, calm drone of voices and discussion which constituted the senate erupted into excited cries of joy. There were flashes of light throughout the senate floor. More of the Beings were appearing, clad in regalia from a variety of cultures and times throughout Earth history.

"What's going on," said Calhoun, his eyes narrowing. "What are you up to? If you're thinking of—"

Anubis took two strides toward him. "You are a most strident and demanding creature for someone who we could obliterate as easily as crushing a bug beneath our feet."

"Anubis . . ." said Artemis, sounding as if she were trying to rein him in.

But Calhoun was barely paying any attention to her. Instead, he holstered his phaser and stood before Anubis, crouched, hands poised as if prepared to throttle the jackal-headed god. "Make your first step," he said.

An angry hissed escaped from between Anubis' teeth, and then Artemis said *"Anubis!"* more sharply than before. For half a heartbeat, something flickered in her face that seemed to border on concern, and then it was replaced by an easy and confident smile. "There's no need for hostilities. Nothing is to be accomplished by it."

"You should have thought of that," fired back Calhoun, "before your people damaged my ship and killed members of my crew."

"And you should think of that," replied Thoth, "before you are foolish enough to challenge us again. No good will come of it, Captain, I assure you. No good at all. You just remember that. Remember how we hurt you, and can do so again. Because as the Beings are my witness, we've no desire to do it again. But," he added after a significant pause, "we will. Believe it. We will."

"His memory is short, Thoth," said Anubis. "Fortunately, a reminder is imminent."

"And we're back to that," Si Cwan said. "What reminder? What are you referring to . . . ?"

Artemis spoke casually, glancing at her fingernails as if she were making a pronouncement as to what style of hat was going to be in style come the spring. "Oh . . . we're simply about to show some intruders the high price of insolence. That our demands are not to be ignored."

And Calhoun promptly got it. Even as Si Cwan was about to ask another question, Calhoun suddenly said, "The Tholians."

"Of course," Spock murmured.

Calhoun immediately hit his combadge. "Calhoun to *Excalibur*. Three—" He glanced at Soleta. "Four to beam up."

Soleta took a concerned step in Thoth's direction, and Thoth said warningly, "Captain . . ."

"Unable to comply, sir," came Burgoyne's voice. "Our shields are up."

Calhoun's voice caught a moment. "Are you under attack?" he demanded.

"No, sir. But the Tholians arrived with their weapons running hot. We're not targeted, but we, along with the *Trident,* raised our shields as a precaution. If you want me to drop them—"

"No. Maintain shields. Are you and Shelby still in communication with them?"

"Aye, sir."

"Patch me in."

"Do not attempt to thwart the will of the gods, mortal," intoned Anubis. "I am the death walker, and I know when little mortals overstep themselves."

"I've walked some death myself, 'god,' " shot back Calhoun, "and it might be wise for little gods to stay the hell out of my way."

"Such challenge!" called out Thoth, but he didn't appear to be talking to Calhoun. Suddenly light flashed once more in a manner that had become all too familiar to Calhoun, and suddenly Thoth was in the center of the senate floor. Soleta was next to him, looking up at him admiringly.

"My people!" he called out, his arms outstretched. "Worshippers of our divinity! Fellow travelers on the road to greatness and glory! We who are bringing your world into a golden age! Do you believe in our vision?"

"Yes!" The cries were ripped simultaneously from a hundred throats.

"Do you believe in our greatness?"

"*Yes!*" The word thundered and echoed from both inside the building and out, and Calhoun realized that Thoth wasn't just there in front of them, but elsewhere as well. Or perhaps others of his fellow Beings were exhorting the Danteri simultaneously with the exact same words. Either way, it seemed the entirety of Danter was rallying behind their gods.

"There are those who don't! What shall we do about those who don't!?"

"Smite them!"

"Fascinating," murmured Spock.

TRIDENT

COMMANDER LYKENE'S VOICE was so shrill and piercing that Shelby felt as if it was going to slice off the top of her head. Nor was his (she thought it was a "he," though with the Tholians it wasn't always possible to be sure) visual presence on the viewscreen much easier to take.

It was difficult to know exactly what one was looking at when encountering a Tholian. No one had ever encountered them face-to-face, in person. On screen, they appeared to be crystalline in nature, with no discernible or moving features beyond that, such as eyes or mouths. It was possible that the appearance they presented as such was a fabrication, designed to make them appear more formidable than they were. Shelby briefly imagined that the Tholians actually bore a striking resemblance to bunny rabbits in pink tutus, and that brought her some measure of relief.

She let none of this show in her demeanor, however,

as she pressed forward with trying to keep a lid on the situation. Burgoyne's face had vanished from the two-way image on the screen. Apparently he'd received some sort of communication from Calhoun and was busy dealing with that. Shelby couldn't help but think that Calhoun was getting the lucky end of the deal at that moment. Why couldn't *she* have been smart enough to make some incredibly stupid and quixotic trip down to the planet's surface?

Keeping her voice calm and even, she said, "Commander, you don't appear to be listening to what Commander Burgoyne and I have been telling you . . ."

"We have heard you," said Lykene, the screen flickering in response to his words.

"Heard, yes. Not listened."

"The mission given this vessel is clear," he said as if she hadn't spoken. "The planet Danter has been declared part of the Tholian Assembly and subject to our laws. As such, all resources utilized by the Danteri are subject to seizure."

"You can't be serious," said Shelby. "How can you possibly suddenly say that Danter is in Tholian territory?"

"Its elliptical orbit brings it to within our boundaries for one solar day every four Tholian years."

"Commander, with all respect, that is the most pathetic rationalization I have ever heard for a clear act of aggression—"

"The planet's orbit is sufficient to be considered Tholian property," insisted Lykene. "In the interest of cooperation, we will put you in touch with the Tholian Assembly for verification."

"No. No assembly is required," said Shelby. "The problem is—"

"Are your vessels here in attempted contravention of Tholian interest in this situation?" demanded Lykene, cutting her off. The challenge in his tone was evident to Shelby, and certainly to everyone else on the bridge.

"We are here pursuing the interests of the United Federation of Planets, under the authority of Starfleet," replied Shelby, not rising to Lykene's arrogant tone. "And I would assume that those interests are identical to yours: namely the existence of a substance called 'ambrosia' which is alleged to have highly beneficial effects. The difference in our respective cases, Commander, is that we're not endeavoring to coopt it or claim it for our own. Instead we simply want to understand it and determine whether or not it poses a hazard."

"You and your Federation need not concern yourselves," Lykene assured her. "All properties of Danter, including ambrosia, will fall under the auspices of the Tholian Assembly. Your interests in this matter are therefore null and void. It is our directive that you depart orbit at once."

"That's not going to happen," Shelby said heatedly, and then reined herself in lest Lykene think he was getting to her. "And furthermore, I—"

"Captain," Takahashi said from ops. "Getting a new hail from the *Excalibur.*"

"Put them on," said Shelby.

Burgoyne's face appeared, looking concerned. Shelby imagined that it was a probable mirror of her own expression. "Captain," Burgoyne said, "I see you're still on with the Tholians. I have Captain Calhoun from the planet's surface."

"We have no need to speak with more representatives of your Federation," Lykene said. "Our directive is—"

"Tell the Tholians to get the hell out of there," came Calhoun's voice without preamble. *"Trident, Excalibur* . . . can the Tholians hear me? I'm blind down here."

"We hear you," said Lykene. "This is Commander Lykene of the Tholian Assembly, and we have no intention of dignifying your threats with—"

"This isn't a threat, you jackass," Calhoun snapped back.

Shelby put her fingers to her temples and rubbed them, recalling why it was that she perpetually felt as if she had headaches during the entirety of her tenure as Calhoun's second-in-command.

"I'm trying to tell you that you're in danger. The creatures down here who introduced ambrosia to the Danteri are planning to make an example of you and your ship, and I very much doubt you're going to live through it. Now if you have a shred of intelligence, you'll put as much distance between yourselves and this world as possible."

"Commander Lykene, I would listen to Captain Calhoun if I were you," Burgoyne now spoke up. "The last time we encountered the Beings, they put our ship into drydock for several weeks of repairs. You will not stand a chance if they decide to focus their energies on you."

There was a long pause, and Shelby could only imagine that Lykene was consulting with his (her?) own people to try and get a reading of the situation. "We can attend to our own affairs," Lykene finally replied. "We do not require your help. We require you to distance yourselves from this world, now. And this pathetic attempt to trick us into departing . . ."

"I'm not trying to trick you into anything," said Calhoun with a touch of frustration. "I'm trying to help you save your own lives."

"Our lives do not require saving."

And suddenly the image of Burgoyne was gone.

So was the visual of the Tholian.

Instead the screen was occupied by the huge head and face of what could only be considered some sort of wolf creature . . . or perhaps a hyena.

It was black, black as death, and the eyes glowed red. It hung in space, miles long, stars filtering through it in places. Its expression was grim, and it said, "Who comes seeking ambrosia?"

Again a pause. Shelby wasn't entirely sure how to respond.

Lykene saved her the trouble. The Tholian's brittle but firm voice sounded over the com systems. If he was at all deterred by the sight of a miles-long-and-wide jackal head talking at him from space, one wouldn't have been able to tell by the unyielding assurance of his speech. "I am Commander Lykene of the Tholian Assembly. I have come here at the behest of the assembly to inform you—"

" 'Inform us'?" said the jackal-headed being. The expressions of his face were quite limited. "Who are you . . . to inform us of anything."

"We are the Tholian Assembly, and we are now informing you that ambrosia is our property."

"Is it. And I, Anubis of the gods, am asking you how you arrived at that conclusion."

"This world is within territorial boundaries of the

275

Tholian Assembly. As such, it and everything upon it is subject to Tholian ownership."

Shelby almost had to admire Lykene. He had staked out a truly idiotic position, but having taken it, he wasn't backing down from it.

"I see," rumbled Anubis. "Well, Commander Lykene of the Tholian Assembly, if it is ambrosia you seek, then it is ambrosia you shall have."

For a heartbeat, Shelby felt a surge of relief. Calhoun had obviously been worried that something bad was going to happen, but it appeared that the Beings were going to cooperate. That relief, however, evaporated as Anubis continued, "Provided, of course, that the entirety of the Tholian Assembly is willing to worship us."

"Worship?" For the first time, Lykene sounded puzzled.

"That's one of their conditions, Commander," Shelby interjected. "They've been fairly consistent about that. In order to avail oneself of ambrosia, one must be willing to worship these individuals as gods. Build temples to them, pay tribute, bow down to—"

"This is not a negotiation," Lykene replied. "We are not seeking the cooperation of these creatures purporting divinity. We, and the members and allies of the Tholian Assembly, are here to claim the substance ambrosia for our own. There will be no worshipping, no tribute, no bowing. We demand that one metric ton of ambrosia be made available to us immediately. This will be due us in no less than one hour."

"I see," said Anubis, his voice continuing to sound within the ship through means that Shelby could not even begin to guess. "And if we refuse?"

"Then the Tholian Assembly will regard such a stance

as a declaration of war, and you will have to live with the consequences of your actions."

"Perhaps we will," Anubis said, and then his voice flattened and his eyes glowed in the vastness of space. "You, however . . . will not."

"Tholian vessel!" came Calhoun's voice, sounding desperate. "This is exactly the wrong tack to take! Stand down if you want to survive! Captain Shelby, make them get out of there!"

"Commander Lykene," Shelby began.

"Captain!" said Gold from conn, and he had never sounded as alarmed as he did just then.

The face of Anubis appeared to be getting larger, and his jaws were opening. Wide.

"Perspective check! Is he coming toward us?" demanded Shelby.

"Negative!" Hash said. "He's heading for the Tholian ship! Changing view angle."

Immediately the viewpoint of the screen shifted, and they now had a true outlook of what was transpiring. Sure enough, the massive head of Anubis was bearing down, not upon the *Trident* or *Excalibur,* but on the triangular Tholian vessel. The Tholian was standing his ground.

"Conn, do we have a phaser lock?"

"There's nothing to lock on to, Captain," said Gold. "Our eyes tell us it's there, but the instruments say it's not."

"Tholian firing," announced Hash.

Sure enough, the Tholian ship was shooting at the giant image approaching them as blue pulses of energy blasted out of the vessel. They passed harmlessly through the great face, and Anubis was almost upon them.

"It went right through him," said Hash. "Is it possible he can't hurt them? That it's just some sort of illusion?"

"I think we're about to find out," said Shelby.

She was right.

The vast jaws of Anubis clamped down upon the Tholian vessel, locking on to it top and bottom. Anubis then shook his head from side to side, like a dog worrying a bone. And the Tholian vessel was rocked, helpless. It continued to fire, but the blasts had no more effect than they had before. But as impervious as Anubis was to being touched, it wasn't slowing him down in the slightest in his endeavors to assail the Tholian ship.

"Elizabeth! What's happening up there?" came Calhoun's voice.

What Shelby was witnessing was so insane, she wasn't entirely sure what to say to Calhoun. And then, before she could answer, the entire thing became moot.

Through with playing with the Tholian ship, Anubis' jaws scissored together. It cut through the hull of the Tholian ship without slowing down. Then the head snapped to the right and left, and the ship came apart in all directions. In the silence of space, an eruption occurred as the internal atmosphere of the Tholian vessel—whatever that might be—rushed out into the vacuum as a fireball devouring the ship and its inhabitants. Then, just as quickly, the fireball snuffed out and was gone.

"Elizabeth!"

"They're gone, Mac," she said tonelessly. And it was obvious from the way she'd said it that she didn't mean they'd beaten a quick retreat and returned to Tholian space.

Slowly the vast head of Anubis swiveled around and was now staring right at them once more.

"We hope that the lesson we have taught here today will not be lost upon you," he said. And then the image disappeared from the screen.

"Son of a bitch," muttered Shelby, the irony of the observation—considering what Anubis looked like— not being lost on her.

She knew that she had no particular reason to care about the fate of the Tholians. They were a belligerent, territorial, and duplicitous race. But needless death remained needless death, even when it happened to someone for whom one felt no affection. And it further underscored the tremendous menace that the Beings represented.

"Captain," said Hash, turning in his chair. He looked slightly pale and shaken by what he'd witnessed. "Just before the Tholian ship was destroyed, they got out a distress message to the Tholian Assembly. They, and their allies, know what just happened here."

"It's going to be all over the ether in no time," Gold said.

"Mac," said Shelby as she stared at the emptiness of space. "Burgy. You still there?"

"I'm here, Elizabeth," came Calhoun's voice.

"Here, Captain," said Burgoyne.

"I'm thinking, gentlemen . . . that we may have a war on our hands."

"Very likely."

It was neither Calhoun nor Burgoyne who had replied, however. Instead a woman was standing on the bridge, clad in a lightweight, Greek-styled toga, with a quiver of arrows slung over her back.

Shelby rose from her chair, knowing instantly. "Artemis," she growled.

"We are fully aware that this assault will likely bring more attackers," said Artemis airily. "That is acceptable. But it will bring more worshippers as well. People who understand what it is we have to offer."

"That being a quick and horrible death to anyone who doesn't accept your word? Who doesn't bow down to you?" demanded Shelby.

"Yes," said Artemis with a flatness that was chilling. "We came with an offer. We were initially rebuffed. But the Danteri accepted us. Others will as well. Those that don't . . . will be annihilated. We will be worshipped. And loved. And respected. And those that don't will pay the price that blasphemers and nonbelievers have paid throughout history."

"That price being having to put up with poseurs laboring under the delusion of godhood?"

"Captain," said Artemis slowly, "do you desire to have your ship encounter the same tragic end as the Tholian vessel just did?" She paused and then repeated, more sharply and with greater warning, *Do you?*"

There was vast tension on the bridge. Her jaw twitching, Shelby said, "No. I don't."

"Ask me not to."

"Are you threatening this ves—"

"Ask me not to."

There was a sudden shaking and shuddering of the *Trident*, and Shelby was almost knocked off her feet, grabbing the back of the command chair to steady herself. Others grabbed at their consoles, and Artemis simply stood there, her arms folded. Alarm systems were going off all over the bridge.

"Don't destroy this ship!" shouted Shelby.

An instant later, the shaking ceased. Artemis smiled then, and took a step back. "You see? That wasn't so difficult. It was almost a prayer. But that will come in time. At least, you'd best hope it does . . . lest it come too late."

And with that, she vanished in a burst of light.

Shelby stood there, her face flushed with humiliation and anger, her eyes flinty and filled with anger.

"Elizabeth," came Calhoun's voice. "Are you still there."

"Calhoun," said Shelby, in as controlled a manner as she'd ever spoken, "round up our people and get back up to *Excalibur.* I'll meet you there. I've had it with these creatures. It's time to kick their asses back to whatever mountaintop they crawled down from."

"Sounds like fun," said Calhoun.

EXCALIBUR

i.

MOKE WAS VERY AWARE that something big was going on.

The atmosphere in the *Excalibur* seemed to have changed. Everyone appeared to be very focused as they went about their duties. There was very little chatter between crewmen, very little of the relaxed mood he'd come to know. The crew seemed very much "all business."

But then Moke realized that it was an attitude that he'd be well advised to emulate. He too had business, after all, and it was up to him to attend to it. And that business very much involved speaking with Mackenzie Calhoun.

He knew that Calhoun was back on the ship. He'd tried to raise him on the com link, but when he'd identified himself, Calhoun's voice had said brusquely, "Moke, is something wrong? Are you okay?"

"Wha—? Uh . . . no," said Moke. "No, I'm fine. It's just—"

"Then I hate to be abrupt with you, but there's a great

deal going on at the moment, so this will just have to wait until later." And with that, he cut the link.

Moke would have been fully aware that there was a lot going on even if Calhoun hadn't told him. Captain Shelby had returned, and she'd brought both Mueller and also a man that Moke didn't recognize. He was the first man whom Moke had ever seen that he would have described as "pretty," and there was something about him that Moke definitely didn't like. Moke tried to say hello to her, but Shelby was too deep in discussion with the man and barely glanced at him.

He didn't take offense. He knew she had grown-up things on her mind. But he also knew that he had to talk to Mac, because "it was time."

Coming from another direction was Zak Kebron. He looked different somehow to Moke. His skin was glistening, almost as if it was brand new. He was holding what looked to be a kind of short, curved sword, swinging it in leisurely fashion back and forth without apparently thinking about it. Several people had to jump out of the way to get clear of it. Kebron didn't seem to notice.

"What's that, Zak?" inquired Moke.

Kebron stopped briefly and held it up. "Well, the science department has gone over it thoroughly in tandem with engineering. As near as they can determine, it's some sort of energy funnel. But it has not storage capability of its own. Nor are they clear on precisely what type of energy it's designed to channel, or what it could be used for. Does that answer your question?"

Moke stood there, stunned. He hadn't anticipated Kebron answering with anything more than two or three words at most, and probably not even that. This copious explanation was entirely outside his expectations or Kebron's typical behavior. All Moke could manage was a nod, at which point Kebron reached out with his huge hand toward Moke's head. For an instant, Moke thought that Kebron was going to crush his skull, but the Brikar simply ruffled his hair with one finger and then continued on his way. Moke was so surprised that he completely forgot to tell Kebron he needed to see Calhoun until it was too late.

He sprinted after Kebron, his shorter legs no match for the Brikar's stride. He got to the turbolift moments after Kebron had already entered it, and even though the next one came along in mere seconds, it seemed an eternity to the boy. Passersby saw Moke saying "I'm hurrying, I'm hurrying!" to thin air and wondered if he wasn't becoming addled in some way.

He stepped into the turbolift and suddenly realized he wasn't sure where to go. "Morgan," he called out.

Morgan's voice promptly filtered into the turbolift. "You're the only one who calls me by name, Moke. It's very much appreciated. What can I do for you?"

"Can you tell me what deck Kebron got off on? Or where Mac is? I need to—"

"Zak Kebron is joining Captain Calhoun in the deck-three conference lounge. Would you like me to take you there?"

"Yes, please."

As he made his way to the conference lounge, he kept running through his mind what he was going to say. The problem was that he didn't fully comprehend it, which was frustrating, because he felt as if he should. Every so often he would mutter back to the empty air next to him, getting more confused looks from crewmen.

Finally he stood in front of the conference-lounge door. It didn't open automatically the way that most other doors around the ship did. He wondered why, and then saw a small steady red light on a wall panel near the door. He correctly intuited that it meant the door was locked.

"Morgan," he called once more.

"Yes, Moke."

"Why is the door locked?"

"Sealing a conference lounge door from the outside is standard procedure for any conference involving two or more commanding officers. It's a safety measure."

"Oh. Okay. Can you open it?"

"For you? Of course."

The light switched from red to green and the door slid open as Moke confidently walked in.

He'd never seen Calhoun looking quite so surprised. He was obviously in the middle of saying something, his index finger extended, making a point. Shelby was there along with the gleaming man and Mueller, and Zak Kebron. Si Cwan was there as well, and Burgoyne, and so was a rather intimidating-looking man who reminded Moke of Soleta. But he sensed the man was much older than Soleta, and much graver of mien.

"Nice security lock you've got there, Captain," said Shelby.

"Moke," said Calhoun, shaking off his initial confusion. "What are you doing here?"

"I needed to talk to you, Mac. It doesn't matter if everyone else is here . . ."

"But it does matter, Moke," Calhoun said firmly. He

came from around the table with the clear intention of escorting the boy out. "We're in the middle of discussing some important things, and—"

"Yes, I know. The dark, one-eyed bearded man told me so. It's been getting easier and easier for me to hear him lately."

There were bewildered looks from around the table. "We're taking time for a young boy's imaginary friend?" asked the gleaming man.

"Quiet, Mr. Gleau," said Shelby. So that was his name. Gleau. Made sense to Moke, since he kind of glowed.

"A one-eyed, bearded man," said the man who somewhat reminded Moke of Soleta. "Captain Calhoun . . . if I am not mistaken, that description roughly matches that of the Earth Norse all-father god, Woden, father of the thunder deity Thor. Under ordinary circumstances, that would be considered—at most—a coincidence. However, when one takes into account the nature of the entities with which we've been dealing . . ."

"Yes . . . yes, I see where you're going with that, Ambassador Spock." Calhoun was still approaching Moke, but his body language had changed. He no longer looked as if he was about to rush Moke out the door. "This one-eyed man . . . tell me more about him. Where did you see him?"

"What do you mean, 'did'?"

"I mean . . ." Calhoun stopped, his eyes narrowing. "Wait . . . are you saying he's . . . he's here? Now? You're seeing him now?"

"Yes. Right over there," said Moke, pointing to a spot at the far end of the room. "He's next to McHenry."

ii.

The meeting had only just begun when Calhoun looked up in surprise at Moke's arrival. The fact that Soleta was not present merely fueled Calhoun's determination to attend to the Beings once and for all, and he was pleased to see that Shelby shared his attitude. It was so rare that they were one hundred percent in accord with one another.

Shelby had offered to bring her science officer, Gleau, along. Calhoun had readily agreed, since Soleta was down on Danter and could hardly be considered in useful condition anyway. However, when Mueller, Shelby, and Gleau entered, he noticed that Mueller seemed to be giving Gleau a wide berth, even looking at him with distaste. He had no idea what the problem was between them, and decided it wasn't really his concern. Whatever it was, no doubt Shelby had a handle on it.

They had gone around the room quickly, each individual describing their encounters and sharing their knowledge in short, concise sentences. Thus in short order they were current with each other's knowledge.

But before they could take the discussion beyond that, Moke had entered, to Calhoun's astonishment. He didn't know what it was the boy wanted and, at that point, didn't much care. But he was brought up short when Moke told them of what he'd been seeing.

"McHenry?" Several voices chorused at once.

Burgoyne's was the loudest. S/he was staring fixedly at the place where Moke had been pointing. "Mark?" s/he said, and s/he squinted and stared, then looked away and then back again, and then s/he gasped, "Oh . . . my God . . . Mark . . . ?"

"Where?" demanded Calhoun.

"Right there!" S/he pointed with quivering finger. "He's right there! I thought I saw him earlier, but I just . . . I thought I was imagining it, thought I was crazy! I figured there was no way. He's still lying in sickbay, he's . . . it isn't possible, is it . . . ?"

"When dealing with the unknown," said the one who'd been called Spock, "it is generally wise to approach situations from the point of view of what is possible, rather than what is not."

"Moke." Calhoun was down on one knee, holding the boy by the shoulders. "Can you communicate with him? The bearded man. Can you ask him if his name is Woden?"

"He can hear you, Mac. He's standing right there."

"Oh. Of course." Calhoun tried to repress a smile and didn't entirely succeed. "All right . . . what did he say?"

"He said yes. Among others."

"Can he restore McHenry to life?" asked Burgoyne with urgency.

Moke listened carefully, then said, "He said it depends upon what happens. With the others."

"I don't understand," said Shelby. "Why is it that you can hear and see him, Moke?"

Moke blinked in surprise. "I dunno. I just . . . well, I just could. I never thought to ask him."

Calhoun marveled at that, although he reasoned that perhaps he shouldn't. Children, after all, were the most accepting of creatures, their reality an ever-changing and fluid environment.

Then he saw Moke pale, and his eyes widen. "Moke?" said Calhoun. "Moke . . . what is . . . ?"

"He . . ." Moke's lips suddenly looked bone dry. "He . . . he said . . ."

Once again Calhoun took him gently by the shoulders, except this time he could practically feel the boy trembling. "Moke . . . what did he s—?"

"He said he's my father."

The words thudded in the air like mallets. Moke began to shake more violently, and it was all Calhoun could do to steady him. He looked in the direction that Moke was staring, as if he could see the elder god himself.

It was insane. It was a completely insane notion.

And then he thought of how vague Moke's mother had been about the boy's patrimony. And of the incredible stormlike powers that the boy had possessed . . . powers that were certainly consistent with someone who had a filial connection to an alleged thunder god.

And just like that, it suddenly became a much less insane notion.

When Mackenzie Calhoun had come to Moke's world, Moke had latched on to him, turning him into a surrogate father even though Calhoun had made abundantly clear to the lad that he was not at all responsible for bringing the boy into the world. That had deterred Moke's devotion only slightly, and when his mother had passed away, she had given the boy over into Calhoun's keeping. He'd done the best he could with him, even though occasionally Calhoun felt utterly at sea.

Yet now, out of the blue, the mystery of Moke's parentage was solved, except all it did was evoke even more mysteries.

Moke looked up at him, wide-eyed, stunned, and obviously not a little scared. "Is . . . can that . . . is . . . Mac, is he . . . ?"

For one of the few times in his life, Calhoun had absolutely no idea what to say. "It's . . . I suppose it's possible, Moke. I don't know. But this I do know," and now he stood and, feeling a bit foolish, addressed the empty air. "These Beings . . . these fellow creatures of yours . . . it's clear that they want to spread their dominion over much more than Danter. The problem is, I'm not exactly sure whose side you're supposed to be on. I swear to God, though . . . if you're ruthlessly manipulating the hopes and dreams of this boy as part of some twisted game . . ."

"It's not a game," Moke said suddenly. Then he said to Calhoun, chagrined, "I . . . I didn't mean to interrupt. I was just saying what he said. He said it's not a game."

"I get that, Moke."

"Why is he invisible?" asked Mueller. "Why is he communicating this way instead of just appearing to us, as the others have . . . ?"

"If we are to believe that he is endeavoring to aid us," Spock said, "then the logical assumption is that this condition was, in some way, inflicted upon him by others of his kind."

"He says that's right," said Moke. "He says you remind him of Pan."

Spock made some sort of odd grunt.

"It's not easy for me to hear him," Moke said. "He kind of . . . of flickers in and out. Sometimes I catch a whole sentence, sometimes only a word. I think he said just now that he's able to talk a little more directly through me because the Beings aren't as strong as they were," Moke continued.

This prompted bewildered glances among the officers. "Not as strong," said Shelby. "They annihilated that Tholian ship with what seemed to be minimal effort. If that's them in their weakened state, I'd hate to see them when they're firing on all cylinders."

"He says . . . What?" Moke was addressing the corner of the room. He looked as if he was straining to hear. "The . . . worshippers are key," said Moke.

"What?" More puzzled looks. "Worshippers are key?" asked Kebron. "Key to what? If—"

"Of course," said Spock in such a way that it was the closest Calhoun had seen the Vulcan come to expressing annoyance with himself . . . or at all. "Of course. It is obvious. Painfully obvious. I am a fool."

"Then we're all fools," said Calhoun, "because I'm still not entirely certain what you're talking about or what's going on."

"You have no reason to feel that way, Captain," Spock told him with certainty, "because you have no reason to have figured out what is happening here. I, however, have no excuse, for I have encountered this before."

Slowly he began to circle the room, and it appeared as if he was talking more to himself than to anyone else at that point. "Going all the way back to the *Enterprise*'s encounter with Apollo, there has been one main area of consistency in the behavior of these Beings. That is their desire to be worshipped . . . prayed to. A wise man once asked, 'What does God need with a starship?' One might also wonder . . . 'What do gods need with worshippers?' "

"But they're not gods," Calhoun said firmly. "They're . . . Beings. Beings of energy . . ."

"In a humanoid form," Gleau chimed in. He had been standing there with a distant, even annoyed air that so much attention was being paid to Moke, and that information was being gathered through this bizarre manner. But with the flow of ideas, he was starting to go along with it, even build upon it. "But even energy beings need sustenance of some sort."

"I have encountered creatures on several occasions," said Spock, "that actually derived nourishment from such things as emotions. Usually negative emotions, such as fear or anger."

Mueller looked at Spock with something akin to bemused wonderment and asked, "Is there anything you *haven't* encountered?"

Spock gave it a moment's thought. "No," he decided.

"Is this right, Moke?" asked Calhoun. "Ask your . . . friend. Is what we're saying correct?"

"He's nodding," said Moke. "I think it's getting harder for him to talk . . ."

"So what we're dealing with here," Shelby now said, "are creatures that draw their power from positive emotions—the worship—that people feel for them."

"And also from doubt," added Calhoun. "If an opponent becomes concerned that the Beings will triumph, they derive strength from that as well."

"If, however, they are of the same type of creature as I have encountered," said Spock, "thriving on psychic energy . . . then their outward appearance is a sort of construct, to provide frame of reference for onlookers . . . not unlike the Organians."

"Mr. Spock . . . I'm sorry, Ambassador Spock," Gleau said. "Not to sound foolish, but I've taken a special interest in your career. In fact, you were the subject of my dissertation at the Academy."

"How exciting this must be for you then," said Mueller dryly.

Gleau ignored her, instead continuing to address Spock. "I remember studying that incident with Apollo. During that encounter, didn't you destroy some sort of 'energy source' of his?"

"Yes. In the shape of a place of worship."

"All right. So I'm thinking," Gleau said, "that the temple was a sort of repository, a final battery of absorbed energy that Apollo had been storing. So I'm speculating that such energy has a shelf life; eventually, over enough time, it dissipates."

"It would make sense," said Spock. "It would explain why he so needed the *Enterprise* crew to worship him. That worship was what he required to sustain his power and form."

"So let's theorize, then, that when the Beings first confronted us, they were in a weakened state," said Calhoun.

Burgoyone looked stunned that Calhoun would even suggest it. "Weakened state? Sir, I seem to recall they came damned close to destroying us!"

"But they didn't," Calhoun reminded him. "They didn't . . . because the *Trident* showed up. Because when the *Trident* showed up, we believed that we'd been saved. That we were going to be able to fight back. And the *Trident* came barreling in with no preconceptions as to whether she would win or lose. They were just determined to win."

"What are you saying, Captain?" asked Si Cwan. "That the *Excalibur* was vulnerable to the attack . . ."

"Because we believed we were. Yes. Because we *believed* we were in danger from them . . . because we believed that they were—if not gods, at least beings with nearly godlike power—that gave them the energy they needed, like vampires. Our own belief in their ability to hurt us . . . gave them that very ability. That's why they're encouraging races to attack them. They *want* word of their power to spread, because the more it is believed that they are invincible, the moreso they will become. Basically they're living incarnations of the term 'self-fulfilling prophecy.' "

"That's a hell of a theory, Mac," said Shelby, looking somewhat dubious. "Moke, what does your invisible friend have to say about all this . . ."

"I . . ." Moke blinked. "I don't see him. He's . . . he's gone. And so is McHenry."

"Where did they go?"

"I don't know!" said Moke with growing urgency. "I don't know!"

iii.

"I don't know . . . how much longer . . ."

The Old Father's words echoed Moke's, except they were outside the conference room.

McHenry had found himself becoming oddly accustomed to his twilight existence, if for no other reason than the constancy of Woden's company. Now, though, Woden was looking shaken and weak, even for a ghost.

They stood in the corridor, and McHenry wondered—not for the first time—how two beings who were insubstantial could stand anywhere at all. But that was the least of his concerns.

"You don't know how much longer what? What's going on?"

The Old Father let out a slow breath, which was rather ironic when one considered that he had no reason to breathe. "The energy of belief that the others are tapping into . . . I can access as well, even from my current state. With greater effort, and not to as impressive an effect, but I can accomplish it. The others, however . . . they're taking a great interest in what transpires on this vessel. I can sense them doing so. I'm doing what I can to block them, however."

"What, you're saying there's essentially a whole battle going on that the captain and the others have no idea is happening?"

The elder god forced a smile. "You would be amazed how often that is the way of things. The truth is that mortals only perceive a fraction of what is happening in the universe. They think they know so much, but truly comprehend so very, very little. It is the job of higher beings to help keep them safe. To protect them."

"We can do a fine job of taking care of ourselves, thanks," said McHenry.

"Oh, and you've attended to that wonderfully in your case, haven't you."

McHenry scowled.

"The problem is, I cannot maintain my defenses indefinitely," said Woden. "I am old and tired, and have not fought in quite some time. It takes a lot out of me.

So we must hope that your associates hurry to their conclusions while still under my protection."

"And if they don't?"

The Old Father stared at him. "They'd better" was all he said.

iv.

Spock was no longer walking around the conference lounge. Instead he was seated, his fingers steepled thoughtfully. "When we faced a creature that thrived on fear," he said at last, "Captain Kirk gave the crew tranquilizers so that the crew no longer feared it—and the creature was weakened. Likewise an energy being that siphoned hostile energy during a manufactured series of battles with a crew of Klingons was thwarted when the Klingons and we ceased hostilities. What we need to do is find a way to sever these beings from their source of strength."

"But it's a very different situation here," Si Cwan pointed out. "In your case, you simply had to deal with the minds and actions of the crew of the *Enterprise.* You're essentially saying that the crews of the *Excalibur* and *Trident,* in going into combat with the Beings, cannot be concerned about defeat."

"Basically, yes," Calhoun said reluctantly. "If we fear failure . . . if we believe that the Beings are superior to us, or can destroy us . . . then we more or less guarantee our own defeat."

"Now, there's a challenge," said Shelby with a significant lack of enthusiasm. "It's like saying, 'Don't think of pink elephants.' "

"But it's more involved than that," said Mueller. "What you've been saying is that the Beings—if we're correct about this—are drawing their strength from the Danteri. It almost doesn't matter if we believe in them or not, because the Danteri do. In order to dampen the strength of the Beings . . ."

"We would have to cut off their energy at the source," said Spock. "We would have to—in short—obliterate the Danteri."

There was a momentary silence, and then Calhoun said what he suspected they all figured he'd say: "I'm not seeing a downside of that."

"Mac," Shelby said, not without sympathy, "I know better than anyone here how you feel about the Danteri. But I can't believe that even you would advocate genocide."

He grimaced and then slowly nodded. "You're right," he admitted. "Besides, just to be pragmatic about it . . . I very much doubt the Beings would simply stand by and allow us to annihilate their root of psychic sustenance. That still leaves us, though, trying to determine the best way to proceed."

"We'd be wise to determine it sooner rather than later," said Kebron. "My suspicion is that the Tholians weren't bluffing. That they've forces and allies who will be showing up here before long to launch a full-out assault. Except they'll already be showing up with the knowledge that the Beings easily destroyed one vessel. That will sow the seeds of doubt which the Beings will bring to full bloom, destroying those who oppose them, elevating Danteri worship, and very likely convincing assorted races that they should join the Danteri in bowing down to this pantheon of gods."

They all stared at him.

"When the hell did *he* get so chatty?" demanded Si Cwan.

"Ah, Si Cwan," laughed Kebron. "How I've missed ou."

"You hate me!"

"Oh, why drag along childish feuds into phases of turity."

Si Cwan turned to Calhoun and, indicating Kebron, d, "Did he eat ambrosia, too?"

"I'll explain it later, Ambassador."

"Yes, it's really an amusing story," said Kebron. "You see, in the life cycle of—"

"Later!" Calhoun said in annoyance. He sagged into the nearest chair. "You know, I'm really of mixed feelings on that. Genocidal concerns aside, part of me would dearly love to just stand aside and watch these angry races show up, trying to blow the Danteri to hell and gone. *Grozit,* we could even justify it on Prime Directive terms."

"Perhaps," Shelby agreed. "But there's every possibility the Beings would triumph, making matters even worse than they already are."

"I know, I know."

"Wait . . . wait a minute," Gleau said abruptly. He pointed at the bladed weapon that Kebron had laid in the middle of the table early on in the meeting. "That thing is one of their conduits?"

"As near as we can determine, yes. But apparently only they can actually utilize it—"

"We don't have to utilize it," said Gleau. "All we have to do is use it to determine the frequency patterns that it operates on and taps into."

"What . . . ?"

"Oh!" Burgoyne's eyes widened. "I see where you're going with this. Once we know those patterns, we can broadcast 'white noise' through the sensor arrays."

"A logical notion," said Spock. "It might very well serve to scramble the Beings' ability to 'feed' off the mental energies of the Danteri. Cut them off from their source of power."

Burgoyne's mind was clearly racing through the logistics. "The thing is, it's going to need both of the starships, one to cover each side of the planet. Otherwise the planet's own surface would block the white noise from affecting that side which is opposite the starship."

"And if we do all that," Calhoun said, "then the likelihood is that the Beings will come after us. Can this 'white noise' be used to block out whatever energies we might feed them ourselves, based upon doubts . . . ?"

"We'd be spreading our resources too thin," said Burgoyne. "We really need to focus on their prime energy source, the Danteri. We try to do too much, we'll wind up accomplishing too little."

"All right then. So they'll be deprived of their initial energy source, but they'll seek to draw energy from our own doubts and beliefs that they're invincible. Is that basically it?"

"Why are you attacking them?" asked Moke.

The question brought everything to a halt. Calhoun looked at the boy and said, "Because they're dangerous, Moke. Because they represent a threat to us . . . to you . . . to everyone and anyone who won't live in a galaxy where the Beings are worshipped. They attacked and killed people on this ship. They've brainwashed

Lieutenant Soleta . . . and an entire world besides. One of them attacked and nearly killed Lieutenant Kebron . . ."

"And Kalinda and I as well," said Si Cwan.

"So you see, Moke, they have to be dealt with, before it gets worse."

"I guess," said Moke, then paused and added, "but it's a shame."

Calhoun tried to come up with a response to that, but couldn't. Because he knew that Moke was right. It was a shame. A damned shame.

But it had to be done.

As long as they didn't get themselves killed doing it.

V.

Mueller stood in the turbolift with Gleau as it whisked them toward the transporter room that would bring them back to the *Trident*. "That was good work you did back there," she said. "I want you to be the point man between us and *Excalibur* on this. Work with Engineering Chief Dunn in making certain that he coordinates with Burgoyne and the *Excal*'s chief, Mitchell."

"This is killing you, isn't it," Gleau said.

She had been staring straight ahead, but now she turned and stared at him in open bewilderment. "Killing me? In what respect?"

"Between M'Ress and her complaints about me, and your own attitudes, you must have been hoping I would step aside, perhaps even transfer off." He gave her a smarmy smile. "Yet now I turn around and prove my worth to the ship. Made myself look pretty good. My guess is that bothers you no end."

"Your guess is completely wrong," she informed him. "All I care about is the well-being of the *Trident.* You're the science officer. You're *expected* to be of use, not to fail."

"Expectations are one things. Hopes are something else. You were hoping . . ."

"Do not tell me my own mind, Lieutenant Commander," Mueller told him stiffly. "My hopes are my own. They are not for public dissemination, and they're certainly not yours to assume. Do I make myself clear? And wipe that smirk off your face before I rip it off."

"Oh, absolutely," he said. The smirk diminished . . . but was still there nevertheless.

vi.

Zak Kebron had remained behind in the conference lounge. He stared at the far wall for a long time, having turned the scythe over to Burgoyne so s/he could study it more closely. He rapped his thick fingers on the table for a while, and finally he managed to say, "I think you should know . . . I'm sorry. Presuming you're still standing there, that is. I'm sorry about what happened to you, Mark.

"The truth is, I had some suspicions about who and what you were, and what you were capable of doing. I *was very* suspicious. But all I cared about was trying to 'catch' you somehow. Instead, I should have realized that you had some potentially great problems and tried to help you deal with it. Not just rat you out. You need a friend, and instead you got a suspicious head of security.

"I'm very, very sorry. And . . . I hope it means something."

Three decks away, watching the internal and external struggles of the Old Father, Mark McHenry was vaguely aware that something had been said that directly pertained to him, but he wasn't sure what it might have been, and then dismissed it as not being of any real consequence.

vii.

Calhoun sat in his quarters on the couch, facing Moke in the chair opposite, watching the boy staring into space. "It's going to be all right, Moke," he said after a time.

"I'd . . ."

"Yes?"

"I'd finally stopped wondering. Y'know? Finally stopped." He looked up at Calhoun with a distant sense of bewilderment. "Spent my whole life wondering what my father was like, but because of you . . . because of how nice you've been to me . . . I stopped wondering. And even in all those years where I did wonder . . . I never thought he'd be . . ." He paused. "What is he? What am I?"

"He's a different form of life, Moke. That's all. Just as I am. Just as this ship is crowded with many different forms of life."

"Yes, but . . . the things he can do . . ."

"I can't do the things that Zak Kebron can do. And Kebron can't do what Dr. Selar can do, and so on. Every different life-form is special, Moke. *Grozit,* even within the same life-form, everyone is special. Everyone has their own unique talents and abilities. There's a lot to learn about Woden, and hopefully we'll have the chance to learn it."

"And me. What about me?"

"You're a boy, Moke. A young boy." He put a hand on Moke's shoulder and smiled. "And you had some abilities that might have stemmed from him. Otherwise, nothing's changed."

"Do you . . . ?"

He seemed stuck for completing the sentence. "Do I what, Moke?"

"Do you think he loves me? Y'know. Dads love their sons. Do you think . . . ?"

"I could lie to you, Moke, but the truth is, I simply don't know."

"Do you think he loved my mom?"

Naturally Calhoun had no more idea of that than the previous question, but there was something in the boy's face that seemed to indicate this answer was even more important. Calhoun nodded firmly. "I'm sure he did. And I'm sure he would have stayed with her if he could," he added quickly, anticipating the next question.

"Do you love me?"

The question caught Calhoun off guard, although in retrospect he realized it shouldn't have. "Me?"

"Well, you basically act like my father. But you don't . . . y'know . . . say it much."

"I've . . . never been that demonstrative about such things, Moke. But . . . yes. Yes, of course, I . . . yes. I do. Like my own son. Actually . . . I hardly ever got to know my own son. So you're sort of a second chance to do things right." He hesitated, then asked, "Okay?"

"Okay," said Moke.

"Uhm . . . look, Moke . . . there are things I have to attend to now. Do you want to head over to—"

"Can I stay here? In your quarters?" asked Moke. "I won't touch anything, I promise. . . ."

"Sure. Absolutely," said Calhoun. "If that's what you want."

"Yeah. I would."

"Well . . . all right." He got up and walked out, leaving Moke still staring into space.

Except he wasn't.

The Old Father stared back at him.

"You shouldn't have left her," Moke said softly. "You really shouldn't. You could've made our lives so much better."

Woden's single eye looked wistful, and then he shrugged. "I'm sorry," he said.

"Yeah, well . . . sorry isn't always good enough," said Moke.

"I know," said Woden. "But sometimes it's all we have."

And then he faded from sight, leaving Moke alone.

Meantime, Calhoun stood in the hallway just outside his quarters, leaning against the bulkhead. He suddenly felt more tired than he had in ages. It was obvious they were about to enter round two against the Beings, and it was more than likely there would not be a round three. There was no margin for error, and literally no room for doubt.

"Are you all right?"

He hadn't even realized his eyes were closed, but

when he opened them, Shelby was standing there. "I thought you were heading back to the *Trident*."

"I was. But I thought I'd swing by on the way over. I'm worried about you."

"About me. Why are you worried about me?"

"Because someone has to be," she said with a shrug. "I figure I'm elected."

He laughed softly and then rubbed the bridge of his nose. "I'm not entirely sure, but . . . I think I may owe you an apology."

"That's impressive," she said, folding her arms. "I don't believe I've ever heard that many qualifiers in one sentence."

"I think . . . in some ways . . . I feel as if I haven't had a chance to get any solid ground beneath my feet since the first *Excalibur* blew up. As if I've just been flailing about, trying to get a hold on something firm, and not succeeding."

She paused. "And is that what our marriage is? A failed attempt to get some footing?"

He chuckled. "No. No . . . that's the only thing I've done in the past year or so that I'm absolutely confident about."

"You're confident in everything you do, Mac. Even when you know full well that it's absolutely indefensible. That's what I love about you."

"What you love about me?" He looked at her skeptically. "I thought it was the one aspect of my personality that always drove you the most insane."

"Calhoun, you've been driving me insane ever since your handling of the *Kobayashi Maru* set my career back a year."

"Ummm . . . yes," he sighed. "I've always felt kind of guilty about that."

"No, you didn't. You still don't, even to this day. Don't you lie to me, you smug bastard," she admonished with mock gravity. "You can do just about anything else, but don't lie to me. If there's one thing I don't deserve, it's that."

"You're right. In fact, if there's one thing you do deserve, it's this."

And he wrapped his arms around her and kissed her passionately.

Passing crewmen slowed, looked, and then walked quickly away, and one was heard to murmur, "Guess yellow alert means something different for officers than it does for us grunts."

DANTER

SOLETA LAY BACK in the field of long grass, staring in leisurely fashion up at the sky. Her clothes were scattered about, but she wasn't the least bit concerned over her lack of apparel. Thoth, similarly undraped, lay next to her, his head propped up with one hand. The sky was clear, no clouds, no hint of storms. It seemed one of those glorious days that would stretch on forever.

"Why me?" she asked Thoth at length.

"Why you what?"

"Why have you taken such an interest in me? Me, of all the females you've encountered . . . of all the ones you could have . . ."

"I was drawn to you by your intellect. And by your hurt. I sensed your inner turmoil and felt that you could truly benefit from the inner peace I could bring you."

"And you were right." She smiled and ran her hand

along the strong angle of his chin. "You were so right. I feel as if I could—"

And suddenly Thoth pitched backward, grasping at his forehead. Soleta immediately sat up, consternation evident. "Thoth? What's wrong? What—?"

He fell forward, gasping, clutching at his chest.

"What's wrong?" she repeated, even more alarmed than before.

"I . . . I don't know. My head . . . feels like . . ." Suddenly he gripped her by the shoulders. "Love me."

"What?" She tried to smile, although it wasn't easy considering his agitated state. "In the mood again already? If you—"

"Love me! Believe in me! Do you?"

"You know I do!" Soleta was completely confused. "How could you not . . . ?"

"I can't feel it! I can't feel you. It's . . . it's as if I'm blind . . . I—"

And suddenly there were flashes of light from all around them. One by one, then by the dozens, the Beings were springing into existence, all babbling in similar agitation to one another. Soleta quickly tugged on her clothes, but Thoth was wandering around, naked, looking like a flummoxed Greek statue, despite the fact that he was Egyptian.

The voice of Artemis cut above the rest of them. "You feel it? You all feel it?!" There were nods, confused babbles of assent.

"Feel what?" Soleta asked Thoth. "I don't feel anything. Nothing's changed. Nothing's . . ."

"Everything's changed! How can you not feel it!" His temper flared and he grabbed Soleta and shook her fiercely. "How is this happening? How is this—"

"Stop it!" Soleta effortlessly yanked her arms out of his grasp. The move sent him off balance, and she came forward quickly and shoved him hard. Thoth stumbled back, and although he righted himself just in time to avoid falling over completely, he still gaped at Soleta as if seeing her for the first time.

Soleta blinked several times, and was then filled with mortification. "I'm . . . I'm so sorry, Thoth. I've no idea what came over me . . . I . . ."

"Maybe she has had something to do with it," Anubis said, pointing an angry finger at her. "Perhaps her dalliance with you, Thoth, has simply been a means of putting you off guard."

"Don't be an ass, Loki."

"Anubis. I prefer Anubis—"

"And I prefer that you go straight to Hades!" shouted Artemis. Nearby her, Tyr the swordsman and Hermes the messenger were nodding in agreement.

"This is no time to turn against each other," began Thoth.

"What's happening?" Soleta interrupted. "Tell me what's happening. Perhaps I can—"

Suddenly the combadge on Soleta's uniform beeped at her. She looked confused, as if she'd forgotten it was there, or what it was for. She tapped it and said tentatively, "Yes?"

"Lieutenant, this is Captain Calhoun," came the familiar voice. He sounded quite calm, even a bit amused. "Are any of your godly friends nearby?"

"We are all here!" shouted Artemis. "Calhoun, are you responsible—"

"For the weakness you're no doubt feeling at the moment? Yes. Yes, I am. Or more correctly, we are."

"You mortal bastard!" bellowed Anubis. "How dare you! Do you have any idea of the forces you're unleashing? The retribution you're bringing upon yourselves?"

"I have a fairly clear idea." Calhoun's voice crackled over the combadge. "You, however, have no idea at all. And unless you and your associates clear off Danter . . . clear out of this sector of space, in fact . . . and take your mind-sapping ambrosia with you . . . then this mortal bastard and his wife, the mortal bitch, are going to kick your pseudo-Egyptian-Greco-Roman-Norse-Mesopotamian asses. Not only that, but we'll tell every other existing race how to dispose of you as well, using the exact same techniques we're using now."

"And unless you, Captain, cease whatever you're doing immediately," and suddenly Artemis' bow was unslung and an arrow was nocked and aimed straight at Soleta, "then your little pointy-eared lieutenant dies."

Soleta gaped, staring at pointed death from less than ten feet away.

"No," Thoth said sharply. "She's an innocent in all this. Put it away, Artemis."

"Stand aside, Thoth!"

"Put it away!"

Thoth stretched out his hand, and energy leaped through the air, enveloping Artemis. She staggered, swung her bow around, and the arrow flew off course . . .

. . . and thudded straight into Thoth's chest.

Thoth staggered, looking down at the shaft protruding from him, even as Soleta let out an alarmed shriek. He sagged to his knees.

310

"Thoth!" cried out Artemis, and she ran toward him. "Thoth, I'm sorry . . . I . . . I didn't mean . . ."

Soleta started toward Thoth, but he held up a hand and shouted "Stay away!" even as he gripped the arrow firmly. He gritted his teeth and then let out a howl of pain as he ripped the arrow from his torso. Soleta saw something glowing from within the hole, some sort of energy that appeared to be seeping out of him.

"You . . . you have to be all right," she said desperately. "You can't die. . . ."

"Oh . . . we can," Thoth said, his voice rattling. "If . . . if we suddenly find ourselves bereft of energy . . . if our own weapons are turned against us . . . we can die quite well . . ."

"Thoth . . . !"

"Get away from him!" shouted Artemis, and she shoved Soleta furiously aside as she knelt down next to Thoth. "Thoth . . . this . . . this can be fixed . . ."

"Can this, I wonder?" said Thoth, and the hand that was still holding the arrow jammed it upward into the pit of Artemis' stomach.

Artemis screamed, a scream heard from one end of Danter to the other, and Thoth, his face a mask of fury, ripped the arrow upward through her body in a move that would have disemboweled anyone else.

But it was not internal organs that spilled from Artemis, at least nothing like any that Soleta had ever seen. Instead it was almost like solid light, twisting and turning from her, and Artemis shrieked and cried out and pounded upon Thoth, and howled at him in tongues that had not been spoken since the dawn of man.

"Artemis . . . my sweet," Thoth managed to say, his

voice choking, "I remain a god of truth . . . and I believe the truth is . . . that we have overstayed our welcome . . ."

Then the very air seemed to crackle, and Soleta fell back as a burst of light and heat blasted her, sending her sprawling flat ten feet away. She gasped, then scrambled to her feet, and she saw the two gods fading, fading . . .

. . . and gone.

The rest of the Beings stood there for a long moment, more stunned than she would ever have thought possible.

"Loki . . . wha . . . what do we do now?" said Tyr.

And Anubis looked heavenward and growled, "We get the bastards who did this. We destroy them, restore the balance to this world, and annihilate any else who come. We build our reputation as gods of destruction! They will fear us and bow down to us!"

"What about this one?" asked Hermes, indicating Soleta.

"Forget her. She's meaningless. Only Calhoun matters. *Calhoun and Shelby and their minions,*" roared Anubis, *"will know the fury of the gods unleashed!"*

And then, from over Soleta's still active com link, came Calhoun's mocking voice:

"I can't wait."

EXCALIBUR

i.

MARK MCHENRY, standing in the sickbay and looking down at his own unmoving body, suddenly staggered and clutched at his chest. He felt as if something had suddenly been yanked away from him, and he had no clue what it was.

Then, suddenly . . . he knew. He didn't know how or why he did . . . but he did.

"Artemis," he whispered.

And from next to him, almost in his ear, came the voice of the Old Father.

"Yes. Artemis," he confirmed. "She loved you, you know. Not in any manner that meets the standard definition of sanity . . . but she loved you."

"Now what?"

"Now," said Woden, "it finally ends."

And that was when Calhoun's voice came across the ship's loudspeaker.

ii.

"I can't wait," said Mackenzie Calhoun.

He was staring at the image of Danter on the screen, turning leisurely in its orbit. Suddenly from the tactical station, Zak Kebron called out, "Captain. Detecting an energy burst from the planet's surface."

The face of Morgan Primus suddenly appeared on the screen. "Confirming," she said. "Energy surge bearing eighteen mark five. Similar to the energy frequencies generated by the Beings in their previous attack."

"You still have firm control of conn, Morgan?"

"Aye, sir."

"Captain," Robin Lefler spoke up, looking distinctly uncomfortable. "For a potential battle situation, wouldn't it make sense to have, you know . . . a living person at that station? No offense, Mom."

"You had a living person at that station," Morgan reminded her archly. "Fat lot of good it did him."

"Captain . . ."

"Lieutenant, your opinion is noted and forgotten," said Calhoun. "Calhoun to *Trident*. Captain Shelby, you ready?"

"Ready, Captain Calhoun," replied Shelby. The *Trident* was out of sight on the opposite side of the world, so her voice was a comfort to him.

"Robin . . . put me on with the crew."

Robin made a quick adjustment at the ops station and nodded. "Go ahead, Captain."

"Attention all hands," said Calhoun after a moment. "This vessel is about to be attacked by the same individuals who damaged us so badly in our previous encounter. We have, however, determined the source of their power . . . and believe it or not . . . the enemy is us. They will feed on any doubts, any reservations we have, and turn those doubts against us. We cannot permit that to happen.

"This ship . . . this crew . . . is more than just a Starfleet crew going through its paces. You are all, every one of you, heroes in your own right. The thing is, even heroes feel fear. They feel it, but they get the job done despite it.

"You have to be more than that. You must feel no fear. You must not waver in your confidence, even for a moment. Each and every one of you must visualize our triumph over these creatures. Visualize it, hold on to it for all it's worth. Use it as a source of strength to overcome any hesitation or fear you might have, or might even think of having.

"And consider this: Throughout centuries, the greatest legends of mankind have been steeped in eras and times when mere mortals threw themselves against the will of the gods and triumphed over impossible odds. Those mortals are among the greatest, most epic of heroes that have ever existed. Rather than have a moment's fear over our present situation, think upon the fact that you have the honor, the privilege, the pure joy of being here on an occasion that is positively epic. We face beings who purport to be gods. We fight a fight for control of our own destinies that began millennia ago and ends this day. And all of you, every single one of you, will cherish this opportunity and be able to hold your heads high and say, 'I was there. I touched greatness. I am an epic hero. I served aboard a ship that carried me to greatness, and I was up to the journey.'

"And I know you are. As your captain, as your leader, as a man privileged to serve with you, I know that each and every one of you are.

"All hands, battle stations. This one is for the book of legends. Calhoun out."

He paused a long moment then, allowing the silence to thicken. Then he said, "Captain Shelby . . . you may want to give your own crew some sort of pep talk as well, just to make sure . . ."

"I simply broadcast yours when you were speaking, Mac," said Shelby, and even though it was only her voice, he could hear the smile in it. "I felt sure you could do the job for both of us. Good luck."

"Same to you, Captain." Then he turned to Ambassador Spock, who was simply standing there, stony-faced, looking at the planet below. "Is that what Captain Kirk would have done?" he asked.

"Perhaps," said Spock. "Either that or he would simply have medicated the entire crew."

"Oh," said Calhoun. "Well . . . that would have worked too, I suppose."

"Captain," came Morgan's voice, "here they come."

She was right.

They were visible on the screen, and it almost seemed a replay of the previous encounter. A sailing vessel of ancient origin, a trireme, coming straight toward them. Its battering ram protruded in the shape of a giant ram's head, and it appeared on a collision course.

"Welcome to the party," Calhoun said calmly.

"Captain," said Spock, "it should be noted that, once

battle is joined, anything can occur. And that the most difficult thing to fight . . . is water."

"Water?" said Kebron from tactical.

"Yes . . . water, Mr. Kebron," Calhoun agreed. "The ocean. The waves pound you, but you can't hit it back because it moves wherever you try."

"Enemy is preparing to engage. Evasive action, Captain?" came Morgan's voice.

"Targeting incoming vessel," said Kebron.

"Don't do anything," replied Calhoun.

"Nothing?"

"Morgan . . . we're going to need you for this, because nothing human can think fast enough. When they start firing, analyze where the missiles are going to hit, and simply roll with it. Preserve the shielding. Captain to all hands," he continued without pause. "Just so you know, we're going to be rocking a bit. But we're not going to be hurt. Nothing they're going to do can hurt us. And we're going to rub their noses in that. In fact, if I were you, I'd start feeling sorry for them. Calhoun out." He turned toward Burgoyne. "Burgy, make sure engineering is keeping the white noise going through the sensor dish."

"Aye, Captain."

"Here it comes!" called Lefler.

Just as before, arrows came hurtling through the ether of space. They hammered into the *Excalibur*'s shields, and the starship pitched and yawed with each new salvo. They did not, however, fire back.

"Status report, Mr. Kebron."

"Shields holding, Captain."

"Calhoun to all hands. Shields are holding firm. They're not hurting us. Not at all."

Again and again, as the trireme hurtled toward them, the darkness of space was alive with the glow of the arrows. And with computer precision, Morgan not only was able to roll with each new attack, but even began dodging some of them entirely. No starship was particularly graceful when it was under impulse power, but in the case of the *Excalibur,* under Morgan's guidance, the vessel dipped, twisted, and turned about like a vast dancer.

Closer and closer came the trireme, and still the assault continued to have no effect. The entire time, Calhoun continued to speak to his crew, to exhort them to be utterly convinced that the Beings had no chance. He extolled their bravery, spoke condescendingly of the Beings, reminded them of all the challenges they'd faced before that they'd come through.

"They thought they could defeat us!" Calhoun called, his voice rising as if he were speaking to an array of troops spread across a field, and for the first time in ages, he felt the blood of what he once was, a warlord of Xenex, pounding through him. So sterile had been his time as commander, operating from a small room rather than being in the midst of his people, waving a sword, shouting encouragement to them and howling that no enemy could possibly stand in opposition to him. He hadn't even realized it was missing until this very moment, but now, now he would never let it go again. *"They thought they could batter us down! But they were wrong! We do not need to believe in them! We believe in ourselves! We will triumph! We will beat them down! We will show them that the United Federation of Planets does not bow, does not break to those who would try to deprive us of our very drive to achieve! Mr. Kebron: All phasers, fire!"*

"All phasers firing!" shouted Kebron, and the *Excalibur* cut loose at the trireme. The phasers cut into the ship and the vessel skidded around, shaken. The Beings were visible upon the ship's deck and they could be seen falling about, utterly shaken.

"No doubts!"

The phasers fired again.

"No uncertainties!"

And again, hammering down.

"No defeat!"

The trireme spun in space, lurching wildly from side to side, as if the invisible winds that propelled it had turned against it entirely.

iii.

In Calhoun's quarters, Moke ignored the rocking of the ship. Instead his entire attention was focused on the bearded man before him. He seemed more robust than before, and told Moke that it was because "the battle was joined," which Moke didn't understand, and that the Old Father could now "fully concentrate on the business at hand," which Moke also didn't understand.

But of all the things that eluded Moke's comprehension, the whys and wherefores of the bearded man's turnaround in ability to communicate was the least of them. He had more pressing problems on his mind.

"Why her?" he asked. "Why my mom? Why—?"

"Because," said the Old Father, smiling benevolently, "in all my travels, in all the galaxy . . . I saw her, and was struck by beauty as I'd never seen. Beauty of face. Of form. And of spirit. Pure."

"Did you love her?"

His great head slowly nodded. "Yes."

"Why . . ." He felt his eyes misting up, and he wiped the tears away. "Why didn't you stay with us?"

"I couldn't. I would have liked to . . . but it wasn't possible."

"Why?"

"Sometimes, Moke," said the Old Father gently, "you have to take certain things on faith. The truth of it is . . . gods make lousy fathers for the most part. But I was watching over you . . ."

"If you were watching over us," said Moke, "then why did you let Mom get killed?"

The Old Father sighed heavily at that. "Sometimes, Moke . . . mortals do foolish things. It would be nice if the gods could stop them from doing it . . . but then mortals would never learn. Unfortunately, because of that, sometimes very good people die."

"I know. But I taught them," Moke said, his eyes glistening once more, but this time there was cold anger and even relishing of what had happened that fateful day. "I taught them. I hurt them. Badly."

"Yes," nodded the Old Father. "You did. Using the power you got from me. That was a gift I was able to give to you. I would have liked to do more . . . but all of us, Moke, all of us . . . mortal or immortal . . . we do exactly and precisely just as much as we can, and no more than that. It's sad but it's true."

"Did you bring Mac to me? To our world? Did he land there because of you?"

"Yes," said the Old Father without hesitation.

And Moke realized that he had no idea whether Woden was lying or not . . . and made the conscious choice, at that point, not to care.

"Thank you," he said. "And . . . thank you for making Mom happy . . . even if it was only for a little while. She needed it."

"You're welcome," said the Old Father. "And Moke . . . I need something, too."

"What is it?" asked Moke, eyebrow raised.

iv.

In sickbay, Mark McHenry screamed.

It was a sound that caught every med tech completely off guard, and a number of them let out similar startled cries as McHenry, who had been lying immobile, in a twilight state between life and death, sat up on the table and gave a startled shriek. Then he coughed violently as air flooded back into his lungs and he fell back.

Dr. Selar, the only person in sickbay who kept her wits about her, ran to McHenry's side and started shouting for stimulants to be pumped into him. The ship continued to rock under the battle that was ongoing in space, but Selar was only concerned with the fight for a man's life that had suddenly reignited in sickbay.

And then his eyes snapped open, and he looked at empty space in front of him, and his voice croaked as he said to nothingness, "Yes . . . I believe in you . . ."

V.

"Yes, I forgive you," said Moke to the bearded man who stood before him in Calhoun's quarters. "And I believe in you."

And suddenly Moke cried out, thrown back like a puppet yanked by a string, and energy seemed to spiral out of him . . .

vi.

And suddenly McHenry cried out, thrown back like a puppet yanked by a string, and energy seemed to spiral out of him . . .

vii.

"Captain," Morgan suddenly said, "something is happening. Some sort of rift is opening in front of us. Readings similar to a wormhole, but with major variances."

"Are the Beings causing it?" demanded Calhoun, sitting forward in his chair.

"I believe it unlikely," Spock said. "Particularly since it appears to be affecting them far more than it is us."

The Vulcan was right. Ahead of them in space, a whirling vortex of energy had opened up and seemed focused on the trireme. The focus on the screen zoomed in on the Beings, and they were running about, looking panicked. Calhoun was able to make out Anubis, and he was shaking his head violently, seemingly petrified by the energy whorl.

"Get me some specifics!" shouted Calhoun. "What are we facing here?"

"All readings off the scales," called out Burgoyne.

"We have *got* to get bigger scales," muttered Kebron.

Some of the beings actually tried to leap out of the trireme, and they were the first to be hauled, kicking and screaming in the silence of space, toward the vortex. The ancient sailing ship shook violently, began to splinter, and then with a rending and tearing of wood-that-wasn't-wood, the ship tore in half. The rear spiraled into the energy whirlpool, and more of the Beings fell in that direction as well. Then the prow of the trireme followed, tumbling, and they could just make out Anubis clutching on for dear life, and then there was a release and discharge of energy so blinding that the screen shut off for a moment to preserve the eyesight of anyone watching.

viii.

In sickbay, Mark McHenry—still with the horrific scars and burns that couldn't be healed—sat fully up once more and swung his legs off the med-lab table.

"Lieutenant, lie down immediately! That's an order!" snapped Selar.

He paid no attention, shoving her aside and stumbling forward, lurching wildly and grabbing for support.

And suddenly everyone in sickbay saw him.

An old man, older than seemed possible, with a vast

white beard and one eye, who wore his years around him like a great cloak that was weighing him down for one, final time.

He sagged forward, and McHenry put his arms out and, much to McHenry's shock, caught him.

"Did it," whispered the Old Father. "As . . . their power drained . . . mine grew . . . used the spark of divine . . . in you and Moke . . . broke free . . . did it . . . can't . . . can't anymore . . ."

"Rest," McHenry urged through cracked lips. "Rest now."

"Oh, I will," and the Old Father had a twinkle in his eye. "For good. Your turn now. Yours or Moke's . . . but I'm thinking . . . yours . . . let him grow up some . . . and . . . and Mark . . . get the job done . . . as I know you can . . ."

And slowly the Old Father began to dissolve.

And Mark McHenry felt him seeping into every pore, every atom of his being. Felt a glow suffusing him, and power and knowledge, and of course, everything made so much more sense now. . . .

The med techs stepped back as the glow spread further and further, seeming to creep into every corner of the sickbay. Dr. Selar didn't even think to call for a security team. For all her Vulcan training, she was watching with as much open wonderment as the most emotional human. She felt an unaccustomed wetness on her face and realized it was tears. Quickly, shamed, she wiped them away.

And then there was a vast release of colors and light, a soundless explosion, and the light was gone.

And so was Mark McHenry.

ix.

"Okay," said Calhoun, staring at the screen, which was devoid of any type of threat. "Would someone care to tell me what just happened?"

"All right," said McHenry.

He had appeared with no warning, no introductory burst of light. He was just there, looking very much like his old self.

There were gasps of confusion, but McHenry held up his hand in a casually peremptory fashion. "The Beings are gone . . . well, not gone, exactly. Imprisoned. Sealed off."

"How?"

"Partly Woden's power, Captain. Partly mine and Moke's. And partly yours." He smiled upon seeing Calhoun's confusion. "Woden was unique among all the Beings, which is probably why he was just about the most powerful of them all, and why the others feared him. See, they could only derive power from people believing in them. So could Woden—or Zeus, or Kris Kringle, or any of the other names that he's used throughout the—"

"Kris Kringle?" said a stunned Robin Lefler. "You mean . . . Santa Claus? You're telling me that the Beings were defeated because we believed in Santa Claus?! Come on!"

"Robin, not now," Burgoyne warned.

"Partly that," admitted McHenry. "But of all the Beings, he was the only one able to draw strength and sustenance from people believing in *themselves*. The fact that you faced down the Beings, that you collectively weren't afraid . . . that gave him the additional strength he needed to break out of the imprisonment that the others had inflicted upon him, and let him turn the tables. But . . ."

"But what . . . ?"

McHenry sighed heavily. "It cost him. Cost him everything . . . except his inner essence, which he placed into me. And the problem is, the Beings can be imprisoned . . . but destroying them is a much more difficult matter. Someone has to remain as a sentinel against their possible return . . . plus as an early warning against other extradimensional threats that could harm all reality . . . or, at the very least, be really, really annoying. And I'm afraid that's gonna have to be me. No more sleeping at my station."

"I don't accept that," said Calhoun. "There must be another way . . ."

At that, McHenry laughed. "Sorry, Captain. There are some things in the universe that are beyond the influence of even the great Mackenzie Calhoun." And very, very slowly, McHenry started to fade. "Don't be concerned: I've always felt such an affinity for the stars. Well . . . now I'll be walking among them."

"Will . . ." Burgoyne sounded as if hir voice was choking. "Will we see you again?"

"You'd better hope not," said McHenry. "Because chances are, if you do, I won't be showing up with good news." He smiled at Kebron. "When we started at the Academy, Zak, bet you never thought you'd wind up serving next to a demigod, huh?"

"McHenry," said Kebron, "there's things that should be said . . ."

"Say them some other time. I'll stumble over 'em sooner or later. Oh, and Robin . . ."

"Mark . . . ?"

He wagged a finger at her. "I'll know if you've been naughty or nice. So watch it."

And he disappeared.

DANTER

Soleta woke up.

She wasn't even sure she had been sleeping. All she knew was that she was lying in a field, and suddenly there was a clarity of vision that she had been lacking before.

And then, slowly, the memories began to creep back to her. The memories of peace of mind, and warmth, and a lack of concern.

And a smiling face above her, and heat within her.

She had lost all of that, and instead her free will had been returned to her.

She should have been happy. And relieved. Even angry.

Instead she began to sob.

TRIDENT

SHELBY SHOOK HER HEAD in disbelief as she and Calhoun walked down the corridor leading to the turbolift.

"So McHenry's gone?"

"That's right," said Calhoun.

"And Soleta's returned to the ship."

"Feeling very bewildered and, I think, rather embarrassed," Calhoun told her. "And the effects of the ambrosia are wearing off the rest of the Danteri as well. They've already been imploring Si Cwan to come back and take another stab at beginning a new Thallonian Empire."

"Let me guess," said Shelby. "He doesn't want any part of it."

"No. The Danteri were no joy to work with even before the Beings got involved with them. Si Cwan is interested in keeping a safe distance from them. I think he's still enchanted with the idea of a new Thallonian

Empire, but he's convinced the Danteri aren't the way to go."

"Our remaining problem is the Tholians," said Shelby. "Fortunately enough, Ambassador Spock is with us. The Tholians are on their way, but we're thinking the ambassador will be able to forestall any problems. Especially when he explains that the downside of ambrosia is that it makes anyone who takes it extremely peaceful. I doubt that's going to be very attractive to the Tholians." She paused just before they got to the turbolift, turned, and said to Calhoun, "I'm very proud of the way you handled everything. I really am."

"Thank you. That means a lot, coming from you. And I love you."

She laughed softly. "You don't initiate that statement very often. And I love you, too."

"Tell me," he said, "do you think they'd miss me back on the *Excalibur* if I was gone for, oh . . . another half hour or so?"

"Even if they did, they'd probably figure out why and have the good taste not to comment on it."

"Your cabin?"

"By all means."

They walked forward into the turbolift, the door hissing open, and Shelby jumped back and barely stifled a shriek.

The ripped-up body of Lieutenant Commander Gleau tumbled out of the lift, staring with lifeless eyes up at them.

"This might take longer than a half hour," said Calhoun.

Look for STAR TREK fiction from Pocket Books

Star Trek®

Novelizations

> *Encounter at Farpoint* • David Gerrold
> *Unification* • Jeri Taylor
> *Relics* • Michael Jan Friedman
> *Descent* • Diane Carey
> *All Good Things...* • Michael Jan Friedman
> *Star Trek: Klingon* • Dean Wesley Smith & Kristine Kathryn Rusch
> *Star Trek Generations* • J.M. Dillard
> *Star Trek: First Contact* • J.M. Dillard
> *Star Trek: Insurrection* • J.M. Dillard
> *Star Trek: Nemesis* • J.M. Dillard

Star Trek: Deep Space Nine®

Far Beyond the Stars • Steve Barnes
What You Leave Behind • Diane Carey

#1 • *Emissary* • J.M. Dillard
#2 • *The Siege* • Peter David
#3 • *Bloodletter* • K.W. Jeter
#4 • *The Big Game* • Sandy Schofield
#5 • *Fallen Heroes* • Dafydd ab Hugh
#6 • *Betrayal* • Lois Tilton
#7 • *Warchild* • Esther Friesner
#8 • *Antimatter* • John Vornholt
#9 • *Proud Helios* • Melissa Scott
#10 • *Valhalla* • Nathan Archer
#11 • *Devil in the Sky* • Greg Cox & John Gregory Betancourt
#12 • *The Laertian Gamble* • Robert Sheckley
#13 • *Station Rage* • Diane Carey
#14 • *The Long Night* • Dean Wesley Smith & Kristine Kathryn Rusch
#15 • *Objective: Bajor* • John Peel
#16 • *Invasion! #3: Time's Enemy* • L.A. Graf
#17 • *The Heart of the Warrior* • John Gregory Betancourt
#18 • *Saratoga* • Michael Jan Friedman
#19 • *The Tempest* • Susan Wright
#20 • *Wrath of the Prophets* • David, Friedman & Greenberger
#21 • *Trial by Error* • Mark Garland
#22 • *Vengeance* • Dafydd ab Hugh
#23 • *The 34th Rule* • Armin Shimerman & David R. George III
#24-26 • *Rebels* • Dafydd ab Hugh
    #24 • *The Conquered*
    #25 • *The Courageous*
    #26 • *The Liberated*

Books set after the series
    The Lives of Dax • Marco Palmieri, ed.
    Millennium Omnibus • Judith and Garfield Reeves-Stevens
        #1 • *The Fall of Terok Nor*
        #2 • *The War of the Prophets*
        #3 • *Inferno*
    A Stitch in Time • Andrew J. Robinson
    Avatar, Books One and *Two* • S.D. Perry
    Section 31: Abyss • David Weddle & Jeffrey Lang
    Gateways #4: Demons of Air and Darkness • Keith R.A. DeCandido
    Gateways #7: What Lay Beyond: "Horn and Ivory" • Keith R.A. DeCandido
    Mission: Gamma
        #1 • *Twilight* • David R. George III
        #2 • *This Gray Spirit* • Heather Jarman

#3 • *Her Klingon Soul* • Michael Jan Friedman
#4 • *Treaty's Law* • Dean Wesley Smith & Kristine Kathryn Rusch
The Television Episode • Michael Jan Friedman
Day of Honor Omnibus • various

Star Trek®: The Captain's Table

#1 • *War Dragons* • L.A. Graf
#2 • *Dujonian's Hoard* • Michael Jan Friedman
#3 • *The Mist* • Dean Wesley Smith & Kristine Kathryn Rusch
#4 • *Fire Ship* • Diane Carey
#5 • *Once Burned* • Peter David
#6 • *Where Sea Meets Sky* • Jerry Oltion
The Captain's Table Omnibus • various

Star Trek®: The Dominion War

#1 • *Behind Enemy Lines* • John Vornholt
#2 • *Call to Arms...* • Diane Carey
#3 • *Tunnel Through the Stars* • John Vornholt
#4 • *...Sacrifice of Angels* • Diane Carey

Star Trek®: Section 31™

Rogue • Andy Mangels & Michael A. Martin
Shadow • Dean Wesley Smith & Kristine Kathryn Rusch
Cloak • S.D. Perry
Abyss • Dean Weddle & Jeffrey Lang

Star Trek®: Gateways

#1 • *One Small Step* • Susan Wright
#2 • *Chainmail* • Diane Carey
#3 • *Doors Into Chaos* • Robert Greenberger
#4 • *Demons of Air and Darkness* • Keith R.A. DeCandido
#5 • *No Man's Land* • Christie Golden
#6 • *Cold Wars* • Peter David
#7 • *What Lay Beyond* • various
Epilogue: Here There Be Monsters • Keith R.A. DeCandido

Star Trek® The Lost Era

The Sundered • Michael A. Martin & Andy Mangels
Serpents Among the Ruins • David R. George III
The Art of the Impossible • Keith R.A. DeCandido

Star Trek® Omnibus Editions

Invasion! Omnibus • various
Day of Honor Omnibus • various

The Captain's Table Omnibus • various
Double Helix Omnibus • various
Star Trek: Odyssey • William Shatner with Judith and Garfield Reeves-Stevens
Millennium Omnibus • Judith and Garfield Reeves-Stevens
Starfleet: Year One • Michael Jan Friedman

Star Trek® Short Story Anthologies

Strange New Worlds, vol. I, II, III, IV, V, and VI • Dean Wesley Smith, ed.
The Lives of Dax • Marco Palmieri, ed.
Enterprise Logs • Carol Greenburg, ed.
The Amazing Stories • various
Prophecy and Change • Marco Palmieri, ed.
No Limits • Peter David and John J. Ordover, ed.

Other Star Trek® Fiction

Legends of the Ferengi • Ira Steven Behr & Robert Hewitt Wolfe
Adventures in Time and Space • Mary P. Taylor, ed.
Captain Proton: Defender of the Earth • D.W. "Prof" Smith
New Worlds, New Civilizations • Michael Jan Friedman
The Badlands, Books One and *Two* • Susan Wright
The Klingon Hamlet • Wil'yam Shex'pir
Dark Passions, Books One and *Two* • Susan Wright
The Brave and the Bold, Books One and *Two* • Keith R.A. DeCandido

STAR TREK
SECTION 31

BASHIR
Never heard of it.

SLOAN
We keep a low profile....
We search out and identify
potential dangers to the
Federation.

BASHIR
And Starfleet sanctions
what you're doing?

SLOAN
We're an autonomous
department.

BASHIR
Authorized by whom?

SLOAN
Section Thirty-One was
part of the original
Starfleet Charter.

BASHIR
That was two hundred years
ago. Are you telling me
you've been on your own
ever since? Without specific
orders? Accountable to
nobody but yourselves?

SLOAN
You make it sound so
ominous.

BASHIR
Isn't it?

No law. No conscience. No stopping them.

A four book series available wherever books are sold.

Excerpt adapted from *Star Trek:Deep Space Nine*® "Inquisition"
written by Bradley Thompson & David Weddle.

2161.01

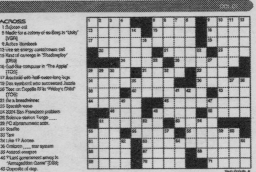